by Scott Ciencin

Illustrations by Mike Fredericks

Random House 🏠 New York

www.randomhouse.com/kids

Library of Congress Cataloging–in–Publication Data
Ciencin, Scott.
Dinoverse / by Scott Ciencin
Includes bibliographical references
Summary: When thirteen-year-old Bertram and three other friends find themselves living in
dinosaurs' bodies sixty-seven million years ago, they discover new ways to think about their lives.
ISBN 0-679-88842-X (trade paper)
[1. Self-acceptance—Fiction. 2. Dinosaurs—Fiction. 3. Evolution—Fiction. 4. Time travel—Fiction.
5. Science—Fiction.] I. Title.
PZ7.C5907Di   1999
[Fic]—dc21
98-41377

Printed in the United States of America 10 9 8 7 6 5 4 3 2 1

To my beloved wife, Denise. This novel is as much a part of her heart and soul as it is mine.

I love you, sweetheart—and literally couldn't have done it without you!

—S.C.

Author's Note

If you're like me, you love dinosaurs. You may even have imagined what it would be like to look through their eyes and listen through their ears.

With the help of project advisor and paleontologist Dr. Thomas R. Holtz, Jr., I was able to take a journey back in time to live with these amazing creatures. Unlike Bertram Phillips, I didn't have access to a machine that would send my mind back 67 million years. So I did the next best thing. I read as much about dinosaurs as I could. What I discovered about their day-to-day lives, I put into the novel you now have in your hands.

You can take that wild and fun trip, too. Your local library has plenty of books about dinosaurs, and there are more being written all the time. The Internet is always buzzing with up-to-the-minute information on new finds. Documentaries and television shows about dinosaur discoveries are frequently being produced.

Best of all, you don't have to settle for just one opinion about anything concerning dinosaurs. Paleontologists often find different ways of interpreting new discoveries, which leaves room for *you* to become a paleo-detective yourself. Check out what they've found, and then form your own ideas.

But you'd better look sharp while you're digging around in the past, because you could get lost back there. Of course, that's really a big part of the fun—that and finding your way back again.

You never know, you might just have the time of your life. I sure did!

—Scott Ciencin

Prologue

The day he'd been waiting for had finally arrived. Bertram Phillips sat at the breakfast table, gazing at the feast he'd spent the last hour laying out for his dad.

Doc Phillips, as his dad liked to be called, was late. No big surprise. Bertram was used to his dad never showing up on time for anything. He made a habit of setting his dad's watch—along with his office and bedroom clocks—fast for that very reason. It still wasn't enough.

Mom had been the only one who could keep Doc Phillips on schedule. But Bertram and his dad had been on their own for a while now, so Doc was always late.

Bertram adjusted his thick glasses. At thirteen, he was small for his age, and a little round in places he wished he wasn't. His soft brown hair fell over his forehead and was content to not get up again. He had a kind face and was a "good-looking boy," or so his relatives would tell him whenever they visited. Which wasn't very often. Today, he wore his favorite outfit: a deep blue V-neck sweater with a powder blue T-shirt beneath, khaki pants, and earth-tone shoes.

1

He glanced up at the wooden dinosaur clock his dad had made. Instead of numbers, the clock's face displayed images of various dinosaurs who'd lived from one end of the Mesozoic to the other. Bertram could name each and every one of them.

He knew all about the Mesozoic, the age of dinosaurs, which so fascinated paleontologists and graduate students like his dad. The big hand was on the Icarosaurus, the little hand the Afrovenator. That meant it was ten past seven. His dad was *way* late.

Frowning, Bertram rose. He stuck the cookbooks back on the shelf and braced them with his dad's Velociraptor bookends. He opened the oven and used the "Bucky the Brontosaurus" oven mitt to take out the croissants—his dad's favorite—before they burned.

He left the kitchen, maneuvering through the small hall and the stacks of textbooks and paleontology magazines that were every-where, and went upstairs. He knocked twice on his dad's door, using the replica Nanotyrannus jawbone door knocker. No reply.

"Um…Dad?" Bertram called. "Dad, it's late. Time to get going!"

Bertram stood there, listening intently. Weird. His dad wasn't answering. He knocked again, then gently pushed open the door. He went inside and saw a heap of wrinkled white sheets sitting in the middle of his dad's abandoned bed.

There was more dinosaur paraphernalia inside, a ton more, but Bertram's gaze filtered out the tyrannosaur headboard and the col-lection of dinsaur models hanging from the ceiling. He figured his dad was in the bathroom, but when he checked, that room was empty, too.

Then he found the note. It was lying next to the lava lamp. He read the note three times, his heart sinking a little more with each go-around. It said:

Yo, Claw-Brother!

I just picked up an e-mail about a breakthrough on the site. It's around three in the morning now and I'm going to check it out with Bobo and Finch. It looks like we might have a pelvis bone from some kind of super-predator, something bigger than T. rex—bigger than Giganotosaurus, too!

I know you have your science fair today, and I'll do my best to be there. Later, you little troglodyte.

—*Doc*

Bertram sank to the bed. Tears welled up in his eyes. He forced them away, but a dead weight remained in his chest.

"He'll be there," Bertram whispered. "He'll be there…"

Putting the note aside, Bertram shuffled out of the room. There'd been no mention of his birthday. None. Worst of all, the note had been signed "Doc." Just *once* he'd like to find a note signed "Dad."

But he knew it wasn't going to happen.

Bertram plodded down the steps. He collected his books and went outside to wait for the school bus. A couple of neighborhood kids circled the wide street on their bikes. One of them noticed Bertram and yelled, "Hey, it's Blurtrum, the intelligent idiot!"

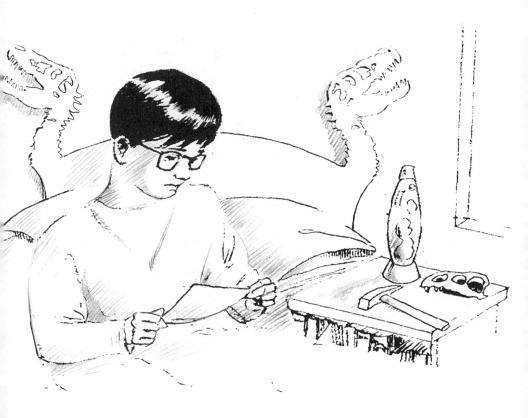

"No!" called another. "It's Bert-RAM—he's got a computer for a brain."

While the first two were taunting him, another let out a blood-curdling cry and sped his bike right at him. Bertram drew back from the charge in alarm. His attacker cut the wheel and blurred past.

A sudden flash flood of mud and gunk rose up, splattering Bertram from head to foot. He hadn't even noticed the puddle by the curb. His tormentors cackled and screamed, then took off in search of other prey.

"Predators," Bertram muttered. He went back in the house, showered, and changed into a plaid shirt—white T beneath—and his *other* pair of khaki pants and earth-tone shoes. By the time he got back out, the bus had come and gone.

He walked to school, arriving a little late. He was surprised to see long lines of students outside. The closest line was made up of kids from his homeroom. One of them, Mike Peterefsky, beckoned.

Mike was tall for his age, handsome, with strong cheekbones, warm blue eyes, and a friendly smile. Mike absently ran his hand through his brownish blond hair, which was cut in the same style as most of the football players. It was short, spiky on top, and shaved a little on the sides. As usual, he wore torn, baggy jeans and his older brother's varsity jacket. Beneath the jacket was a Tigger T-shirt.

A few of Mike's friends groaned as Bertram approached. One of them, Sean O'Malley, glared. Sean was tall enough to pass for a high school kid. In fact, he was the tallest guy in their entire junior high, and Mike's only real competition for the title of star football player. Sean had a little scar on his chin. His eyes were small, mean, glacier gray. Today he wore a tank top that showed off his muscular arms and shoulders, and he acted as if the cold didn't bother him.

Bertram froze.

"Come on," Mike said. He gestured for Bertram to come closer. Next to him, Sean shook his head and turned away, smacking Mike with his shoulder.

Mike looked at his teammate and buddy. "What?"

"Survival of the fittest. Remember that."

Mike frowned as Sean and a few of the other guys from the

football team drifted further up in line. Bertram moved closer, and Mike put his hands on Bertram's shoulders, then guided him into line ahead of him.

"Ms. Carol's gone to see why we haven't been let back in," Mike explained.

"Yeah, but I'm late," Bertram said. "I've gotta get a pass and—"

"You leave that to me," Mike promised.

Bertram knew he could trust Mike. Still, there was something in Mike's eyes. He seemed troubled. Bertram wondered what was wrong, but he didn't feel like he could just come right out and ask. Instead, he gestured at the line and said, "So what's going on?"

"We don't know if it was a fire drill or a false alarm."

A feminine voice intruded. "*Or* the real thing."

Bertram looked up suddenly. He nearly choked. The prettiest girl in the eighth grade was looking over from another line. Candayce Chambers.

"I mean, we can hope, right?" Candayce said.

Bertram gasped. He always gasped when she was near. Candayce was radiant. Bright, naturally blond hair trailed midway down her back, elegantly styled as always. A mild tan from her summer vacation in Florida. Rosy cheeks. Perfect teeth. Glittering green eyes.

Next to her was Tanya Call. Tanya's red beaded tank top exposed her temporary mehndi tattoos.

"How ya doin', ladies?" Mike asked.

Candayce absently brushed something from the shoulder of her pretty green and aqua blouse. "Looking forward to this geeky science fair thingee."

"Really?" Bertram asked. His heart rose.

The dark-haired Tanya leaned forward. "It gets us out of class, nimsey-doodle."

"Right," Bertram said. He looked away, stared at his shoes, knowing they weren't geek shoes, but feeling as if they were, since *he* had them on.

Suddenly, at the edge of his vision, he noticed Candayce was straightening her cloud-print skirt. He stared, feeling himself getting lost in those clouds. He hauled his gaze to her emerald eyes and watched as she confidently tossed her hair.

Spotting one of her rivals, Candayce frowned, her serene, heavenly expression turning to pure evil. Bertram knew it was time for Dish 101.

"Look, there's Plastica!" Candayce said, loud enough to make sure she was heard.

Tanya joined in. "Hey, Pam! Nice nose job!"

Their victim scurried away, cutting nervous glances over her shoulder while she cupped her hand over her nose. Mike sighed disapprovingly, but Candayce had gone into Terminator mode. She would *not* be stopped.

"Did you know she wears butt pads?" Candayce asked.

"Are you kidding me?" Tanya replied with predatory interest.

"About something like that? No way. And I saw little Miss Wombeley in the girls' shower the other day. Stretch marks *and* cellulite. Guess where."

Bertram tried to tune out what they were saying, but it was impossible. Candayce was the prettiest girl he'd ever seen, a goddess on the outside—but within, she was a carnivore. That particular knowledge was among the saddest he'd ever acquired.

"Oh, God," Candayce said. She covered her face with one hand. "*Major* loser alert."

Bertram looked up and saw Janine Farehouse approaching. She was short, with kind of a stocky, compact little rectangle of a body, black hair she seldom did anything with, and dark, knowing eyes that never missed a thing—though you wouldn't know that from the way she almost always seemed to be looking somewhere else. She was pretty, though Bertram knew better than to ever say that to her face. He tried not to even think it in her presence.

Janine wore a flannel shirt, blue jeans, and black boots. Her heavy key chain *chonked* and *chinged* as she walked by. She held it by the steel wolf key ring and flicked her keys on their long chain. Behind her was a teacher, Mr. Graves, hands on his hips, gaze cast down at his own lengthening shadow, head shaking violently from side to side.

Bertram didn't need to hear a word of what had been said to guess that Janine had been blamed for the fire alarm—and that she had talked her way out of it.

"Oh, look, it's the girl most likely to be living alone with five cats by the time she's twenty," Candayce muttered.

"I wish *I* could spend all my time changing sheets," Tanya added.

Bertram frowned. Janine's mom ran the Autumn's Fest bed-and-breakfast on the outskirts of town. Janine spent most of her time there or at school. Or getting into trouble.

Janine stopped and looked at the pair of girls. Candayce and Tanya tried to look tough, but each of them took an involuntary step back. Janine seemed to be doing more than looking at them. She was looking inside them. Making them shrivel. Words would have been redundant.

Smiling, Janine moved on, watching over her shoulder for a little while, until she cut through another line of students and disappeared.

"How do you ward off the evil eye again?" Candayce muttered, trying to make a strange symbol with her hand and fingers.

"No, like this, like *this,*" Tanya said.

Ms. Carol came to their line. She looked pretty distracted, even before she spotted Bertram.

Mike stepped forward. "Yeah, I was wondering why you didn't count Bertram present before. He raised his hand and everything."

"Oh," Ms. Carol said absently. "Um, sorry, right…" She turned. "Okay, class, it was a false alarm. They'll be letting us back in any time now."

Bertram turned to Mike. "Thanks."

Mike shrugged. "It's nothing."

Bertram smiled at Mike. That wasn't exactly true. The simple gesture of friendship had meant the world to Bertram.

By the time the students were let back in, it was almost twenty minutes after eight. Bertram was excused so he could go to the science fair. He got to the gym and made his way through the various exhibits until he came to the small tent Mr. London had helped him set up two nights before. With breathless anticipation, he slipped inside the tent and surveyed his masterpiece.

Bertram's M.I.N.D. Machine, his Memory INterpreter Device,

was a fabulous contraption. It stretched ten feet across, was eight feet high, and went back six feet. Dozens of computer screens were imbedded in its mishmashed mess of a face. Cables as thick as a man's arm and corrugated metal sleeves connected one mechanism to another.

At its center was a used office chair that had been cleverly disguised and remade as the Launch Seat. Rows of push-button controls and a pair of joysticks adorned the arms. A canopy of gadgets sat over the headrest, with little wires and suction cups dangling from them.

Bertram smiled. He'd seen many of the other exhibits. They were nothing compared to his masterpiece. So what if it was all an illusion?

Nearly every component in his machine was there just for show. At its heart was a simple biofeedback machine and a single functioning home computer. The PC was equipped with a CD-ROM that would feed images to the center monitor depending on what impulses were sent through the biofeedback sensor.

All the other computer screens had been rigged with monofilaments that would light up like bright Christmas tree lights, blinking and changing patterns—but not really doing anything at all. The rest of his machine had similarly been scavenged from junkyards and the garbage cans of computer stores across three counties.

Bertram had wired and welded together motherboards and various circuitry panels. He'd soldered discarded chips and cracked disks, making a monstrous, towering edifice that amounted to nothing more than a magic trick. But then, he'd learned all too well that appearance was everything. Adults liked to tell him it wasn't. But in his experience, it was.

Bertram frowned. He couldn't shake the feeling that the machine still needed something. But what?

Then it came to him. He pushed his collar back, pulled out his silver chain, and carefully removed his good-luck charm. It was a tiny T. rex bone his dad had found at their current site. Bertram opened a panel, slipped the charm inside, and sealed it again. He felt better. Now he knew the machine had every chance of working. His dad would be impressed.

Bertram could hear students being let into the gym. The tent flap rustled and Mr. London appeared. The science teacher had a receding hairline and sharp, hawklike features. But his stern looks were balanced by a warm smile and good sense of humor. Today, he wore a white shirt and a Coca-Cola Bears tie.

"Ready for the big day?" he asked.

Bertram nodded eagerly.

"Then let's take this tent down and get to business."

From somewhere close, a booming voice announced, "I am the Great and Mighty Groz!"

Bertram stuck his head out of the tent and took a peek at the exhibit at the next table. He saw a fortune-telling machine with a light sensor. Kids passed their hands over a violet ball and the model of a wizard turned from side to side and made pronouncements.

"Ask me your questions and I will reveal your destiny!" Groz gloated.

"Is Karl a doofus?" a boy asked.

Bertram heard the wizard turning. "You betcha!" Groz cried. Kids roared with laughter.

Bertram snickered. *This* was the competition? He had nothing to worry about.

Bertram hit a switch on the generator, kicking in the power supply. A low, rumbling *thummm* sounded. Lights blinked. Digital arrays raced back and forth. Strange images formed in the fake computer screens. The harsh fluorescents above dimmed for a moment. Then Bertram's M.I.N.D. Machine came to wonderful, glorious life!

A crowd gathered as Bertram and Mr. London completed the unveiling. Bertram shrank inwardly as he surveyed the sea of faces before him. He knew so many of these kids, but there was no one he could really call a friend. He looked beyond the clutch of fellow students, hoping to spot his dad, but he was nowhere to be seen.

His father's words rang hollow in his memory: *I know you have your science fair today, and I'll do my best to be there.*

"Everyone, um, hi. Thanks for coming," Bertram said nervously. He tried to recall the lessons Mr. London had given him about public speaking, but it didn't help. He felt so nervous he thought he might pass out at any second. His head was light, and he fought a rushing wave of dizziness.

Then, in the crowd, he spotted Candayce. She wasn't saying anything. Just smiling—at him!

No, not at him. Movement out of the corner of his eye alerted him. Bertram looked to a nearby window and saw Mike and a bunch of his buddies on the playing field, goofing around during their gym period with only some of their padding on. Mike caught a football and two guys tackled him in a classic hi-lo. Bertram had read all about the various plays. He winced as Mike went down hard, then sighed with relief as the two guys got off him and Mike popped up again with the ball.

Mike was *fearless*. He could take a hit, no matter how hard, and just keep going. Bertram wished he could be like that. He also wished, despite it all, that Candayce would look at him the way she was looking at Mike.

Someone off to his left cleared her throat. Bertram looked over and saw Janine. She was looking right at him, right into him, and somehow, it calmed him. He sensed she wasn't judging him. She understood. Understood *what* exactly, he wasn't quite sure. But she understood, and that was enough. She winked and made a subtle gesture, letting him know he should get on with it.

He nodded, bounced in place a little, then leaped into his speech. "Memories and dreams. We've all got them. For some, they're a secret thing. My machine, the Memory INterpreter Device, makes dreams a reality. It looks inside people, analyzes their memories, and shows you their dreams. So, who wants to go first? Volunteers?"

The mood among his spectators changed in a heartbeat. Suspicion replaced interest. Some kids started walking away.

"I'm not putting those sticky things on my head," Candayce said. "It'd ruin my makeup!"

Celia Brooks and her trademark Big Hat leaned over Candayce's shoulder from behind. The hat was at least a foot and a half high. "Yeah, and all the thing'd show is a blank screen."

Before Candayce could say anything, a shriek came from the audience. Joey Cirone's bare legs and boxer shorts immediately became the center of everyone's attention as he struggled to pull up his pants.

"Joey's low-riders fell down again!" someone hollered. Everyone started laughing.

Bertram knew he had to do something. Fast. "Just to show you how safe this is, I'll go first."

He turned and wired himself into the machine. All the biofeedback device could *really* do—so far as he knew—was send a signal that became more or less intense depending on his brain activity. The calmer he was, the slower the pulses the machine would spit out; the more upset, the faster. Bertram had rigged the PC at the heart of the M.I.N.D. Machine to roll various images from its writable CD-ROM, depending on how slow or fast the pulses were. Fast ones got more chaotic, crazed images, like mountain goats butting heads and football players doing the same thing, and slower ones triggered images of sparkling streams, cloud formations, sunrises.

Bertram strapped himself in with a seatbelt he'd taken from an auto graveyard, then quickly applied the little black suction cups to his temple. He took his glasses off and handed them to Mr. London. His teacher smiled, his face beaming with what Bertram took as genuine pride. It filled him with encouragement.

Bertram used the remote control on the chair's arm to engage the machine. Trumpets sounded. Music exploded. Lights whirled. He looked into the blur that was his audience and sensed that he had them. Every one of them.

Bertram hit another switch and began the flow of images. He heard laughter and applause from the audience, and the occasional hushed sounds of awe. It was working!

If only he knew *which* images were being projected. He couldn't control that, but he could control what kind of pulses his brain was sending out. He and Mr. London had worked out a routine.

First, Bertram thought of a place he'd like to go. A secret place. In his mind, Bertram pictured the tall, strange standing stones from the Late Cretaceous period that had been excavated near his dad's dig. It was the very place where his dad had found the tiny T. rex bone Bertram had placed inside the machine for luck. Doc Phillips spent his weekends there with his buddies, and he sometimes let Bertram come along for their "Brew and Bones" parties, though naturally Bertram wasn't allowed to drink.

He pictured being alone with his dad at the mysterious standing stones. He concentrated on the mental image. It was a peaceful waking dream. Heaven.

"Cool," someone said in the audience. Bertram smiled. He didn't know what the others were seeing on the main screen, but whatever it was, it had their attention.

Time for a change of pace. He decided to think about someone he admired. Someone he'd wished he was like. A little envy to speed up the action.

Bertram thought of Mike out on the playing field. Scoring a touchdown. Surrounded by pals. A jealous little spur formed in his heart, then was replaced by his admiration for what a decent guy Mike was. As the crowd around Bertram started cheering, thoughts of Mike faded into memories of Candayce. Her windswept hair. Glowing smile. Perfect eyes. Tingling, his heart racing, Bertram heard a bunch of guys hooting and hollering. The cheerleader reel must have gone up.

Bertram made the mistake of thinking about the things Candayce had said this morning. She was beautiful—the most beautiful girl he'd ever seen—but inside, she wasn't so pretty.

Gasps came from the audience. Bertram realized he had to get back to something more fun. He thought of Janine and wished it was possible to put what was inside her into the body of Candayce Chambers. One had the perfect body, the other the perfect soul.

Chill, Frankenweenie, he told himself. But from the oohs and ahhs of the crowd, he knew he'd chosen well.

He felt a strange warmth in his body and realized he was covered in sweat. His heart was really racing now. His mind followed. What was *happening?*

Suddenly, at the edge of his vision, he saw a man approaching. *Dad?* he wondered. Bertram didn't have his glasses on and couldn't see very far. All he could tell was that the man was short and had dark hair.

"Hey, it's going too fast!" a guy shouted from the crowd. "We can't see the pictures!"

Bertram only barely registered the complaint. Fear gripped him. Something was going wrong and his dad was going to see it! This couldn't be happening!

The M.I.N.D. Machine started shuddering. Bertram craned his neck to look at it. He squinted. Each dormant computer screen was broadcasting images. The images went past too quickly for him to make them out very well, but he had a sense that he was looking at dinosaurs. And all from the same period.

"That's...that's impossible. It doesn't make sense," he whispered. He hadn't put any images of dinosaurs on the CD. And he hadn't rigged those particular screens to show anything at all. Ninety-five percent of the machine was just junk!

Yet every single bit of the machine was in operation.

Terror overtook him. He unstrapped his seatbelt and reached for the sensors still clinging to his forehead—but it was too late.

A blinding light filled his vision and an explosion roared in his ears. Bertram was shocked to see tendrils of white flame reaching from his hands. One struck Candayce, another Janine, while a third and final bolt of rippling energy raced toward the window, where Bertram had seen Mike, and shattered it.

Bertram heard screams and the sound of breaking glass. Then he felt as if he was at the center of a tornado, being ripped and twisted away from all he knew. He was falling, tumbling, flying!

Then he was gone.

P
A
R
T

O
N
E

Cretaceous
Crunch

YOU ARE HERE

Millions of years ago	245	Triassic	208	Jurassic 145	Cretaceous	67

335 First reptile	230 First pterosaur	225 First dinosaur	145 First bird	65 End of dinosaurs	1.5 First man

Chapter 1

Bertram

South Dakota
67 million years ago

Bertram woke to find himself in total darkness. It took him a moment to get over the feeling of falling and accept that, for better or worse, he'd landed.

He smelled moist earth, rich leaves, and pungent moss-encrusted bark. His throat felt dry and scratchy. His skin felt odd. Kind of numb. And thick. Rubbery. All around him, insects buzzed.

It took him a moment to realize that his eyes were squeezed shut. That's why it was dark. Nervously, he opened them and found himself in a small clearing on a bright, sunny day. Around him were thick, round stumps and fallen, shattered trees.

What was he doing outside? he wondered. He tried to stand up and found that he couldn't. He was on his hands and knees, and his limbs were like four stone pillars. He was trying to understand what had happened to him when he noticed the trees some twenty feet ahead.

He was seeing the trees with perfect clarity, even though he wasn't wearing his glasses. That was jarring enough, but the true shuddering impact came when he *identified* these particular trees.

They were 200-foot-tall needle-encrusted Sequoiadendrons. In other words, they were twenty-story-high redwoods. Not the usual thing one saw in Montana. Or in the twentieth century.

Bertram squeezed his eyes shut and shuddered. *This is not happening. This is* not *happening!*

Then he heard a roar.

He opened his eyes.

He didn't see anything, but could *feel* thudding, jarring footfalls through the damp earth.

Whatever was making those sounds was coming this way!

Suddenly terrified, Bertram looked around for a place to hide. He was struck again by how acute his senses had become. His gaze locked on a beehive that hung fifty feet up on a redwood's limb. Bertram could smell honey. Racing along a lower branch, an opossum looked for midges and beetles to eat. And Bertram could see it. Smell it. Almost *taste* it.

The roar came again. Closer this time. The footfalls were getting louder. Bertram tried again to get up—and couldn't! He looked down at his feet, and what he saw nearly made him faint.

His feet weren't there. Instead, spaced farther apart than humanly possible, were two gray-and-orange wrinkled, scaly boots! Except—they weren't boots. They had nails at the end of them, like an elephant's feet.

Bertram tried to move his right hand, and one of the big, round feet stirred and came up off the ground!

His entire body quivered as he focused on the footprint that had been left in the earth. He now had a very good idea of exactly what had happened to him. But knowing a thing and believing it are two different matters entirely. Bertram *knew* he was a kind of pudgy eighth grader from Montana, yet he could barely *believe* that anymore, considering the evidence to the contrary. And that evidence now included slamming, crashing footfalls, which were coming closer.

Dead ahead, smaller trees toppled, then a dark shape appeared. A very *large* dark shape. It blocked a space between a pair of redwoods, avoiding the luscious streaks of emerald and amber light carving their way through the dense forest.

With a roar, the towering Tyrannosaurus rex burst into the clearing. In a blur of gray-and-blue scales, the predator came charging right at Bertram. He saw the rex's huge flashing teeth. There was no time to run, nowhere to go!

Bertram wanted to shrink down inside himself. Consequently, that was exactly how his body responded. His torso hunkered close to the ground, his chin mashed against his chest, and his arms and legs folded up beneath him. When the T. rex's maw came toward his face, he squeezed his eyes shut. The rex's breath *stank*. The predator roared again, and the sound was deafening!

Bertram shuddered inwardly. His backside automatically quivered. Then something attached to it rose up and slammed to the ground hard enough to make the earth tremble!

Silence filled the clearing. Bertram opened his eyes and raised his head. Just a little. The T. rex came raging at him, his massive jaws snapping.

"No, no, no, no, no!" Bertram screamed as he tucked his head back down. He made his body shake and shudder until *the thing* that was attached to his backside whacked the ground again. It kicked up dirt, causing the rex to jump back and away from him.

I don't like this game. I don't like this game, Bertram thought wildly. And yet there was a part of him that *did* like it. A brave, defiant part of him knew he was tough enough to handle the rex, as long as he didn't give in to the fear. He had no time to really think about that strange *other* part of himself he'd suddenly discovered. He had to *do* something.

Okay, then. Bertram was willing to accept, in light of not having become the T. rex's breakfast, that there was a reason his attacker hadn't just taken a bite out of his shoulder or back while he cowered on the ground.

Then it came to him: *He can't.* There was something there. Like armor.

His thoughts were a whirl: Tyrannosaurus rex. Lived sixty-five to sixty-seven million years ago. The very end of the Cretaceous period. What dinosaur at that time in history could actually give a T. rex a decent battle?

An Ankylosaurus. A club-tail. That had to be it! He was in the past, in the body of an Ankylosaurus, and the massive spikes covering his back and head were protecting him. A good thing, too, considering he was fighting for his life!

"Can't be any worse than junior high school," he muttered. The T. rex roared again and snapped his mighty jaws close to Bertram's face. "Forget I said that. I'm sorry, I'm sorry!"

The rex faded back a little. Bertram opened his eyes to a narrow slit but didn't raise his head this time. He watched the Tyrannosaurus peering down at his sides, where his vulnerable belly would appear if he stood up. Bertram slapped his tail on the ground and the rex backed off.

Whoa, Bertram thought. He could hardly believe he'd actually seen that. *He* had made a *T. rex* back away.

Bertram allowed himself to really feel his new body for the first time. He knew that an Ankylosaurus weighed about three or four tons, and that he was a plant-eater. That meant this body was all muscle. Not one ounce of fat.

Cool.

Not that he really wanted to find himself tossed back in time like this. Not really. But if it had to happen, it could have been worse. An Ankylosaurus could take care of itself. That was a lot more than Bertram had ever been able to do before in the pudgy little human body he'd left behind.

How could this have happened, he wondered. *Did the M.I.N.D. Machine—*

The T. rex roared and flew at him. Bertram realized that he'd raised his head. He tucked it down, closed his eyes, and whacked the earth with his tail again. The T. rex came close, but the spikes on Bertram's head prevented the predator from chomping down on him.

All right, Bertram told himself. *Think. There are only two options. Break this stalemate, or wait it out.*

As afraid as he was, he didn't think he could stand doing nothing. So he made his decision.

Bertram opened his eyes. He looked beyond the pacing, agitated T. rex. Only twenty feet ahead, past the mass of fallen trees and wide splintery stumps, was the forest from which the rex had sprung. *No way out there.* Bertram knew he would have to inspect the rest of the clearing.

Taking a deep breath, he rose up suddenly and attempted to spin himself around in a quick one-eighty. Moving in this body was a lot harder than he thought it would be. He wasn't used to the weight, or the power. He tripped over his own feet and went down hard. Miraculously, he didn't break any of his limbs. He hunkered down fast.

The rex was on him again, roaring and spitting and bellowing in hunger and rage. Bertram beat his tail on the ground and whipped it high in the air. The rex backed away.

Bertram had moved only a few feet, but it was enough. Now he could see a wall of tangled vines, dense bushes, and very tall trees. Between the lower reaches of the thick, high trees, roots and branches clung to one another to form a terrible barrier. But at the center was a way out. Sunlight poured through a single very low opening that screamed *Freedom! Escape! You can get through here, but the big guy can't! He'll be trapped on this side!*

All Bertram had to do was get there without getting eaten. If only there was some way he could distract the T. rex...

An idea flashed in his mind. Bertram concentrated, and managed to raise his tail straight up. The T. rex leaned his head forward and appeared to zero in on it. Then Bertram got his tail to sway gently from one side to the other. The T. rex's head followed the movements perfectly.

Suddenly, Bertram rose up and rushed forward, beating his tail on the ground as he charged the T. rex. He hollered defiantly! Startled and distracted, the predator leaped to one side to get out of the way.

Bertram saw the opening come closer, and he halved the distance separating him from it before the T. rex roared and came at him again. Bertram hunkered down and whipped his tail around. It smashed into the remains of an old tree trunk, sending chunks of wood flying, and distracting the T. rex once more.

Bertram lunged for the opening, but moving in this body was like scrambling on his hands and knees in a human body. He was slow—so slow compared to the blinding movements of the rex. As his head brushed against the curtain of leaves at the end of the corridor, he heard the rex's jaws snapping behind him. Quickly, Bertram pushed through the opening. The harsh sunlight on the other side blinded him. Even though he couldn't see what was ahead, he scrambled forward.

Suddenly, the ground tilted violently. His tail whipped around, striking a tree and sending wooden shrapnel high into the air. Then, with a shrill cry, he was sliding down a sharp incline.

Trees lining the hill whipped up in front of him and snapped as he struck them. His body banged against heavy rocks as he tumbled end over end, and he felt every bruising, jarring impact. Finally, he skidded toward the base of the incline. He flipped over one more time, onto his spiky back, his tail curled up and trapped under him. A cloud of dirt rose up as rocks and debris scattered down around him. Then it was over. He'd landed belly-up.

Bertram tried to move, but all he could do was make his front and rear paws wriggle in the air. An image came to mind: a sixteen-wheeler flipped onto its back, its wheels spinning helplessly. He wasn't going anywhere.

From somewhere above and behind him, Bertram heard the T. rex roar in frustration. All right, he thought, he'd gotten away from the rex. At least he had *that* much to be grateful for. Only—he was vulnerable like this, with his belly completely exposed. He tried to free his trapped tail, but all he could do was make it twitch.

Looking down, he saw that there was a small clearing at the base of the incline. It bordered another deep woods filled with Araliopsoides, which were lush, leafy ginseng trees rising about thirty feet.

Suddenly, he smelled something. A powerful scent similar to the rank odor of the predator from which he'd just escaped. Bertram gasped as heavy footfalls came his way. The ground shuddered. Thick tree branches snapped like twigs.

"No…" Bertram pleaded. "Please, no."

A shape appeared between two of the trees. Another T. rex! This one was emerald-and-rust-colored. But he looked just as big, just as fierce, and just as hungry as the last one.

"Please," Bertram whispered.

The T. rex lumbered closer. His maw hung open. He was drooling. The claws of his tiny little arms were making strange little clicking noises. Unlike the other rex, he didn't roar. He just kept coming on, closer and closer, the sunlight glinting off his dagger-shaped six-inch-long teeth. Bertram had seen fossils of teeth like these. He knew that each inch-wide tooth was able to saw through meat and puncture bone. The Tyrannosaurus's jaw was powerful enough to tear off as much as five hundred pounds of flesh at one time!

"Please!" Bertram yelled. "Don't eat me! *Please!*"

The T. rex came at him quickly now, opening his maw even wider. His teeth were inches from Bertram's exposed, quivering belly! Bertram squeezed his eyes shut.

"Pleeeease!"

He waited. And waited. Finally, he heard another voice. "Bertram, is that *you* in there?"

Bertram froze. His gaze locked on the rex's face. "Mike?"

The T. rex slowly nodded. Bertram's entire body sagged with relief. Tears formed in his eyes as he began to laugh.

He was no longer alone.

Chapter 2

Mike

Mike stared down at the vulnerable club-tail. Bertram looked so pitiful, wriggling there on his back, his belly exposed. He listened patiently as Bertram went on about his science fair project and some dinosaur bone he'd used.

"It was supposed to be for luck," Bertram said, shaking his enormous head. "But if my Memory INterpreter Device came to life and matched what it found in my subconscious with patterns from the molecular composition of that bone, well, that might explain why it sent us here."

"You mean you *wanted* to come here?" Mike asked. "You wanted this to happen? Why?"

Bertram snuffled. "I don't know. It's just a theory. Mr. London and I talk about that kind of stuff all the time. The collective unconscious. And the possibility of its extension to an organic memory. How the cycle of life on a molecular level stretches back to the origins of life in the universe. I mean—I didn't mean—I'm *scared*, Mike!"

Mike couldn't follow what Bertram was saying. He looked down at his tiny, scaled arms and shook his head, which whipped back and forth so quickly he became dizzy and wanted to sit down. Only he didn't know *how* to sit down as a T. rex. Or how he'd get back up again.

This world was so strange. The air was dense with insects. He didn't know if he could get used to the constant buzzing and humming. Bees landed on him. Bugs crawled all over him. Ants. Cockroaches. Disgusting! He shuddered and stamped in place, trying to knock them off.

Suddenly, a nearby movement, seen out of the corner of his eye, arrested his attention. A pair of rabbit-size hoofed animals moved closer. They looked part cat, part rat, and, well, part horse, tiny as they were. They crawled onto Bertram's belly and snatched away large leaves that were stuck to him. Then they kind of *galloped* away.

"Bertram?" Mike asked. "What was that?"

"A pair of Protoungulatums, I think. Forerunners of horses, antelopes, camels, and so on. Extinct now. I mean, then. Uh, later." Bertram growled with frustration. "In *our* time."

"Oh."

Silence walled itself up between them for a moment. Then Bertram said, "What if there is no way back? What if we're stuck here forever? What if—?"

"Listen to me," Mike interrupted.

"What if—?"

"*Listen to me.* You designed this machine, right?"

"Yeah, but not to do what—"

"Would you have built a machine that could only send us one way? Is that how you would have designed it?"

"Wha—uh—"

"I don't believe you'd have done that, Bertram. You're too smart. So there's got to be a way back. There must be. We just have to figure out what it is."

Mike felt a sudden rumbling inside him. A low growl came from his stomach. He was hungry. Without thinking, he took a step toward the writhing hot lunch before him and opened his gigantic, razor-lined maw.

"*Mike!*" Bertram screamed.

Mike stopped and got ahold of himself. "Sorry. Instinct."

"Uh-huh. Right. No problem," said the Ankylosaurus, but he was visibly trembling.

Mike closed his eyes. He wondered if now would be a good time for a nervous breakdown. This was crazy. How could he buy into any of it? An hour ago, by his reckoning, he'd been an athlete. The next Steve Young. That had been his dream. To one day measure up to his idol. His human body was a finely honed machine that had never let him down. He wanted it back.

And yet…a part of him was almost *relieved* to be here instead of in his own time, in his own body. So long as he was here, and not there, he didn't have to worry about the *Big Event* his buddy Sean had planned for today's practice after school. Mike had known about it for weeks—and had been sick over the whole thing just as long.

"Mike?" Bertram asked, sounding excited.

Mike opened his eyes. "Sorry. A lot on my mind."

"I think I've worked out how we're communicating. You're not really *hearing* anything when I talk, are you? We're like…made of thought. Pure energy. We're just brainwaves. And somehow we can hear each other. Guess it had something to do with the M.I.N.D. Machine. It linked us up."

"Okay."

"We still move our mouths when we speak, but it's just habit. If we make any sound at all it's just…" The Ankylosaurus made a weird clicking, grunting noise.

"Gotcha," Mike said.

Bertram suddenly waved his paws wildly. "Um, uh, Mike, listen. You think you could help me up? I mean, I can't stay like this. What if some other predator—"

"I'm not a predator," Mike said sharply.

Bertram trembled. "Mike, *please.*"

Mike nodded his head. He had to stop thinking about Sean. Sean and his talk of how they were all *predators,* and that, without a killer instinct, none of them would survive. Not one single member of the team.

"All right, let's get you on your feet." Mike reached out with his hands, forgetting they were now tiny two-fingered claws, and found he couldn't reach very far. He leaned forward, grasping with his claws, and banged heads with Bertram.

"Ow!" he cried, expecting a surge of pain in his skull. All he felt was a dull thud.

"I didn't feel much of anything," Bertram said thoughtfully.

"Huh!" Mike said. "Me either, really. Let's try it again."

"Um...okay."

Mike thrust his skull forward, colliding with Bertram's. There was a sharp crack.

"Cool!" said Mike. "It's like wearing a football helmet!"

Mike whonked his head against Bertram's several times and started laughing. "This is really something!"

Bertram rolled his eyes. "I hate being stuck like this."

"Oh, right. Sure."

"Hmmmm," Bertram said, "I was thinking...How about using your feet to turn me over? You've got those powerful legs. You can put your tail down and use it to balance. Try that."

Mike looked behind him and saw that he'd managed to keep his tail up. Some things just came naturally.

Mike forced his tail down on the ground, hoping to use it like a tripod, as Bertram had suggested. Then he balanced on one leg and dug his opposite foot into the pile of rocks and debris surrounding Bertram.

The moment he tried to kick upward, Mike lost his balance. He tried to use his tail to compensate, but, in his panic, he moved it in the wrong direction. The world spun. He hollered. A fierce roar escaped his throat as he pitched backward and landed with explosive impact, a cloud of dirt and rock flying up around him.

For a moment he just lay there on his back. *Some athlete I am,* he thought. Then he sighed and tried bending at the waist to reach a sitting position. It didn't happen. Instead, all he did was yank himself partway up, as if he were trying to perform a sit-up, then flop back to the ground. A deafening thunderclap of noise marked the attempt. He rolled to his side and tried to push off that way, but his arms were too little to be of much help. He gave a low growl of frustration. He tried again and again, but couldn't find a way to get up.

Mike lay back, panting. "I feel like such a loser."

"You're not a loser. If you were a loser, you'd have enough free time on your hands to memorize the names of every tree, shrub, and creepy-crawly thing in the Mesozoic."

"Bertram..."

"Forget it, Mike, just let me think. There has to be a way."

A minute went by, then Bertram said, "Try getting on your belly."

Mike slowly turned. It was difficult at first, because his tail kept getting in the way, but finally he managed it. He immediately tried pushing up with his claws, but all he managed to do was lift himself slightly. He flopped back to the ground and growled. A nest of cockroaches scattered. Things in the nearby woods shook the branches and made shrill sounds. Mike didn't want to know what they were. He sighed.

"It's okay, it's okay," Bertram said. "Don't worry about your hands. Your claws. Whatever. Try and get your legs up underneath you. Pretend it's track. You do track, right?"

"Sure. Football, baseball, track. Football's what I really love, but I've got to keep myself in condition—"

"Pretend you're trying to get into the starting position, only without your arms. Just your legs."

"Okay, I get it." Mike moved one leg, then the other. He drew them up under him, then managed to haul one foot under his belly, planting it firmly on the ground.

"There you go, you've got it!" Bertram cried.

Mike pushed off, and tried to get his other foot up in time. He swayed, slammed his tail down for balance—and lost it completely. He stumbled to one side, a nearby tree racing toward him. He put up his claws, hoping to grab hold of the tree for support. But when his full weight struck it, the tree bent backward, splintered with a high crackling, and fell over. Sharp bits of wood flew into the air. Mike roared with frustration as he hit the ground with the fallen timber.

"Chill," Bertram said. "This is doable. It's just going to take a few tries. Go on, give it another shot."

Mike tried twice more. He almost had it on the last attempt, then he went down.

"Come on, Mike. A winner never quits and a quitter never wins. You know that."

"Coach Garibaldi!"

"That's right."

"How do you know about that?"

"I've been to some games."

"Really? You?"

"Yeah, me. Even geeks like football."

Mike looked over at Bertram. "I never called you that. I never even thought that. Don't put words in my mouth. Especially not words like *that*."

"Sorry," Bertram said. "I hate being helpless like this. I feel so stupid."

"You're *not* stupid. Just wait."

It took Mike five more attempts before he managed to get to his feet. He tottered for a moment, then straightened himself out. *"I did it!"*

"All right!" Bertram cried. "Hey, tail off the ground!"

"Right. Thanks." Mike lifted his tail. "Now what?"

"Now flip me over!"

Mike's broad shoulders sagged. They were right back where they had started. Then he saw a three-foot-long turtle with a golden shell, peppered with pockmarks, ambling toward the trees. It had a long neck and a pointy nose, and it gave Mike an idea.

"Wait a minute," Mike said. "One time our whole family was camping. We found this turtle flipped over on its back, just like you are. When we tried to grab its shell to help it, the turtle snapped and bit at us. It didn't understand we were trying to help."

"So what'd you do?"

Mike walked over to the fallen tree. He glanced back to Bertram. "How strong would you say I am?"

"Plenty strong. Your arms can lift over 450 pounds."

"Good." Mike stomped the branches on the ground, breaking

them off. Then he bent low, wrapped his tiny arms around the log he'd made, and lifted it up.

"Tell me you're not..." Bertram said.

Grunting, Mike shoved the log up against the club-tail's flank. "I weigh too much!" protested Bertram. "This won't work! I'll end up being a shish kabob!"

"An Ankylobob, you mean," Mike teased giddily as he worked the makeshift fulcrum under Bertram's bulk.

"It's not going to work," Bertram repeated.

"Don't be such an Eeyore."

"Whaddya mean?"

"You know, in *Winnie-the-Pooh*. Eeyore. The donkey. The one who's always gloom and doom."

"The realist."

"Okay, that's it," Mike said with a laugh. "Now you're about to get a positive experience whether you like it or not!"

Mike dropped down onto the exposed end of the log. He knew Bertram was right—too much pressure and the wood would shatter. So he heaved his bulbous, flopping belly onto it and sank to his knees, driving most of his weight onto his end of the seesaw. Incredibly, Bertram's right side was lifted up into the air by several feet.

"Whoa!" the Ankylosaurus hollered. The log began to crack. Mike had been expecting this. He shifted his weight and, avoiding Bertram's spikes, drove his shoulder into the hard shell of the Ankylosaurus. He pulled one foot up under him, then the other, and heaved with all his strength!

"*Miiiiiiiiiiiiiiiiiiiiiike!*" Bertram wailed.

Bertram was now teetering on his side like a quarter that had fallen onto its edge. His legs were shaking. His head whipped from side to side. So did his tail.

"Bertram, you're going to hit me with your tail!"

The tail froze. Mike watched as the Ankylosaurus teetered one way, then the other. Mike had to do something. What?

An idea came to him. He went down on his knees again, knowing full well that if his new plan failed, he'd never be able to get out of the way in time.

Picking up the log he'd used as a fulcrum, Mike thrust it like a spear at Bertram's shell. It connected just as the club-tail's body began to sink back in his direction.

"Oh, no," Mike whispered. He stood up, putting all the power he had left into one final push.

A moment later, Bertram flopped over, onto his belly! He landed with a yelp of surprise, the ground thundering to mark his arrival.

Mike's tiny arms flew into the air. He whooped as he hopped from one foot to the other, slapping his tail on the ground in a victory dance. "Ooh, yeah! All right! Can't touch me tonight! Nuh-uh!"

Bertram watched, his head happily bobbing up and down. Then Mike's stomach growled again and Bertram stilled. "Okay, what do we do about *this?*" asked Mike. "T. rexes are meat-eaters, right? I mean—a part of me wants to eat *you!*"

Bertram took a half-step back.

"You know I won't," Mike assured his friend. "It's just—I'm not eating the locals. I don't care *what* this body wants. I'd rather starve. Really."

Mike looked at all the greens surrounding him. "Hey, I can just go vegetarian, right? Have a salad."

Bertram shook his head. "Your body won't run on vegetable matter. It can't digest it. That's why there were carnivores who ate meat and herbivores who ate plants."

"So what do we do?"

Bertram appeared lost in thought. Then his eyes lit up. "You and your family ever go fishing?"

"Um…sure."

"Then that's what we'll do. First, we have to find salt water. In the Cretaceous period, an inland sea divided the land that would become the United States. My new nose is pretty good, and I smell something that makes me think we're near the shore. But you're a lot higher off the ground. You should be able to figure out the exact direction. Your nose knows."

"My nose knows?"

"Your nose knows. Trust me."

Mike looked at him funny. *Your nose knows.* What did he mean by that? Mike took a deep breath—and found out.

"Whoa!" Mike cried. So many strange scents—information overload! His chest heaved and his body trembled as he tried to make sense of all the smells.

"Trust your instincts, Mike. It's just like you're playing football. Relax and go with your gut."

Mike's new Tyrannosaurus gut was the last thing he wanted to trust. But he was hungry, and a rough, growling, animal part of his brain was ready to separate all of those scents he'd just experienced into two essential categories: food and non-food. Bertram fell into the first category.

"Sea water…it's salty. Smelly. Think about that," said Bertram. "Try to concentrate on that."

"Okay," Mike said. He took another breath, not quite so deep this time. He pictured the beach, the tang of sea water, then he pointed with his stunted little arms. "The water's that direction. It's a ways off, but I can smell it."

His stomach growled. It was a low, deep, reverberating sound.

"We'd better get going," Bertram said.

Mike sniffed again. "That's weird. I'm smelling—don't laugh—"

"Tell me."

"I'm smelling *fear*. Something really terrified. Coming this way."

Bertram nodded gravely.

"And it's not alone. Whatever's scaring it is coming toward us, too." Mike sniffed one more time. "Bertram, the *whatever* that's scaring it?"

"Uh-huh?"

"There's a lot of *whatevers* on the way."

They both looked to the brush. A handful of blurry shapes were racing toward them.

Chapter 3

Candayce

Help meeeeeeeeeeeeeeeeeeeeeeeeeee!

Candayce Chambers plunged through the dense, buzzing, insect-infested woods, monsters at her heels.

Things that might have been roaches or rats scurried at her feet, but she didn't look down. She had a sense that other *things* were watching her from the trees and beyond, but she couldn't concern herself with them right now. Her pursuers were dinosaurs. T. rexes. Just like in the movies. Except—and this would have been the funny part if she'd been in a mood to laugh instead of scream—they were just little guys. Pint-sized!

Ha-ha. Big funny. They were trying to kill her!

All right, Candayce, she commanded herself, *you're going to wake up. Now!*

She didn't. So she ran. Branches snapped against her body, but she felt no pain, only a weird bloatedness. Ahead, she saw flashes of brown and green and amber. Tangled roots and soft blue-white daggers of sunlight. She sniffed. The whole area smelled bad. As if a thousand dogs had just been walked and there wasn't a pooper-scooper to be found.

Her legs moved awkwardly as she continued her flight. They

33

were strong and powerful, but thick and squat, like stumpy little tree trunks, if that made any sense. Of course, this was just a dream, and dreams didn't have to make sense.

Turning, she looked over her shoulder at the rexes heading her way. They were green-and-gray, their scales spotted and striped with dull purples and yellows. Their maws hung open, revealing rows of glistening razor-sharp teeth. Saliva sprayed in every direction. The monsters grunted and growled like football players chasing cheer-leaders after a winning game. Disgusting!

She ran faster than she ever had before, but it wasn't enough. She'd managed to outdistance her pursuers so far by going low and ducking through tangled networks of underbrush where they couldn't follow. But they always caught up.

She burst into a wide-open area at the foot of a large drop-off. Another pair of monsters rose up in front of her. One was short and squat, covered in spikes. It looked a little like a turtle, only it was about thirty times the size of any turtle she'd ever seen. The other was a giant T. rex. It was easily *twice* the size of the creatures closing in behind her.

She was trapped! No, she wouldn't accept that. Her sensei's words came to her: *In a crisis, always do the unexpected. Zig when your opponent expects you to zag.*

Under normal circumstances, Candayce wouldn't pay a whole lot of attention to the life lessons her sensei imparted. To her, mar-tial arts was just exercise. Punching and kicking. It was trendy, it was fun, and it let her get some of her anger out.

But these were hardly normal circumstances, so this time she listened. Tearing *between* the T. rex and the big spiked turtle thingee, Candayce was past the monsters and at the bottom of the incline in only a few seconds. She'd been hiking up and down mountains half her life and she wagered the dinosaurs chasing her wouldn't be any good at it.

"Candayce! Stop, wait!" the club-tail yelled.

She froze, but just for a second. It was a dream, so *of course* the big spiky turtle-looking guy would know her name. Why question any of it?

She resumed running, thinking about her therapist. Her therapist got a hundred dollars an hour, and part of his duties included helping her dispel bad dreams. He'd given her techniques for guiding the course of her night visions—staying in control of them.

None of the tricks she'd learned were working. The nightmarish scene remained in place.

"Candayce!" another voice. *Mike's voice.* It had come from the T. rex. She looked back despite herself.

Over her shoulder, she saw Mike—no, that couldn't be right, not even in a dream, it was just too weird—confront the half-sized rexes. He let out a roar that made her sink to her knees and place her hands over her ears.

Weird how clammy her skin felt. And dried-out. What she wouldn't do for some moisturizer. In fact, all of her skin felt hard and callused. And what was that weird *weight* she felt on her behind?

Something told her not to look, but she did anyway.

A long pastel-colored tail stuck out straight between her hips. It was attached to a reptilian-looking spine. Both were mustard yellow with pimento red toppings: stripes on the tail, spots on her back.

She looked down at her thighs and nearly gagged. What had happened to her? Her thighs were *enormous!* And she had a pot belly! And her chest was *flat.* Not to mention scaly. She had wrinkles and rings and lines and dents! And she was naked!

An instant before her mind could give out totally, an idea came to her: Someone had dressed her in a weird costume for this dream, that's all it was.

Well, she didn't like it one bit!

A chorus of growls dragged her attention away from what was *usually* her favorite topic—herself. And for once, she was glad. At least for a nanosecond or two.

She saw that forty feet away, Mike the T. rex was kicking rocks at the smaller rexes, scattering them. The spiky turtle guy was attacking them, too! He swung his club-tail and a couple of the little guys went flying!

Mike roared and slammed his tail onto the ground. The earth beneath Candayce shuddered. She heard a sliding sound from above and turned as rocks trickled down from the incline. He'd started an avalanche!

"Yow!" Candayce hollered as the rocks hit her head. Weird how the stones felt so light. They hardly hurt at all when they connected. The "avalanche" ended quickly. She studied the incline. It was constantly shifting. No way could she get a decent foothold. Looking back again, she saw the smaller rexes fleeing.

The big one turned toward her. Candayce was paralyzed by his gaze. She wondered if the only reason he'd fought off the other creatures was so that he could have her for himself. For breakfast.

You're not going to faint, she told herself, even though her head was feeling light. *You're not going to do anything that—that—girly...Do you hear me?*

Girly? she immediately chided herself. *If Mike Tyson was looking at* that, *he'd be laid out, too!*

The giant T. rex took a step her way. "Candayce, it's me. It's Mike. You don't have to be afraid."

This was too funky. Too much for anyone to expect her to be

able to handle. Why couldn't she wake herself up from this bizarro dream? The T. rex came a little closer. The ground shuddered with his approach.

Candayce suddenly became aware of two very different sets of instincts within her. One set of instincts told her to trust Mike. He was always a nice guy. Too nice for his own good half the time, but that was another story altogether.

The other set of instincts told her to run like the wind and not look back under any circumstances.

One set of instincts was hers. The other wasn't.

Candayce stood still. "Mike?"

"It's me. The guy with the tail is Bertram."

"But you're dinosaurs."

"Yeah. It's going around."

Candayce wondered what he meant by that. Then she looked over her shoulder and down at her tail once more. The tail was twitching. *She* was making it twitch.

"Oh, no," she whispered. "No, no, no…"

Candayce held her hands up to her face. They weren't hands. Not exactly. They were scaly paws. Or claws. Kind of. Three sharp fingers and two other stubby things that formed a, well, a *hoof*. Like a horse might have.

She tried touching her face. The hardened scales were there, too. She had a ridge over her forehead. Like an upturned collar. Her jaws were like a set of pliers, only sharp at the tip. She had some kind of beak or something. Her lips were gone. Her hair was gone. Her pert, petite little nose was gone.

Her head felt light again. She sank down and landed on all fours. That *other* set of instincts inside her told her this was a natural position.

"Oh," she said. Followed by an "I," then a "what?" followed by a handful of words she never used when other people were around, ending with a strangled, tear-filled cry.

"I'm ugly and I'm naked and I'm covered with bugs. There are bugs crawling all over me!"

"I know. It's annoying."

"Annoying? Annoying doesn't begin to cover it! What am I, some kind of *animal?*"

"Actually—" Bertram began.

"Shut up! Just shut up!" Candayce wailed. She fell back and squatted, trying her best to cover her chest. "I'm a monster."

"Actually," said the club-tail as he came forward, "you're a Leptoceratops. A crested dinosaur. Distinguished by the parrotlike beak and the Triceratops-like body construction."

"No, no, no," Candayce repeated. "This is a dream and I'm going to wake up."

"It's not," Mike said. "It's not a dream. I'm sorry. We're...we're stuck here. At least until we can figure out a way back. It's a long story."

"No, no, no," Candayce continued.

In reply, the spiky turtlelike club-tailed meandering know-it-all dinosaur thingee said, "Just in case you were wondering, those dinos who were chasing you were Nanotyrannus. Pygmy dinosaurs. There's speculation as to whether they're just young T. rexes or a separate genus. *Controversy,* actually, but with paleontology, that kind of thing happens."

"No, no, no," Candayce said once more. She suddenly felt as if her mind was lost in a whirlwind.

"Help! Help! I can't fly! Help!" The sharp, piercing cry came from above. Candayce didn't look up. She knew that voice. It was *Janine.*

Suddenly, Candayce realized she was trapped. In the past. In the body of a gross little dinosaur. With Mike. And some geek. And Janine, the Wicked Witch of the Eastern Flats.

"No, no, no," Candayce chanted again. She wanted to run. Only her feet wouldn't move. Her body wouldn't move. Her eyes just went kind of glassy.

No, no, no, she thought.

Then she didn't think anything else.

And she was happy.

Chapter 4

Janine

Janine Farehouse could see her reflection in the waters below. She knew what she had become. And she knew she wasn't dreaming.

She was a Pterodactyl. Her wings were dark crimson and Day-Glo blue, and they stretched fifteen feet from tip to tip. She had claws—but no teeth.

And she was flying. Or so she'd told herself, until she realized that she had confused *flying* with *falling*. Even though she was soaring evenly through the air, she was also descending rapidly—at high speed. The world was flashing past in a near blur.

She screamed!

Panic took over. She flapped her wings, an activity that hadn't even occurred to her until this very moment. The world flipped over a half-dozen times and she plunged straight down like a heavy weight tossed out of a 747. She would have screamed if she hadn't suddenly felt so sick to her stomach.

The water reached up for her, glassy and smooth. Hard as diamond. She could see her own reflection perfectly—or the reflection of the sleek, magnificent flyer in which she was unfortunately residing. It was like falling into a mirror.

A crazy thought came to her. She wished she had her markers, her spray paint cans. Her fat Magnum 44 black would be choice. Or maybe something in a German Fat Cap. She wanted to cover the flat surface barreling up at her with graffiti. She could turn it into a real burner, a true piece of art. She could picture it now: This solid wall, covered in wild colors. She'd be proud to leave her tag here, just the way she did on the buses and buildings back home.

The surface of the water rippled. The hypnotically pleasing illusion of a solid surface melted and vanished as two huge emerald-and-onyx bumps rose from the waters. Then a twenty-six-foot-long neck unfurled, writhing and whipping about like a snake. The head at the end of the neck snapped its mass of shining, needlelike teeth at the precise spot where Janine would soon plunge.

Janine freaked. She twisted and turned. She wriggled her long arms, and by extension her wings. She tried to flap, tried to sail, tried to soar, but she couldn't break free of this terrible descent. The sea creature below snapped its maw a few more times and ground its teeth together in anticipation.

Without warning, Janine went cold. Her emotions turned off. Her fear cut out. She studied the situation calmly, determined to think of something.

This sort of thing had happened to her only twice before in her thirteen years. Once, when news came that her father had been killed overseas and she had to be strong to hold her mom together. And another time, when she and her older cousin were on the Hi-Line, good old Highway 2, and a blowout sent them careening toward a Montana double-date—two guys and two dogs sitting in the cab of a midnight black pickup truck. Without a single tremor of fear, she'd analyzed the situation, seized the wheel from Margie, and saved both their lives.

It was time to grab the wheel again. She looked calmly at what was happening: She was in the body of a Pterodactyl and she was falling to her death. *She* didn't know what to do. But there was a safe bet that this body still held a prior occupant. If so, it was the only chance they both had now.

Janine searched inside. A consciousness rose up. It was the buried mind of the Pterodactyl. Janine surrendered herself totally. The Pterodactyl inside her sensed a current of air ten feet over the snapping head of the sea creature. The flyer spread her wings and angled herself into the draft.

This is going to work! Janine told herself.

There was a sound, like a parachute suddenly opening, or a massive sheet being whipped by the wind—

Thhhhhhhhhhhhhhwwwwwwaccccccccccck!

Then came a yanking, a jerking, and the rustle of wings, and Janine was being lifted up and away from the danger! She heard the angry cry of the sea creature, and an incredible splash below. Out of the corner of her vision, she saw a mighty shape burst from the water—but she didn't care. She was sailing away, the wind catching hold of her hollow bones.

The momentum she'd gained from the sudden nosedive robbed her of the chance to ascend toward the heavens. All she could do was glide to a landing, skipping along the frothy water, until she came to a rest on the surface.

She spun in a slow circle, relief flooding through her. Then, slowly, a nightmare came into view: The sea creature was only a hundred feet away. Its head and neck were raised, its rounded back arched in a hump. Pairs of flippers in the front and the rear slapped at the water.

Janine had seen this particular monster before. Or something just like it. Images from grainy old photographs entered her mind.

Nessie. *The Loch Ness Monster.* A prehistoric creature, where Janine came from. A not-so-friendly native here and now.

Janine dimly recalled reading a book when she was nine about a pair of children who had wondrous encounters with Nessie. Somehow, that book had left out a lot about the Elasmosaurus's predatory nature and very, very sharp teeth.

Janine's calm vanished. So did the mind of the Pterodactyl. Logic told her that if there was any way out of this, the Pterodactyl would have at least dropped a clue before it split.

It hadn't. She was fish food.

Suddenly, a shadow fell upon her. It wasn't the Elasmosaurus. Janine looked up and saw another Pterodactyl whipping over her, flying straight for the sea monster's huge head!

The newcomer was golden with streaks of gray, blue, and

scarlet. He loosed an ear-piercing scream and soared to the right, and then to the left.

Nessie was fascinated. The creature turned to see the new Pterodactyl sail past, spin, then perform a perfect figure eight. Nessie snapped and bit furiously, but the tricky newcomer always remained out of reach.

"Janine, swim for it!" someone called. She recognized the voice. She was about to reply, "Bertram?" when it occurred to her that it didn't matter who was delivering the advice—she'd better just take it!

Paddling, she turned herself in the water and looked toward shore. In the distance, she could see a T. rex and an Ankylosaurus trying to get her attention.

She didn't know much about paleontology—not like Bertram—but she knew enough to recognize that the rex and the club-tail were natural enemies, stemming from very different branches on the tree of life. Yet there they were, standing side by side as if it was the most natural thing in the world. What the heck was going on here?

A roar sounded behind her. She craned her neck and looked back to see her tricky Pterodactyl friend dive right into the Elasmosaurus's reach, then dart away at the last second.

Nessie looked frustrated. The game was no longer fun. She wanted prey she could actually capture. She wanted *Janine*.

Janine swam. She paddled and kicked, nearly submersing herself twice. She heard the sighs of the waves turn to hisses and roars as they rose and fell angrily behind her. She could almost *feel* the Elasmosaurus closing in.

Suddenly, a pair of fins cut through the water beneath her raised wing. A dark gray shape glided beside her, and something slapped her back. Janine froze as the waves revealed an Ischyrhizz, a seven-foot-long saw shark.

Oh, good, she told herself, *a killing machine with a Ginsu knife attachment. Mother Nature must have been in a funny mood the day she created this one.*

The shark dove beneath the water. Janine relaxed but only a little. The waves were driving her to shore. She looked back and saw the other Pterodactyl, whom she now thought of as the Trickster, diving in close enough to scrape at Nessie with the tip of his wing.

Enraged, the Elasmosaurus forgot about her pursuit of Janine for a moment and went back to snapping at the Trickster. She nearly snagged him with her first try, and Janine suddenly feared for her mysterious savior.

"Over here!" she hollered at Nessie. "You stupid old, stupid…"

She couldn't come up with an insult. Not for a fish. Or a water-bound mammal, or whatever it was. People—fine, no problem. But trying to dis a fish was beyond her.

It didn't matter. Nessie heard her insults. Or she heard *something*, anyway. Janine understood that she wasn't making human sounds. She was making the same piercing cries as the other Pterodactyl.

Nessie turned toward Janine. Another great tidal wave rushed up, carrying Janine a dozen feet into the air. Like a surfer, she was hurled over the water for an instant, then slapped down and nearly tugged under.

A pair of five-foot-long sharks sailed beneath her, apparently fed and disinterested. Thank goodness.

Slow-moving, four- to six-inch-long invertebrates in mother-of-pearl shells swam by, their cilia flickering. The sun bounced off their iridescent shells, creating a rainbow of color. Eight-inch-long lobsterlike Linuparus with spiny, armored segmented bodies drifted near. A school of blue-colored fish sped around her. Their jaws were filled with curved and interlocked elongated teeth. They attacked smaller jelly-bodied fish.

Janine wanted out of there! She kept swimming, hard and fast, watching the sand beneath the water rising up, higher and higher...

Finally, she looked back and saw the Elasmosaurus stuck several yards back in the deep. She wanted to laugh and cry in triumph! She'd made it. She was safe!

Then, Nessie's great neck suddenly extended, all two dozen feet of it, and the hungry head came down at Janine.

Janine screamed! And the T. rex let out the loudest, most frightening roar Janine had ever heard. Nessie froze.

"Janine, now!" Bertram's voice cried. "The shore! Now!"

Using her wings as paddles, Janine covered the last few feet separating her from the beach. Trembling, she walked onto shore with her spindly but strong rear legs, then folded her wings around her like a cloak.

Shells of every description littered the shore, painting it in stunning colors. Funnel-like shells, clam-shaped, teardrop-shaped, and a few that looked like small round castles, all mixed together with wreaths of coral. Her feet crunched as she walked. Tiny hermit crabs, little more than an inch long, scampered nearby. Mollusks, limpets, snails, and a few of the lobsters were scattered about.

She turned back to look at Nessie, who railed in frustration, snapped her jaws at the other pterosaur, then slipped back beneath the waves.

"Are you okay?" Bertram asked.

Janine faced the club-tail and his T. rex companion. For the first time she noticed that another dinosaur lay at their feet. It was an ugly, squat, garishly colored little thing with a parrotlike face and a nasty set of thunder thighs. Its eyes were glassy and it drooled a little.

"Yeah," Janine said. "I'm okay."

Above, a great sharp *caw* sounded. Janine looked up to see her new friend circling overhead. The Trickster looked down at her, then regarded her companions with a look that Janine somehow felt was disdain. With a snort, he flew off, dive-bombing the Elasmosaurus one last time for good measure.

Janine looked nervously at the T. rex, then back to Bertram. "Friend of yours?"

The Ankylosaurus angled his head in the T. rex's direction. "Mike Peterefsky. Yeah, he's friendly enough—for a predator."

"I'm not a predator," Mike automatically said with a weak sigh. Then he looked with concern toward the small, lumpy, yellow-and-red dinosaur at his feet.

"I hope I wasn't too rough with her," the T. rex began. "I had to carry her in my claws, y'know, by the leg, upside down, the whole way. I didn't know how else to get her to come with us. I couldn't just leave her."

"You should have seen it," Bertram said, "Mike dragged *me* the whole way by putting my tail in his mouth. He chipped a bunch of teeth doing it, but—"

"We're dinosaurs," Janine said.

"Yep," replied Bertram.

Janine gestured to the glassy-eyed Leptoceratops. "Who's Thunder-Thighs?"

"Candayce Chambers," Mike said.

Janine's head sunk to her chest. The rustle of wings surprised her, but only a little. She was already getting used to this. "What happened to her?"

Mike threw his little T. rex hands into the air. "She just kinda…checked out. I'll carry her, though. It's no problem."

Janine looked back to the horizon, where the Trickster was heading. "So who's he?"

"What do you mean?" Mike asked.

Janine gestured in the other Pterodactyl's direction. "Which lucky eighth grader is that?"

Bertram cleared his throat. "I believe he's indigenous."

Janine was surprised. Her savior was the real thing. An actual Pterodactyl. "Smart sucker. Tricky."

She looked back at the Elasmosaurus frustratedly kicking around the waves. Then she saw its head dip beneath the water and come up with a wriggling four-foot-long shark. It turned, happy enough, it seemed, and swam off.

"Yeah," she said, "this place is really crazy, I'm really enjoying myself…so will someone *please* tell me what we're doing here, why we can understand each other when we're not really talking out loud, and what we have to do to get home?"

The T. rex and the club-tail were silent for a moment. Bertram spoke first. "We're working on that."

Suddenly, a crackling sound made everyone jump. Janine looked up, expecting to see lightning streaking across the sky. But there was nothing. No, that wasn't entirely true. She heard a low, deep humming, and it was accompanied by a tingling at the back of her skull.

"Guys? Do you feel—"

Before she could finish, a second crackling and the sense of some alien force rippled through the air all around them. It was electric. Terrifying!

A voice rose out of the crackling:

"Bertram! Bertram, can you hear me? I pray that you can. This is Mr. London. I know what's happened—and I think I can help..."

Chapter 5

Bertram

Mr. London's words energized Bertram. "I can hear you!" He waited. There was no reply. "Mr. London, I can—"

The crackling came again.

"I don't have much time. I don't know if this will work or not. It's a one-way transmission, so don't bother trying to respond. Just listen."

Bertram fell silent and waited, the gazes of the others upon him. As usual, Janine's seemed to penetrate his soul.

The voice went on:

"Bertram, what I'm about to say may sound odd, even confusing at first, but hear me out. If my calculations are correct, then for you, the accident that sent you and the others into the past has just happened. But for me, it occurred over sixty years ago. I'm not the Mr. London you once knew. I'm a very old man. I'm from what you would think of as the future. One possible future, anyway.

"In my reality, after the lightning struck you and the other students, all four of you collapsed and appeared to be in comas. For the past sixty years of my time, you've remained that way."

"No," Bertram whispered. He looked at Mike, Janine, and Candayce. They appeared equally shocked.

"You can't just tell us that," Mike hollered. "You can't—"

"There's no hope," Janine whispered.

"Stop it!" Bertram cried. Mr. London was still talking and he was missing things that were being said.

"I've spent my whole life trying to understand what caused your M.I.N.D. Machine to evolve and transform into a vessel capable of extracting the true essence of a human being from his or her body and sending it elsewhere in time to live in the physical form of another. From the machine's records, I know that's what happened. Even so, the closest explanation I can come up with is the theory of the twelve monkeys."

The twelve monkeys. Bertram and Mr. London had discussed this. He knew precisely what his teacher meant, but this was no time to dwell on it.

"The most important thing for you to understand is that my time is not the only time. My reality is not the only reality. According to the M.I.N.D. Machine, no transmission from the past, present, or any possible future ever reached you in the Late Cretaceous. That means if you are hearing this message, the past has already been changed. Your course has been altered. It's proof positive that the last sixty years I've lived can be undone. Now it's up to you.

"Bertram, for you and the others to get back home, you must find the Standing Stones, and you must do it

quickly. You don't have much time. If my estimates are correct, you have about ten to twelve days and a great deal of ground to cover. Along with this message, I'm downloading a map that may help you."

Bertram could feel something entering his mind.

"As to how accurate this map is, I cannot say. All I can do is wish you luck and say that I believe you can do this. Try, Bertram. For all of us, try and change the past.
"There's one more thing I have to tell you, something you must know, or else you may not make it back! Remember—"

The crackling faded. The transmission suddenly stopped. The teenagers stared at each other. They waited for the transmission to continue, for a second message to arrive.

The silence deepened.

"I think that's it," Janine said.

"Wait!" Bertram cried. "I know Mr. London. He wouldn't leave us hanging like that."

They waited. The silence became monstrous. It weighed on them, pressing down upon them from every possible angle.

"Comas," Bertram whispered. "We end up spending our whole lives in comas. We miss everything." He looked around frantically. "My dad. My dad can't manage on his own, he—"

"That's only if we don't make it back," Mike said firmly. "We will. Don't doubt that for a *second*."

Bertram nodded slowly. Mike sounded so confident. Bertram wanted badly to believe him.

Then Mike looked away and hung his wide head. "Course, if we don't..." He shuddered. "My dad—my dad'll be okay. He'll just keep going, put all his energy into the business. Construction business, y'know? Peterefsky Builders. But my mom. And Lee. My older brother, Lee, will probably have to come home from college. Probably *has*. I mean, it's already happened, right? We've already failed—"

"Stop it!" Bertram said, terrified. "Please."

Mike looked up at him. "Sorry. Guess I kinda lost it there."

Janine opened her wings. "I don't want to think about this, I don't want to talk about this. It doesn't do us any good. We know what's at stake. What we have to figure out is what's our first move."

A loud rumbling slowly erupted from Mike's belly. Janine and Bertram looked his way. The sound came again. Even louder this time. Janine started to laugh.

"Stop it, we have to be quiet!" Bertram snapped.

"Tell *him* that." Janine broke into a loud guffaw as Mike's stomach again made its presence known.

Mike looked away. "This is so embarrassing…"

"You're embarrassed?" Janine asked. "At least you're a T. rex. I'm a flying reptile who doesn't know how to fly. A Pterodactyl who can't—"

"Actually," Bertram said distractedly, "you're a Quetzalcoatlus. Fairly young, I'd say. Your wingspan full-grown would be about thirty-six feet. You're the last and the most perfect of the pterosaurs. The pinnacle of evolution. And, as far as flying is concerned, you should try to get used to gliding first."

"Oh." Janine blinked. "Oh, okay. The *pinnacle,* huh?"

"Yes."

She nodded toward Candayce. "And what's she?"

"A Leptoceratops. Fairly common."

"Really? Hmm. This might not be so bad after all."

Bertram looked around forlornly. "There isn't any more to the message, is there? That's all Mr. London could transmit?"

"My guess is for now, yeah," Janine said.

Bertram was silent for a long time, taking that in.

"What did he mean about the twelve monkeys?" Janine asked.

Bertram blinked. "There's an old saying. If you put twelve monkeys in a room with twelve typewriters for a thousand years, eventually one of them will write *Hamlet.* It's about random chance. I think what Mr. London was getting at was that if I'd tried to build a machine that could do what the M.I.N.D. Machine did, the odds would have been a trillion to one against it. Probably a lot worse than that. But somehow, without even trying, I put together all the right parts, in all the right ways. Just by pure random chance, I beat the odds. Still, I can't help but think that there's more to it than that. In fact—"

"Listen," Mike said sharply. "Coach Garibaldi has a saying: 'What is, is. Deal with it.'"

"That's progressive," Janine muttered.

Bertram bobbed his head. "Actually, it is."

Mike's stomach growled again. He turned away and slapped his tail on the shore.

The impact made Janine stumble from her feet and land on her back.

"Oh, no, not this again," Bertram muttered, recalling his own painful and frustrating attempts at righting himself.

Janine popped back up without hesitation.

"That's amazing!" Bertram exclaimed. "How'd you do that?"

Janine looked at him strangely. At least, it seemed strange to him. "I just...stood up. It's no big whup."

"This is incredible. You must have established a much greater rapport with the resident mind in your host body than either Mike or myself. This is wonderful. You can help us—"

"*Bertram,*" Janine said.

"Um...yeah?" asked the excited club-tail.

"I stood up. That's it. Let's not throw a parade over it, okay? We've got bigger issues to deal with."

"Right, right, right," Bertram said.

Mike's stomach went again. He shuffled a few yards from the others and shook his tiny claws in the air. "Oh, man!"

"Okay," Janine said in a take-charge tone, "the way I see it, we need to get him fed so he doesn't go native and start picturing us wrapped in hot-dog buns—"

"Hey!" Mike said.

"No offense," Janine added. "But my host, or whatever, is pretty passive. I have the feeling yours isn't."

Mike's head sunk low. "Yeah."

"She's right," Bertram said. "Our bodies are like massive engines. Like any kind of engines, they require fuel."

Janine nodded. "Yeah, I could go for a little something, too.

Nearly dying and everything was kind of exhausting." She laughed. "Once we get some grub, or maybe on the way, we can talk about all this. I'm assuming you've got some idea what direction we need to go to reach the Standing Stones, whatever they are."

"Yeah," Bertram said. "In fact—"

Suddenly, a lower, bassier growling sounded. Bertram almost dismissed the sound, assuming it was coming from Mike. Then he identified the direction of the noise and looked over at Candayce, who was staring out at the waves.

Janine looked sharply in her direction. So did Mike.

Candayce's beak was opening and closing wordlessly. A tear was forming in the corner of her eye.

Images of food registered in Bertram's mind. He could *see* steam rising off a plate full of mashed potatoes. He could *smell* the rich aroma of sautéed mushrooms and onions spread over an expertly cut filet mignon. *Taste* the sweet perfection of a crushed watermelon ice drink…

Snap out of it! he chided himself. He shook his head and dismissed the images. Mike and Janine's mouths were literally watering. Their eyes appeared a little vacant.

"Guys?" Bertram squeaked.

Janine looked over dreamily. Mike's upper lip curled back, showing his shiny teeth. He stared at Candayce as if she were the meal that had apparently just been projected into all of their minds.

"*Guys!*" Bertram hollered.

Mike started, then drew back in alarm. "Oh, *man*…"

Janine looked over. "Hot-dog buns?"

Mike nodded, and Janine tapped Mike's back with one wing. "Look, Mike and I are the meat-eaters. You and Candy Cane over there are the plant-eaters, right?"

Bertram nodded. Janine's ability to plumb the knowledge of her host's mind was astounding. That—or she had read up on paleontology. Either way, she was dead on.

"Fine," Janine said. "You take Sleeping Beauty into the woods, get her to eat some greens. Mike and I will stay here and do some fishing."

"Okay," Bertram said. He was edgy, still waiting, still *praying,* that more of Mr. London's message would arrive. But somehow Janine's calm attitude was becoming infectious. He looked at Candayce, hoping he wouldn't have to drag her the way Mike had earlier. "Come on, Candayce. There's a nice garden salad waiting for us this way."

He took a few slow steps toward the trees in the distance. Candayce's head wobbled in his direction.

"Do they serve Caesar? I like Caesar salads," Candayce murmured hazily.

"You bet," Bertram said. "Come on."

"Okey-doke." Candayce rose unsteadily and followed Bertram. He took one look back at Mike and Janine, then walked with Candayce into the woods.

It occurred to Bertram, for only a moment, that this was kind of like a date. He'd known Candayce all his life, but this was the first time he'd really been alone with her. Though the circumstances couldn't have been any more bizarre, he was actually looking forward to the experience.

Chapter 6

Janine

The sun torched the horizon as Janine walked toward the water with Mike beside her. When a birdlike cry rang out, she looked up, wondering if the Trickster had returned. He hadn't. Instead, from far down the beach, a pair of purple ducks waddled toward her and Mike. Only they really weren't that far away after all.

"They're *huge*," Mike said.

Janine nodded. "I think they're called Hesperornis." The purple ducks were over five feet long. They had sharp teeth in their beaks. Mike growled at them, and they changed direction. They moved into the water, swam out a decent distance, and dove as if rocket-propelled. Moments later, they emerged with mouthfuls of fish. Then something huge—a gray blur with bigger teeth—exploded from the water, snatched them up, and hauled them under for good.

"There's probably some smart remark I could make here," Janine said.

"Duck?" Mike offered feebly, lowering his head a little.

"Right." Janine glanced back to the trees in the distance. "Do you really think Bertram and Candayce will be okay?"

"Oh, sure. If they run into anything, all they have to do is yell.

We'll hear 'em. I'm fast. To be honest, I can't believe how fast I can go in this." He gestured down at his emerald-and-rust-colored bulk. "And Bertram's got that tail. He could use some practice swinging it."

Janine laughed. They waded a few feet into the water. "Keep an eye out for me, okay? I saw sharks before."

"All right," Mike said.

A strong wind rushed over the crashing waves. Janine looked down, and a rainbow of color flashed beneath her. She poked her gigantic, storklike beak into the waters.

"Ow!" she hollered as her beak struck a rock. The jarring impact reached all the way back to her skull and stunned her.

When she looked back to the waters, the fish were gone.

"Sorry," Janine said. "I'm not used to judging distances too well."

"It's okay," Mike said. "We're all gonna need some practice sessions before we make this team."

Janine felt a sudden unease, but didn't know why. It wasn't because of being in this strange new body. She was adjusting to that. So, what was it?

She looked over at Mike and saw something in his eyes that told her exactly where this feeling had come from. She was getting a sense of his emotions. It was actually pretty overwhelming.

"Do you want to talk about it?" Janine asked.

Mike looked startled. "What?"

"Something's bothering you. I can tell."

Mike's little claws went up. "It's this whole thing…"

"No. There's something *else*. I noticed it before the accident, even. When you were outside the school, with Bertram, Candayce—"

"Really, there's—"

"—and Sean."

Mike turned away. Janine felt a hostile flare of emotion stab at her from her companion.

"It's nothing," Mike said.

"Oh." Janine had a definite sense that she had gotten to the root of the problem when she had mentioned Sean. Everyone knew that Mike and Sean O'Malley weren't as close as they used to be. But no one—except the two of them, maybe—seemed to know why. Janine decided not to push it.

Suddenly, Janine saw a long silver-blue shark coming her way. She shrieked and darted back from the water.

Mike opened his maw and plunged his head into the cool shallows. There was an explosion of froth. Janine's vision blurred. She couldn't see what was happening as she raced back to the shore. Then her sight cleared and she saw Mike staring quizzically at the waters.

"I think it's unconscious," Mike said. "I head-butted it. Now it keeps knocking into things. Wait a minute, okay, there it is, it's moving, now it's going away. Yeah, you can come back now. It's safe."

"Oh," Janine said. She gingerly stepped into the waters again, scrutinizing the shallows as she progressed.

"Janine, Janine—there, look!"

She saw it. Four little blue-colored fish. Her beak darted into the water. It opened, taking in the bitter tang of salt water, then it closed swiftly, like a steel trap. She pulled her head out of the water and said, "I don't think I—"

A sudden, disturbing sensation came to her. Something was swimming around in her mouth!

"*Blllllawaaaaaaaaaaaaaaa!*" she screamed, opening her maw and shaking her beak frantically. She heard two small splashes, then couldn't keep herself from swallowing.

"Oh, no," Janine whispered. "I swallowed them. I don't have any teeth, I guess that's what I'm supposed to do, but...this is so *gross*. I can feel them sliding down my throat!"

Mike's tiny arms drew up against his body, his shoulder went up, and he nodded a little too swiftly for the gesture to be casual. He looked wigged out, too. "Yeah, I can see them—little bumps going down your neck."

"Oh! Ah! Jeez! Yuck!" Trembling, she turned away. Then she felt movement in her gullet, slower, slower still, and finally, just a slight relief to the hunger pangs she'd been feeling. She faced Mike again.

"Are you okay?" he asked.

"You're gonna think this is disgusting," she said.

"Try me."

"It's really not that bad."

"Okay," he said, as he looked down at the water again. His stomach growled.

"You really have to eat something, Mike. You do."

Looking amazingly timid for a T. rex, he bent low and studied the water. He took a few loud sniffs. Then he went a little farther out. Something about that disturbed Janine. She wasn't sure what exactly. Just something. She said, "Stay close to shore."

"They're coming! A whole school. Dozens. Maybe hundreds."

"Just be careful." She wondered what danger she'd sensed.

"This is no worse than going to a lobster bar," he muttered.

"What?" she asked.

His little hands gestured helplessly. "You know. Fresh fish. Seeing the little guys looking at you. With their tiny eyes and stuff." He hesitated. "I don't want to do this."

"You've never been fishing?"

He shook his head. "I told Bertram I had. I don't know why. I guess I didn't want to look—I dunno, like I couldn't handle it."

"Bertram would never judge you. You've seen the way he looks up to you."

Janine's words seemed to trigger that same strange unease in Mike once more. Weird. Sean, okay, Mike clearly had problems to work out with him, but why should talking about Bertram get Mike upset?

"Whatever," Mike said quickly.

Janine decided that she had to do something for this guy. It was funny. Mike Peterefsky didn't even know she was alive back in the real world. But here, it was as if they were suddenly best friends or something.

Mike sniffed again, then drove his head savagely into the water. Orange-and-red fish flew up all around him as his maw flashed and his teeth glistened. This time, Janine darted back before the impact of the waves could knock her down.

Terrible chomping sounds followed as Mike lifted his head. He took another step, drove his massive skull downward again, and roared with delight.

She waited on the shore until he was done. He came stomping up to her.

"Feel better?" she asked.

"Bones," he said, moving his jaws from side to side. He turned back to the water, buried his head beneath it, then carefully lifted it with water trapped in his mouth. Throwing his head back, he gargled, then spit. The spray was like an uncapped fire hydrant. "That's better."

"Oh, good."

Janine spotted a couple of the lobsterlike critters shambling past. On instinct, she tried to snatch one of them up with her beak. It slipped out, and she caught it in her claws. She popped it apart and munched.

"Ummmm," she said. "Needs butter, and maybe some Cajun seasoning, but I'll live. It's good. You should try some."

"Another time," Mike said.

"And these shells," Janine said. "I can think of uses for them, too. Hmmmm…"

Mike shook his head. "Can I ask you something?"

"Sure."

"How is it that you're coping with all this so well? I mean, one second you're at school, the next you're here, not even yourself anymore, but you seem okay with it. How are you doing that?"

"Hmmmm," Janine said. "I hadn't really thought."

That wasn't entirely true, of course. She had a very good idea why she was able to handle this. But she wasn't exactly in the mood for sharing.

"I think *you're* handling it really well," Janine said.

Mike's head bounced from side to side. Janine could feel the swell of pride and genuine gratitude radiating from him. She almost felt guilty. Complimenting him was a cheap dodge, an easy way to get out of talking about her feelings. But at least she'd meant what she'd said.

"Thanks," Mike said, then he grew still. He sniffed the air, and his dark eyes clouded over.

"What is it?" Janine asked. "What are you sensing?"

"A couple of miles down the shore. See where the shoreline reaches inland? We can't see too much because of the trees."

"Okay," she said. "So what's going on?"

Mike seemed transfixed. "We've gotta get over there. We've gotta do something!"

"What *is* it?" Janine asked. "Is it Bertram? Did he—"

"Now!" Mike growled and raced ahead, moving so swiftly he was down the shore, around the curve, and out of sight before Janine could cover even a quarter of the distance.

She looked at her useless wings, wishing she could fly. She sighed, then ran as fast as her spindly legs would carry her.

Chapter 7

Mike

The scents of fear and blood that Mike had detected on the southern stretch of the shore had given him some idea of what he would soon be facing. He told himself that he would be prepared for what he'd find. But he wasn't. Not for any of it.

On the shore, dozens of giant sea turtles had been laying their eggs. The turtles were each a good eleven or twelve feet long, and they were mostly green, with spots and streaks of yellow. Their shells were thick, rubbery skin, not horn. They reminded Mike of leatherback turtles, with their weak, toothless, and friendly-looking hawklike beaks and their big, floppy paddlelike limbs.

The giant turtles were under attack, brutal attack. Their nests were being terrorized as well. The predators were tyrannosaurs, like him. Mike counted four on the shore. Three were his size. They were unremarkable, their flesh a mix of green and gray.

One, however, was a giant. Mike stared at him with wonder and fear. He was perhaps twenty feet tall. His flesh was a deep forest green, with black stripes. His eyes seemed to blaze crimson, but Mike suspected that was simply a trick of the light, a reflection of the terrible trauma he had inflicted upon the dying turtle at his feet.

The giant fell upon his victim. Mike watched as he bit hard into the turtle's flank and cracked open its shell. Then Mike turned away.

He didn't know what he thought he could accomplish here. This was the natural order of things. The predators stalked their prey. It was as simple as that. Just like Sean always said. The strong survived, the others didn't.

Others meant kids like Lowell Kramer, the one player on their team who Sean had identified as the source of all their problems. Lowell was a little smaller, a little slower, a little weaker than everyone else. He was also supposed to be the guest of honor at Sean's planned *Big Event*.

Mike shuddered and turned his attention back to what was happening on the beach. Every now and then, a turtle would snap or bite at an attacker. But the T. rexes always leaped out of the way in time.

A roar came from the midst of the carnage. Mike looked up.

The giant had seen Mike. He stared for a few moments, then went back to his feasting.

All around the T. rexes, dozens of turtles struggled to flee the beach and reach the relative safety of the water. Dozens more had been trapped while still laying their eggs.

They were defenseless.

Mike Peterefsky knew that he was no longer living in the twentieth century, and that he was no longer housed in a human frame. He knew what he was now. The meal he'd just consumed was still warm in his belly. Despite all that, he was disturbed by the spectacle before him.

Inside, Mike was still human. His reaction was exactly what it might have been if he'd been on vacation, wandering on some beach, and had come across these monstrosities and their feeding frenzy.

Mike let out a fierce roar. He didn't think. He didn't agonize over it the way he had with the Lowell Big Event, which he'd known about for weeks. He just acted.

The giant looked up lazily from a new turtle he'd taken. He seemed intrigued, perhaps amused, by Mike. But he didn't stop. He ambled over to a fresh turtle and descended on it without missing a step.

The other three T. rexes watched the giant. They seemed to gain some understanding of his actions right about the same instant as Mike: The giant wasn't just killing what he needed to survive. He was progressing systematically through the turtles, wounding each severely, taking a small bite, a nibble, then moving on. He wanted to make sure that as few as possible escaped his little party. He didn't have to do this. He just wanted to.

Mike couldn't believe what he was seeing. The other three T. rexes *could* believe it, apparently. They began to do the same thing. It was too much for Mike. He roared again, then broke into a frenzied run into the ranks of the turtles.

He didn't care that he had no idea how to fight in his new body. It didn't matter in the slightest to him that all four of his enemies would have no qualm about killing—the evidence of that fact was strewn all about them—or that they didn't seem at all worried about his approach.

Even the giant was nodding, as if in approval.

They think I'm coming to join them, Mike realized. If he'd been thinking more clearly, he might have considered how he could use this knowledge to his advantage. How he might draw the others away. Or set some kind of trap for them. He could have planned it as if he was running a play during a big game. But the only thing on his mind was his anger. He led with it, understanding, yet not caring, that it was likely to get him killed.

"You're history," he whispered, half-crazed. And he was so intent on reaching the giant rex leader that he paid no attention to the smaller three. He zigzagged through the field of turtles, nearly flopping down in the sand a half-dozen times.

He passed one of the smaller T. rexes, and a kind of instinctive silent alarm went off in his mind. He disregarded it. Big mistake.

A grunt sounded from behind him, which he also ignored. Then came a host of strange noises. A second alarm. This one not so silent. It hadn't come from within Mike. Nor had it been meant for him.

My scent, Mike realized suddenly. *The other one is downwind of me now, catching my scent, and he knows—he understands—I'm not like them.*

The second of the smaller green-and-gray T. rexes rose up before him, his maw opening wide as he tilted his head to one side and drove it forward with unexpected swiftness.

My throat, he's going for my throat!

Mike reached up with his strong arms, hoping to grab hold of the oncoming powerhouse as if he was an opposing linebacker. The part of him that *knew* he was still a human being thought the idea was crazy—it was like trying to reach out and stop a speeding train that was barreling at you. But he did it anyway. His claws went up—

And didn't reach. His tiny little arms didn't do him a bit of good. He saw a blur of teeth—row after row of shining ivory incisors. He smelled the fetid breath of his attacker, sensed the heat of its body as it moved to take him in a terrifying embrace.

He tried to dive out of the way. It was a human maneuver. Something he might have done on a football field. But his new body wasn't exactly built to handle the move gracefully. His legs launched him forward with incredible power, but his head and left shoulder collided with the scaly monstrosity barreling at him. There was a jarring impact. Mike was certain every bone in his body was going to shatter, every tooth in his skull would be splintered and shaken loose. Neither happened.

Instead, he heard the steel-trap chomping of the other T. rex's jaws clamping shut on thin air as the two of them went down in a confused tangle, then fell away from each other. Mike was aware of the world spinning, a wall of gray-green scales and rippling muscles, then an abrupt view of the sky. He was on his back.

Without losing a second, he turned to one side, flopped onto his belly, and brought his legs up under him. He stood on the first try—and was just in time to confront a pair of T. rexes who were racing toward him from either side.

He had very little time to think, to plan. He saw that the T. rex he'd collided with was still on the ground a few yards away, his tail and head lolling.

One down.

Mike figured that a typical T. rex would probably stand still, target one or the other of his two attackers, and simply try to give as good as he got. But Mike wasn't a typical T. rex.

He waited as the T. rexes were almost upon him, then he darted back, allowing them to collide! Their heads smacked together with a sharp *crack!* They latched onto one another with their small but powerful tearing claws. Each growled and wailed.

All thoughts of Mike appeared to instantly flee from their brains. Their anger now firmly directed at each other, they bit and clawed, and butted and shoved! Their tails rose and slapped the ground. One nearly tripped Mike, and he stumbled backward, so distracted by the warring rexes that he failed to register the thundering footfalls behind him.

Coach Garibaldi would be proud, Mike thought as he took another step back and bumped into something. He turned, expecting it to be a twelve-foot turtle.

It was the giant T. rex. He roared and Mike again forgot that he was no longer a human being. His reason dissolved, his fear became everything.

A second roar came, this one of challenge. Mike was stunned to realize that it had come from *him*—he had gotten in touch with his inner T. rex. His primal Tyrannosaurus instincts issued a roar that declared he wasn't backing down.

Footfalls now came from behind. The T. rex he'd stunned earlier was on his feet. Closing in on him. Mike wondered if he could get away with the same move twice and pit the giant and the other T. rex against each other. He was able to picture easily enough what he wanted to happen: The T. rex behind him would come racing forward to bite him or knock him down with a rear attack and he would dart out of the way, leaving the giant to fend off the attack.

Simple. Only he could sense that the giant would attack *before* the T. rex behind him was close enough for his plan to work. He had to keep that from happening. He had to distract the giant. Mike screamed! Dancing and hopping and banging his tail maniacally on the ground, he waved his little claws and bellowed, "Wahhhhhhhh-hhhhhhhhhhhh!"

The giant froze and stared at him as if he'd gone mad.

"Wugga-wugga-wugga-wugga-wugga!" Mike hollered.

Then he heard it. The footfalls behind him stopped, too. His distraction had worked on *both* T. rexes!

The giant roared. His head lunged forward, jaw snapping just inches in front of Mike's face. Mike froze and fell silent. He took a step back, keeping his tail up so that he wouldn't trip over it. The giant matched his stride.

Mike took a few more steps backward, turning so that he could now see both of his adversaries at once. Behind them, the other pair of T. rexes were still engaged in a savage ballet of tooth and claw.

Mike knew he was overmatched. This was an enemy he could not fight. Not *fairly*. This was a mystery he had to solve. Fast.

A mad jumble of ideas and images flooded his mind. Mike had been assigned a Sherlock Holmes story for English a few weeks before, and he'd liked it so much that he'd gone out and bought all the books. Getting lost in those stories had been about the only escape he'd had from thinking about Sean and what he planned to do to Lowell.

A scene from one of the coolest stories came to him: Sherlock Holmes fighting Professor Moriarty. They were locked in a mad dance of death, about to tumble over Reichenbach Falls. The falls. The water. He thought of Janine. The way she warned him not to wade deeper into the water. She was concerned for reasons she didn't understand, not consciously.

Why? Out of the corner of his eye, he saw the turtles scurrying into the water, where they'd be safe. *Why?*

Mike decided to find out. Darting to one side then vaulting forward in the opposite direction, he faked out Moriarty—the giant T. rex, the pack leader, his enemy.

Mike raced for the water. His rex instincts, the ones that came with his new body, screamed at him to stop. Not in words. Just in a gnarling feeling in his gut that told him this was *wrong*. He ignored it.

Thunderous footfalls sounded behind him. Moriarty and his henchman were closing in. The shore was dead ahead. Mike pictured a goalpost at the edge of the water. Only a few more strides and—

Pain lanced into him, and he shrieked! Moriarty had bitten his tail! Mike tried to pull himself free, but Moriarty's hold was too strong. He stumbled and fell, only a few feet from the water. He scanned the shore. All he could see was turtles. He was on the sand and they were all around him. Moriarty and his pal closed in from his left flank. There was nowhere to go. No way to escape.

As the flashing maws of Moriarty and the smaller T. rex gleamed in the bright sunlight and came down upon him, Mike struggled and kicked, thrashing about frantically, in pure primal terror. His foot hooked under something, and suddenly a gigantic almond-shaped *thing* rose up before him. It blotted out his vision, then went crashing right into Moriarty!

Bertram? Mike wondered. He'd dimly been aware of some kind of shell. No, one of the turtles! He'd kicked it right into Moriarty! Mike heard a roar of frustration. A wail of confusion. It was the break he needed.

He turned onto his belly, brought his feet up, and burst forward in a frantic run toward the water. One yard. Two—then a great splash as the water rose up around him. He felt its chill on his feet. His legs. Up to his thighs.

He waded in deeper, his tail flashing and splashing! The water rose up to his belly and began to engulf it. He took another step, sinking deeper into the frothy waves, and turned to look behind him. Moriarty and his henchman were on the edge of the shore, staring at him in disbelief!

"Come on in, the water's fine!" Mike shouted deliriously. "Come on, ya big wussbag! Come on, show me how tough you are!"

Moriarty grunted. His companion grunted. They came a little closer, stepping tentatively to the edge of the water. Then they stopped and would go no further.

"Wimps!" Mike shouted. "Wussies! Cowards!"

Moriarty and the other T. rex just stared at him.

Suddenly, Mike felt it. He looked down and finally understood why Moriarty and his pal hadn't followed him: He was sinking. The soft pull of the sand was yanking him down. He tried to take a step forward, but the sand was swallowing him up, like quicksand! It was because he *weighed* so much! Tons! "Oh, no…"

Moriarty and his minion bobbed their heads a little, then turned and stomped back down the shore, toward their interrupted meal.

"No!" Mike shouted. He drove himself forward, but the sand beneath him gave no purchase and he only sank deeper. He dimly became aware of other shapes in the water. Long, cylindrical objects. Swimming quickly and with purpose. Sharks. While on the shore, Moriarty drew close to another defenseless turtle, his maw opening wide.

Enraged, Mike thrust his head into the water and closed his teeth around the body of a shark, which was about to bite his tail where it had been wounded. He yanked it out of the water, whipped his head sharply, and sent the flailing shark flying in the direction of his enemy. The blue body of the shark glistened as it soared through the air.

"Catch that pass!" Mike hollered.

With a harsh slap, the shark smashed Moriarty right in the face. Moriarty snuffled and sneezed. His companion let out a loud, disgusting sound that might have been a burp but also sounded strangely like laughter!

Moriarty turned and growled. Then he charged into the water!

Now what? Mike thought.

He tensed and braced himself as best he could, as if the league's biggest linebacker was on his way and there was no one to receive a pass, and no time to run. Moriarty was on him in a heartbeat, foam rising about him in the water, teeth flashing, a savage roar bursting from him.

The giant rex crashed into Mike, the impact hurtling them both further into the water. The deep blue closed in on them like a fist. As they struggled, bit, and clawed at each other, bubbles rose all around them. Mike tried to hold his breath, but Moriarty was all over him, tearing and slashing, and they were drifting farther and farther back, sinking deeper, the sparkling sun on the surface of the water dwindling, fading.

Then something struck them! Mike caught only a brief glimpse of a dark shape, some kind of leviathan with monstrously huge fins, curling and moving in the water. The impact separated him from Moriarty. He tumbled end over end into the deep blue-and-black murk surrounding him. Flailing and kicking, his lungs aching, he was desperately certain that he would drown.

A streak of crimson passed before his eyes. He looked beyond it and saw Moriarty with his maw sunk deep into the flank of the sea monster that had struck them. There was a blur of movement, then a wave rushed at Mike, striking him hard, sending him back toward the shore!

Mike saw the bright glow of the sun on the surface of the water above, then sank again. His feet struck something hard, a stone buried in the sand, and he vaulted off it, propelling himself up and forward. The surface thrust itself at him, and his head burst from the water! He gulped at the air greedily, his lungs on fire, his little arms pistoning, though they did him no good.

A wave rose and crashed down upon him, driving him closer to shore. His head and neck escaped from the water, but when he kicked at the sand, his feet sank in. He was trapped again!

"Here!"

Mike flinched as something splashed into the water before him. Bertram's tail!

Mike used the last of his strength to open his maw and snag the club at the very end of his friend's armored tail. His vision was going dark, but he held on. The waves behind him kicked up again, shoving against his all-but-limp body. Mike kicked with his feet and was stunned to find them leaving the hungry sand.

The sparkling white-and-blue haze of the surface rushed at him—he was free!

He sucked in air without letting go of Bertram's tail. He could see Bertram, Candayce, and Janine on the shore, the club-tail laboriously pulling himself forward. Mike's feet hit the beach again.

Shivering, he let go of Bertram's tail and took a few steps upon the shore. Out of the corner of his eye, he saw a shape coming toward him from behind. Moriarty. The waves had blown *both* of them back!

Mike was so startled that he allowed his tail to get tangled between his legs. He fell onto the shore, belly-up, helpless prey, just as Bertram had been when he first encountered him in this frightening new world.

Moriarty shook off the bitter salt water and took another step onto solid ground.

"Mike! Look out," Janine shouted. Moriarty's mouth plunged toward Mike's stomach—but Bertram's tail whipped out, smashing him in the mouth.

"No more!" Bertram hollered.

Moriarty's head was flung to one side, shattered teeth flying. He stumbled back as Bertram slammed him twice more. The giant fell into the water—and got up again. Mike rolled onto his belly and quickly rose. Moriarty snarled.

"We're dead," Bertram whispered. Beside him, Candayce whimpered. Janine stared defiantly.

Mike had a feeling they weren't dead at all. An incredible splash sounded from behind Moriarty and a beast out of legend rose from the water. Surf, sand, shells, and tiny predators fell away from the dark, round humps of the creature's body. On its side, Mike saw the ragged wound from Moriarty's attack. Then an incredibly long *neck* whipped upward.

Nessie, the Elasmosaurus, opened her maw and brought her head down upon Moriarty. Her snakelike neck whipped around the giant T. rex, and she dragged him toward her. He kicked and roared, but she held fast, sinking back beneath the churning waves with a lazy, smugly triumphant ease. Moriarty thrashed about, but it did him no good. His body was hauled beneath the water. Then they were gone.

Mike wanted to cry out in relief, in triumph, but he knew there were three other rexes to worry about. Turning back to land, Mike's vision was consumed by a field of turtles ambling toward the water. A few yards behind them, two of Moriarty's henchmen abruptly broke off their battle and looked his way. The third rex shifted his attention from a turtle and glared at them.

The rexes sniffed the air and studied the odd pack of travelers who stood together. Shuddering, they turned and loped off the other way.

"Our scents are confusing them," Bertram said. "They don't want anything to do with us. And they've fed enough."

Mike looked at the Ankylosaurus. "You saved my life. I don't know what to say…"

"'Thanks' would be good," Janine said. Candayce nodded.

"Thanks," Mike said softly. He felt weak, shaky, and ecstatic just to be alive!

Bertram nodded, but he seemed more engrossed with the sight stretched out before him. He walked right up to one of the turtles and looked her in the eye. "Archelons. Cool."

Mike shifted his gaze to stare at the pudgy little Leptoceratops. She was wearing *something*. Clothing? No, it was leaves, very large ones, and they were stuck to her body with sap or something. Two on her chest, one lower, like a bathing suit.

"Candayce? Are you all right now? What happened—"

"I—I—oh, don't even speak to me!" Candayce snapped. "Let's just get out of here!"

"She's got a point," Bertram said, turning away from the turtle. "We've got a long haul in front of us if we're going to reach the Standing Stones in time."

"You know which way to go?" Mike asked.

"I've got an idea. We should follow the shoreline to the river, then head west to get back to Montana. Right now, we're in South Dakota, and—"

"How do you know that?" Janine asked.

"Oh, jeez, here we go," Candayce moaned, plopping down on the sands.

Bertram's head bobbed. "The inland sea, the coal beds we passed, and...I just know. I can feel it. Mr. London really did bury a map in my subconscious. We're in what will become South Dakota, and we have to head west, follow the circumference of the earth."

"Huh," Janine said. "So when you move back in time you also move in space. The earth is constantly rotating, so even though we didn't move, the world did. We ended up on the same latitude, but only—"

"Two hundred and forty-nine miles," Bertram said.

"Yeah, just a little east of where we should have been dropped off. It could have been worse. We could have ended up halfway around the world—or right in the middle of the ocean!"

"Or we could have missed the earth's revolution around the sun completely and been left sitting in outer space," Bertram said.

"At least that would mean no one would see me like this," Candayce growled.

"I wonder what the future Mr. London has learned about—"

"Let's *go*," Janine said. "We've got to make twenty-five to thirty miles a day. That's not gonna happen if we stand around talking."

"Right," Bertram muttered. "We should be walking really fast and talking."

Without another word, the small group turned from the shore. Mike looked at the turtles, many of whom would now be going home because of him. He felt good.

A sound came from somewhere far off. A Tyrannosaurus roar?

He looked back to the water. It was still. Moriarty was gone. He wasn't coming back. He *wasn't*.

Mike looked away once more, wishing he could believe that.

Chapter 8

Bertram

Night was falling. The sky was a deep, rich blue, with a dark purple band at its highest reach. Stars and the moon were out. There was still enough light to see, but just barely. All four travelers were winding down. Janine was sitting alone by herself, working on some kind of project. Candayce was with Mike and Bertram, rooting around in the sand, selecting among the cornucopia of large, beautiful shells.

"This is like the first summer I went to Florida," said Candayce. "My dad's an airline pilot. He's really great, but he's not around much. Sometimes we go on trips with him. Anyway, everything's so different in Cocoa Beach. It's hot and humid, you can feel the air pressing in on you like it's got you in its wet hands... But at the beach, everything changes. The winds are soft, the water's cool, the sun's like the best thing that's ever happened to you."

A sharp *pock* came from Janine's little spot close to the waters. A high crack. Then a caw and a muttered curse.

"*What* is she *doing?*" Candayce asked, suddenly inflamed.

"Don't worry," Mike said. "I'm sure it's nothing."

Candayce shook her head. She used her beak to pick up a large shell. "This one's good. Now I just need one more."

"You know what I wish?" Bertram asked.

"I can *imagine,*" Candayce said.

"I just wish…it's silly, but I wish there was a boardwalk. Someplace that sold hot dogs, Cokes, fries…"

"Uhhhh," Mike slobbered. "Don't do that to me."

"Me, either," Candayce said. "An all-veggie diet. Yuck."

"Sorry," Bertram said, lowering his head.

"Don't be," Mike said. "*I* could go for some ice cream."

"*Ice cream,*" Candayce moaned. Bertram wasn't sure if he'd ever heard a more mournful tone.

"Yeah. With lots of nuts and crunchy stuff on top."

Candayce sighed. From down the beach came another *pock!* Then two more. *Pock! Pock!*

Candayce sprang to her feet. "What are you doing, you stupid social *reject?*"

Janine started to sing. Bertram didn't recognize the song.

"*My little buttercup…has the sweetest smile…My little buttercup…won't you stay a while?*"

"She's impossible," Candayce snarled. Mike laughed.

Bertram looked down. "Candayce, be careful!"

"What?" Candayce asked, shifting her weight to look at him. A grinding, crackling sound rose in the night. "My shell! Bertram, look what you made me do!"

Bertram winced. She'd ground it to dust underfoot. "Sorry."

"You should be!"

"Why?" came a fourth voice.

Bertram looked up to see Janine approaching. A strange sound came from her. *Cha-ching. Cha-ching!*

"Oh, no," Candayce whispered. "Not that sound."

Janine held something odd in her right claw. It was a collection of shells and hard platings from the "lobsters" they'd found. Holes had been poked through the shells, presumably with Janine's beak, and a vine had been run through the holes. It was tied at one end. The other end was for Janine to twirl. The *cha-ching* was the sound of the shells and platings clapping together.

Janine had remade her key chain!

"That's really something," Bertram said. "I'm impressed."

"You would be," Candayce muttered.

Bertram smiled inwardly, still delighted to actually be with Candayce, despite her terrible mood.

Candayce turned to Janine. "So what were you saying?"

"*You* smashed the shell," Janine said. "Bertram was trying to warn you. You were making him apologize for *your* mistake."

"Actually—" Bertram began.

"I didn't *make* him do anything," Candayce said, "you—"

Janine whipped her chain. *Cha-ching!* Candayce froze.

"Well, if you couldn't *make* him do anything, how could he have made *you* do anything?" Janine asked.

Candayce stared at Janine, chest heaving, her beak trembling as if she was desperately attempting to come up with some reasonable answer.

"Losers," Candayce said finally. She turned her back on Janine and went back to looking for shells.

Janine watched her for several long seconds. "You want to do a Little Mermaid here, don't you?" Janine asked levelly.

"Go ahead," Candayce said. "Mock me."

"Her leaves fell off," Mike said. "The sap dried out."

"I can help," Janine said. "Find your shells. I've got more vine."

"What?" Candayce asked.

"I'll help."

"Liar." Candayce looked up and found Janine staring at her. Bertram knew that look. Even trapped in the body of a Quetzal-coatlus, Janine could look inside a person.

"Oh, gross! She's doing it again!" Frantically, Candayce tried to make the sign to ward off the evil eye, but her claws were too awkward for the task.

"Come on," Janine said. "It's what you want. Let me help?"

"Really?"

"Yes."

Candayce and Janine went down the shore together. Mike and Bertram sat quietly. They heard Janine and Candayce talking, heard a shriek of glee, then a couple of *pocks!*

"Can I admit something to you?" Mike asked.

Bertram was surprised. "Sure."

"I'm scared. I'd give anything, to like, go over some rise and see a Blockbuster. Or a McDonald's."

"Me, too," Bertram said. "But we *can* do this."

"If we can keep from being eaten."

"Yes…"

"And if we can figure out the other thing we have to do, what Mr. London didn't tell us."

"We'll figure it out."

A scrambling sounded from down the shore. Janine came running. "You guys have to see this!" She looked back.

Candayce raced to them and stopped, proudly displaying herself. On her chest was a makeshift brassiere, a pair of shells tied together with a vine. Another shell was draped beneath her belly. It was the most absurd and yet strangely comforting sight Bertram had ever beheld.

"Finally," Candayce said, "a little bit of civilization!"

"I like it," Mike said.

"Me, too," Bertram agreed.

Candayce went prancing down the beach. Janine stayed behind and said, "Being back here does have its moments."

Bertram finally laughed. He looked to the midnight blue of the sky and the sparkling stars that were brighter now. In the morning, they'd be at the river, and soon after that…who knew? But eventually—and he prayed it would be in time—they'd reach the Standing Stones. What would this world have done to them by then? he wondered.

He sensed that nothing would be the same again for any of them.

Scales Are a
Fashion Disaster!

Chapter 9

Candayce

Candayce Chambers was dreaming. In her dream, she was lounging on a deck chair, and her bathing suit, what there was of it, had attracted the attention of at least a half-dozen guys around the pool. They stared in awe at her long, beautiful legs, soft and tanned, her tiny waist, her flowing golden hair.

Their girlfriends glared, but Candayce didn't mind. Closing her eyes, she reached back and stretched, luxuriating in the bold warmth of the blazing sun overhead. Heat radiated through her. She lapped it up like a hungry kitten.

She was a goddess and she knew it.

Opening her eyes, she felt a momentary confusion as the dream fell away and she was confronted by the sight of star-shaped palm fronds waving lazily to her from high above. She followed the leaves down to a fat trunk decorated with diamond-patterned bark. The tree was ten feet high, and it leaned a little to one side. But…there weren't any trees near the pool. What was this?

She felt a cool breeze upon her bare chest.

Bare?

Candayce sat bolt upright, her arms moving to cover her chest, as a scene that couldn't possibly be real catapulted into view: She was sitting on the edge of a pond, being gawked at by a group of slack-jawed dinosaurs!

The dinosaurs had fat little bodies, parrotlike beaks, and little crests for foreheads. They were only about six feet long, and most were dirt brown or stone gray. Two had purple-and-gold streaks and splotches. Another was emerald. To Candayce they were utterly repulsive—but at least they were keeping their distance.

"Good dinosaurs," Candayce whispered. She wondered if any were behind her, or if she could just turn and make a run for it. Only one way to tell…

She spun, her brain commanding her body to bring her long, sleek legs up under her in a runner's starting position. She imagined the whole thing in a heartbeat: How her legs would piston, how she'd launch herself to safety.

It didn't happen. Instead, she fell over onto her side, her tail caught between her legs. Tail?

Candayce looked down at her scaly body. She put her hooflike hands before her face. She screamed—for all the good it did her. She was a Leptoceratops. Just like her admirers. No amount of hollering was going to change that.

She screamed anyway. The other Leptoceratops tilted their heads this way and that. They made odd clicking sounds among themselves. A few touched tails.

Candayce stopped screaming. She kept *doing* this to herself. Three long days now in the Late Cretaceous, and she couldn't even begin to get used to this new and stubby little body she'd been given.

She looked at her "admirers." The Leptomaniacs weren't trying to hurt her. In fact, they had maintained a respectful distance from the moment she became aware of them.

She surveyed the ground, trying to find the bikini top Janine had helped her to fashion out of shells and vines. It was gone! The same with the bottom! It'd been important to her to keep herself covered, even though a part of her knew full well that it was a pointless gesture. There was nothing left to cover up.

"All right," she said. "What do you losers want, anyway?"

The Leptomaniacs didn't answer. Couldn't answer, of course.

They didn't understand English. And Candayce, even though she was in the body of a Leptoceratops, couldn't speak Leptoceratopsese.

Two of the group broke off suddenly and planted themselves on all fours. The first put his head down. With a loud chuffing and a series of shrill cries, he charged a nearby tree!

Candayce watched as the Leptomaniac bashed himself into the weird leaning palm—and brought it down! The tree fell with a terrible thud. Then the second Leptomaniac launched himself at another tree. Again, there was a sharp high crackling, and the tree toppled.

This one collapsed only a dozen feet off to Candayce's left. A few of its branches fell within a yard of her. The sight of the rich green leaves was too much for her. Though she couldn't quite believe she was doing this, Candayce went on all fours to the branch and gobbled up a couple of leaves.

They were *delicious*.

Out of the corner of her eye, she saw the second Leptomaniac ram his shoulder against the flank of the first. As she ate, she studied this second one a little more closely. He had a little scar on his chin, kind of like Harrison Ford. The first one had dreamy, soulful eyes, like Brad Pitt. It was Han Solo and the Bradster. Not bad, not bad...

It occurred to her that she was feeling some modicum of attraction for each of these guys at exactly the same time she felt something *crawling* around inside her mouth.

There'd been a bug on one of the leaves! One of those real big ones!

Eeeeeeeooooooouuuuuuugggggghhhhh!

Candayce choked and spat out the leaves, shaking her head and collapsing with an inner sob.

She *hated* it here. She just wanted to go home!

A chuffing came again. She looked up to see the first guy, the Bradster, ramming his shoulder into Han Solo's flank.

This is what she'd found cute just a moment before? Gross! What could she have been thinking?

It came to her: *It's not what you're thinking, it's what the dino inside you is thinking. What it's feeling.*

Too weird.

She rose up on her hind legs. No way was she going to walk on all fours. Especially not in front of these guys.

All the plain-looking Leptoceratops got on their hind legs, too. Candayce froze. They froze. Oh, no. This was bad. She'd seen this kind of thing before.

A third Leptomaniac, this one a bit more portly than the others, broke from the formation. With a running leap, he toppled another tree. The tree crumpled and sank to one side. For a terrifying instant, Candayce was convinced it was going to come down right on her!

Turning, she ran a few feet and stumbled on a rock. A shadow came crashing down upon her. She didn't have time to scream!

Then she heard a great splash and felt a spray of chilly water cover her dumpy little body. She looked up and saw that the tree had fallen into the pond separating her from the Leptoceratops clan.

Suddenly, a dozen Leptomaniacs were all around her. They made cooing sounds of concern. A few snatched branches from a nearby tree and tried to dry her. They seemed nervous, yet strangely excited to actually be so close to her.

Oh, yeah. She had definitely seen this behavior before.

Candayce stared incredulously at the Leptomaniacs ringing her in. Brad and Han were at the front of the crowd. The portly one was in the back, his head down, looking mortified. A few of the others jostled him. The brightly colored Leptoceratops stood close to the rear of the group. Strange high shrills erupted from the Leptos as they moved their heads from side to side, their beaks clacking a mile a minute.

Candayce rose and took a step back from the group. She held her head high and kept her claws before her. It was as dignified a pose as she could muster.

"I'm going now," she said, hoping that she sounded at least a little calm and in control. "I'm going and I expect each and every one of you to stay here. Is that clear?"

Candayce took another step. Her companions gave her some room. A few chuffed. One actually sniffed her.

She tried not to think about that.

Instead, she kept backing away, moving slowly and testing each spot before she placed her full weight upon her stubby feet. Her gaze drifted down to her ringed, elephantlike thunder thighs, and she shuddered, wondering how much cellulite she had on her now.

She didn't want to think about that, either. She didn't want to think at all, but she couldn't help it.

As she slowly made her strategic withdrawal, she watched the expectant faces of her companions. They doted on her every move. They stared at her as if she was the answer to their dreams.

Candayce Chambers knew what they desired. She'd dealt with it before, countless times. They wanted her to be their queen!

Chapter 10

Bertram

Bertram was just waking up when Mike came thundering through the clearing they had designated their "camp" the previous evening. His Tyrannosaurus body made the ground shake and the diamond-shaped leaves of the nearby Williamsonias quiver.

Mike opened his mouth and spat out some fish near Janine.

"For me?" she said. "You shouldn't have."

Bertram watched as Janine unfurled her wings and yawned. In another time—his time, to be precise—he might have been fascinated by the opportunity to study, up close and personal, the actual manner in which a nearly full-grown Quetzalcoatlus yawned.

Not today. He looked away as she had breakfast. He sank down on his haunches and closed his eyes, wishing he could sleep a little longer.

"Come on, come on!" Mike growled in an encouraging tone. "We've been doing great the last three days! A good twenty-five miles a day, by all estimates. That's terrific. But today, we're going to do even better! So wakey, wakey, rise and shine, come on in, the water's fine!"

Bertram was in no mood for this. His tail swung lazily from one side to the other. He opened his eyes and looked back to Janine, who was just finishing her meal.

"Come on, everyone," Mike cheered as he wandered a few yards off and started doing deep knee bends, "we've got a lot of distance to cover and we need to get *to* it!"

Janine shook her head. "Who put the batteries back in the bunny?"

Bertram looked at her. "Huh?"

She angled her long beak in Mike's direction. He huffed and grunted as he worked out.

"It keeps going and going…" she joked.

"Right. Whatever," Bertram muttered.

Mike finished his exercises and looked around. He sighed and shook his head. "Candayce took off again?"

"It's what Leptoceratops do," Bertram said absently. "They sun themselves in the morning, soaking up the energy from the rays to get them going."

Mike gazed up at the open space that was visible through the trees. Bertram automatically did the same. Sunlight streamed into the clearing. Soft, gentle breezes drifted by. It was a little chilly, not unlike New England in late spring. Sweater weather. But nice. Certainly not the hot, steaming, soggy weather any of the others said they'd expected in the Late Cretaceous. Bertram had explained that this environment was seasonal, and while they wouldn't get snow, they were heading toward the cold season. This morning, the sun's warmth was welcome.

"She could have sunned herself here," Mike said.

Janine shrugged. Her wings rustled. "Guess she doesn't like the scenery."

Mike sighed. "Somebody's got to go get her. Janine?"

"That's my middle name," Janine said. "*Somebody*. You know, this is the third time in a row I've been *Somebody*. Maybe it's time for someone else to be *Somebody*."

"Candayce won't argue with you. She's scared of you."

Janine seemed to come fully awake with that one. "True," she said, springing to her feet and walking with a bounce in her storklike step. She snatched up her key chain and whipped it back and forth, *cha-ching, cha-ching.*

Bertram knew Candayce hated that sound and would know Janine was coming. And be afraid.

Janine went off happily in search of her prey.

Mike looked over. "Bertram, I'm gonna go study that bark while the ladies are away. I suggest you do the same."

"I went already." Bertram felt a sudden flush of anger. "I mean, I know I'm just a moseying, slothful creature, but I *do* think from time to time, I *do* remember to take care of certain things without having to be reminded."

"Hey, it was just a suggestion." Mike put up his tiny claws.

"All right, then."

Bertram watched Mike go deeper into the woods and shook his head. *I should have been the T. rex.*

All his life he'd been an Ankylosaurus. Dull, plodding, yet powerful—in his intellect, at least. But in all other ways, he'd always been unable to catch up. He was the one people had to protect or make excuses for, never the one who was admired and in control. It just wasn't fair.

Of course, none of this had been his idea. Not really. Sure, he'd built the machine that had yanked their conciousnesses out of their bodies, transported them to the Late Cretaceous, and dumped them into the hulking frames of dinosaurs. Fine. He was guilty of that much. But he hadn't done any of it on purpose. That the machine had attained miraculous powers was purely random, a one-in-a-billion-billion shot. If he *had* planned for it, he would have put himself in the body of the T. rex. No question.

He could still recall when he'd been five, out walking with his dad, and he'd go into Tyrannosaurus mode. His eyes would glaze over. He'd sniff the air for prey. And he'd walk with his hands held close to his chest, three of his fingers tucked in, the other two tapping together like the two-fingered claws of a confident, alert T. rex.

His dad had always smiled lovingly at this. He would say, "You've got a sense of wonder, Bertram. In this day and age, that's the most important gift any of us could be given. Don't ever be ashamed of it. Don't ever run from it. Just enjoy it."

Then, even though they were usually out in public when Bertram went into dino mode, his dad would drop onto all fours and wave his butt in the air, shouting, "I'm an Ankylosaurus! I'm lunch if you can catch me!"

And they'd chase each other, and they'd laugh, and they'd be happy.

I should have been the T. rex.

"Heads up!" Janine called from a few hundred yards away. "Incoming!"

Bertram slowly turned and saw Candayce barreling toward him. A pack of Leptoceratops were chasing after her.

"Help! Help! Help!" Candayce demanded.

"Get on top of me," Bertram said.

Candayce stopped dead. "Yeah, right. In your dreams."

He shook his head. "*Climb* on *top* of my *shell.* Look *out* for the *spikes.*"

"Jeez, you don't have to be so—"

"Now!"

Candayce carefully scrambled up Bertram's shell. Bertram waited until the Leptoceratops had him ringed in. He saw a few of them go down on all fours, as though they were getting ready to spring at him. Oh, right. That would be smart.

Bertram raised his tail and brought it down hard. The ground shuddered. A few of the Leptoceratops fell over. Others reached for one another.

"Whoa! I almost fell!" Candayce yelled.

"So be more careful," Bertram muttered. "Or deal with these guys yourself."

"Okay, okay," Candayce said. "Jeez. What *hasn't* gotten into you?"

Bertram moved in a circle, smashing his tail to the ground in warning. The Leptoceratops withdrew to a safe distance.

"I can still see them," Candayce said.

"Get off me, will you?"

"Right. Sure. I—wait!" Candayce exclaimed. "What's this?"

"What?" asked Bertram.

Candayce stepped down, stomping on the back of Bertram's head in the process.

"Hey!" he yelled. "That hurts."

"Good," Candayce said. She was holding something in her claws that clacked and banged. "Don't look at me!"

He turned away, though he had no idea why she had asked him to.

"All right. You can look now."

Bertram turned back to find Candayce crouching low, holding her shells before her.

"Do these look familiar to you?" she asked, pushing the shells forward just a little.

"Yeah," Bertram said. "What about them?"

"You might have noticed that I wasn't wearing them when I ran to you, asking for help. I was *naked!*"

"Candayce, we're all—"

"My shells were hooked on one of your spikes! You stole them from me when I was sleeping!"

Bertram shook his head. He had no patience for this right now.

Janine approached, slapping her shells. *Cha-ching, cha-ching.* "Hey, Candy Striper. Want me to tie those for you?"

Mike appeared from the woods. "I heard all the noise. What happened?"

Bertram nodded in the direction of the Leptoceratops pack, now quaking at the sight of the T. rex.

Seeing the pack's fear, Candayce moved over to Mike. "Hey, this is more like it," she said.

Mike looked down. "What's with the shells?"

Candayce strained to look up over her shoulder. In her most sultry voice, she said, "Zip me up, dear."

"Huh?"

"Just tie it," she hissed.

"Oh."

Mike bent and went to work on tying together the lengths of vine Candayce had shoved underneath her arms. He fumbled for a while. Finally, Janine had to come help.

When it was done, Candayce eased back and leaned against

Mike. "And at least I know I can trust you not to pull any funny stuff."

Mike looked at the club-tail. "Bertram, what'd you do?"

"Nothing."

"Then let's get to walking," Mike said.

They set out on the path Mike had cleared for them the night before. Fallen Pityostrobus, sixty-five-foot conifers, with pine cones, lined the path on both sides of them. More rose behind, like endless ranks of soldiers standing at attention. The pack of Leptoceratops trailed behind them, scrambling between the trees. Bertram barely noticed. Instead, he watched how closely Candayce stuck to Mike.

"Figures," Bertram said. He wondered what advice his mom might give right about now. Of course, the last time he'd seen her was just before she took off for San Francisco and that "Limited Awareness Seminar," where she met Fred the Real Estate Guy and didn't come back.

Janine came running up to him. *Cha-ching, cha-ching.* "Hey, sunshine!"

Bertram sniffed the air. "Actually, I think there's a cloud front coming in."

Janine shook her head. "Hey, why ruin things while we're behind, right? Why don't we make it a flash flood?"

"Flash floods happened a lot in this era," Bertram said glumly. "I don't see why it wouldn't be possible."

Janine danced around him as they walked. "I know why you're so crabby."

"Really?"

"Sure. I know a lot of things. Like these trees, they're 'pityohs'—or in your case, 'self-pity-ohs.' But it's not the flora that's got you down."

"It's not?"

"Nope. It's the lack of fiber in your diet. Actually, it's the lack of *anything* in your diet. You haven't eaten. At all. Not since we got here."

Bertram tensed. "Just not hungry."

"It's been days."

"Not...*hungry*. What part of that didn't you understand?"

"I think it's more than that."

"Really?"

She bobbed her head. "I've *read* about Ankylosaurus. I know what happens when they eat."

Bertram's tail whipped out so sharply he smashed the low-hanging branches of a nearby tree into twigs. Janine danced out of the way, nearly dropping her chain. *Cha-ching!*

Mike and Candayce looked back. "You two okay?"

"It's nothing," Bertram sniffed and looked back at Janine. "Did you steal Candayce's shells?"

"No. Wish I could take credit, but sadly, no."

"Then who?"

A caw sounded from above. Everyone looked up to see a second Quetzalcoatlus flying overhead. "Loki!" Janine called.

The Trickster bowed his head, sailed in a lazy circle, then flew off.

"Loki?" Bertram asked.

"You're changing the subject," accused Janine.

"You *named* him?"

"Hey, if Mike can name his, I can name mine."

Bertram shook his head. "Nessie. Moriarty. Loki. What's next? The Grinch?"

"You're still changing the subject. Or trying to, at least. I know your secret, Bertram. I know that if you don't eat something soon, you're going to slow down even more."

Bertram felt panicked. "What do you want me to do?"

Janine looked around, her head bobbing, her tiny claw scratching her elongated chin. "Oh, I dunno. How about...*eat something!*"

Bertram looked up in alarm to see if Mike and Candayce had heard her. They were about a hundred feet ahead, and lost in some conversation of their own.

"You have to," Janine said. "We both know that."

"Not necessarily," Bertram said. "There are theories that many dinosaurs could eat huge meals and store them in their bellies, in their tails, and slowly use up that energy—"

"If your body was digesting, we'd know it," Janine said. "It's not. That means you need to eat."

Bertram felt like he wanted to cry. "Come on! Isn't this humiliating enough? Walking on all fours? Being as wide as a car and as fat as—"

"A car without any fuel ends up on the side of the road. I don't want that happening with you."

"You don't?"

Janine shook her head.

"I guess I gotta do it sometime. It's probably why I've been so short-tempered. So irritable."

"Probably."

Bertram waddled off to the side of the road. He strained his head and went to work on a low-hanging branch.

"Hold up, everyone!" Janine called. "Chow break!"

Mike and Candayce stopped. They didn't wander back. They were completely engrossed in their talk.

Bertram hated to admit it, but he felt jealous. He knew the kind of person Candayce was. And in this body, she was hardly a beauty anymore. Still, there was something about her that made his heart race.

He chomped away on the leaves, ignoring the twigs he snapped up and crunched. It was delicious! He'd almost never tasted anything so good! He had no idea exactly how hungry he'd been until he started eating!

"Bertram!" Mike called some time later. "Come on, we need to get going!"

Bertram shook himself. It was as if he was waking from a dream. His eyes focused and he saw that he had grazed through four trees and over a dozen bushes and shrubs. He'd even knocked down a couple of thirty-foot-tall Araliopsoides to get at the leaves. And the greens from the ginseng trees had been very tasty indeed. As he munched, he'd kind of checked out, and become unaware of any action but eating. Freaky. But he did feel better.

Suddenly, he became aware of sounds from all around. "Company," Bertram warned.

"It's the Leptos," Janine said from behind him. "They never

really left, just hung back. Now they're all around us."

"Hmm," Bertram said. "Hey, guys, don't worry about it. I think I know a way of getting rid of them."

"You're kidding," Candayce said. *"Really?"*

"You bet," Bertram said, exchanging a sly conspiratorial glance with Janine. "You bet."

Chapter 11

Janine

Bertram's plan took effect about an hour later. One moment, the group was ambling down the "dirt road"; the next, they were under attack. Only the attack didn't come from without. It came from within. Within *Bertram*, to be exact.

"Whoa!" Mike hollered. "What'd somebody step in?"

"That *smell!*" Candayce wailed.

Janine shook her head and glanced over at Bertram. He looked as though he wanted to drag his head inside his protective shell, like a turtle. Then a strange thing happened. He held his head high and began to lecture them.

"The digestive process of an Ankylosaurus is quite different from that of human beings. It's much more similar to that of rhinos, horses, cattle—"

Brrrrrrrrrrrr-UPPPPPPPT!

"Was that what I thought it was?" Candayce said, gagging.

Mike was looking unsteady on his feet. "That wasn't a fart! That was the queen mother of all farts!"

"I'm afraid I'm just getting started," Bertram said.

"Oh, no!" Candayce wailed.

Janine smiled inwardly. She didn't like the stink any more than the rest of them, but she knew it couldn't be avoided. "Hey, it's not all bad. Look around."

Cha-ching! Whipping her chain, Janine gestured to the trees flanking them. The pack of Leptoceratops was running for cover.

"See, Candayce?" Janine said. "Bertram did you a favor!"

Brrrrrrrrrr-rrrrrrrrr-rrrrrrrr-UPPPPPPPPPPPT!

Janine had seen Bertram's backside wiggle a little before the last one. She'd already moved herself upwind of him.

"You see," Bertram went on in a serious tone, "because my frame is so large and my stomach so huge, parts of my insides are separated into special compartments. Bacteria living within my stomach serve to break down tough woodlike materials within the fermentation chamber and—"

"It's not bad enough you're the little geek who got us into all this," Candayce wailed between coughs. "It's not bad enough you're slowing us down! No! Now you have to hit us—"

BRRRRRRR-UPPPPPPPPPT!

"Ugh!" Candayce wailed, teetering.

Bertram lowered his head shamefully. "Sorry."

"You should be!" Candayce hollered.

Janine had witnessed about enough. She ran forward and used the tip of her beak to snap the vine that was holding Candayce's shells on her ugly little body.

"Hey!" Candayce cried, trying to catch the shells. They dropped to the ground and Janine snatched them up.

"Catch me if you can!" Janine sang as she ran ahead into the woods. *Cha-ching, cha-ching, cha-ching!*

The tangled brush beneath Janine's feet nearly tripped her up a few times, but she managed to reach the top of a rise before Candayce's thumping footfalls caught up with her.

"Give—them—*back!*" Candayce demanded.

"Oops," Janine said, tossing the bikini top over the rise. Candayce raced after it—and stopped just short of going over the edge. She watched as her shells fell hundreds of feet and smashed on a rock.

"Fine," Candayce said, her hooves covering her scaly, flat chest.

"I'll just get some leaves and glue 'em on with sap again. Leaves are all around. Then I won't have to deal with you fixing me up anymore."

Candayce turned her back to Janine and started hunting for leaves.

"Excuse me," Janine said.

Candayce ignored her.

"Hey, *butt-face!*"

The other girl slowly turned. "What did you call me?"

"You're the one who turned around."

Candayce chuffed. Her gaze fixed firmly on Janine. She lowered her head.

"That's right. Drop to all fours and try to knock me down like a tree or something. Just forget you're the most popular girl in the eighth grade and start acting like a butt-faced dinosaur. That's what you are, after all."

Trembling, Candayce looked down at her plump little body. Her shoulders sank. Her head dropped down onto her chest. Her tail sagged. "I am," she said at last. "Aren't I?"

"A butt-face, you mean?"

Candayce raised her hoofed claws. "Just—just *stop.*"

"When are *you* going to stop with Bertram?"

"Huh?"

"Bertram. The one with the crush on you. Heaven knows why."

Candayce looked startled. "He's—he's got a...on me?"

Janine nodded. Candayce straightened up and began to laugh. Now it was Janine's turn to be startled. Candayce's howls caused her to double over. She fell to all fours, then rolled onto her side.

"It isn't funny!" Janine whipped her chain. *Cha-ching!*

"Oh, this is going to be *great!*" Candayce shrieked. Her guffaws caused her entire body to quake.

"Bertram's a decent guy," Janine said. "You'd better not—"

Candayce screamed and giggled. "Entertainment! Oh, thank you, finally, some entertainment!"

Janine stared as Candayce giggled like the cruel little witch she'd always been back in their own time. Janine knew her mistake. She'd tried to appeal to Candayce's good side. She'd assumed such a thing existed.

"My mistake," Janine muttered. She moved forward, slapping her chain. *Cha-ching!* There were other ways of making sure Candayce didn't do anything else to make Bertram feel bad…

Before Janine could reach Candayce, the trees at the edge of the clearing shuddered. Janine and Candayce looked up sharply. There was a sharp crack and a tree toppled off to their left. Another crack, and a tree sank down to their right.

"Oh, no," Candayce said. A second later, the entire pack of Leptoceratops burst out of the woods and came charging their way. Janine eyed the nearby precipice. The drop was sharp. Dangerous. She pictured the charging pack accidentally driving Candayce and herself over the edge.

Instead, the gang came to a thundering halt and ringed in Candayce. "Um…Janine?" Candayce called.

Janine tried to think of what she could do. Though her wingspan was incredible, her body was hollow-boned and scrawny. The Leptoceratops, on the other hand, were like minivan versions of Triceratops. Smaller, compact, and without the horns. But still heavy and strong.

Janine looked to the sky, hoping to see Loki watching over them. The sky was sleet gray—and empty. The Leptoceratops ringing in Candayce moved closer. The more brightly colored of them approached. They nudged her. Firmly.

"What do they *want?*" Candayce cried, terrified. Janine tried to get a little closer, but two of the plain-colored Leptoceratops turned and shot fierce growls her way. Janine let out a high caw that startled several of them.

Including, unfortunately, Candayce.

Janine sighed. "You were supposed to make a run for it. I was trying to give you a diversion."

"I didn't know! How was I supposed to know?"

The portly Leptoceratops flung himself at Janine. She darted back. He lowered his head and did it again. This time, she side-stepped, and he flopped to the ground. Several of the other Leptoceratops turned his way. They bobbed their heads and shoved at one another. Their tails lazily slapped on the ground.

Candayce suddenly sprang into action. She vaulted forward, aiming herself at a breach between two of the Leptoceratops. Janine was amazed. She had made it through!

Then four more Leptoceratops rose up and moved in upon her, gently but firmly butting her flank and driving her to the ground.

"That's it!" Candayce cried. She got up and did something odd with her claws. They flashed, and she whacked herself.

"Oww," Candayce murmured. Shaking her head, she tried to kick with her stubby little legs. And fell down.

Don't hurt yourself, a petty and very pleased voice deep within Janine's head whispered. Then the seriousness of the situation impressed itself on her, and Janine felt ashamed.

"What are you doing?" Janine asked.

"Defending myself," Candayce hissed.

"It looks like you're falling down."

Candayce got up again, and this time used her head as a weapon. She targeted a reddish-colored Leptoceratops and rammed the joint of its left shoulder and neck. It seemed surprised and stared at Candayce quizzically.

"Clavicle, knife-edge strike!" Candayce screamed. She turned, oblivious to the lack of effect her move seemed to have had upon her intended victim. She lowered her head, hooked it in front and beneath the jaw of another Leptoceratops, and brought it up sharply. This dinosaur's head slapped back. He tottered for a moment, and fell against another of the Leptoceratops.

"Palm heel underneath to chin!" Candayce barked.

This little move did not go over well with the Leptoceratops. They crowded in on Candayce en masse. Janine tried to get close, and two Leptoceratops rushed at her. Dropping her chain, she scratched at them but somehow hit Candayce instead, raking the vine that held on her bikini bottom. The shells fell away and were ground under the feet of other Leptoceratops. Then a bunch of the gray guys were in Janine's face, driving her back to the edge of the abyss.

With a shrill cry, Janine toppled back—and fell into the waiting arms of nothing at all. For a moment, she forgot to be afraid. A part of her sensed that this free fall was the most natural thing in the world for her to experience. Then she panicked. Her body flipped over in midair and she saw the ground rushing upward. *Open your wings, stupid! Do it!*

She spread her wings and was surprised as she caught an updraft. The thermal carried her a hundred feet above the ground in a graceful arc. Her head was thundering, but the feeling was exhilarating. She was flying!

She turned back in the direction of the drop and angled her wings just a little, and she started to rise.

An earthen wall approached. It was the hill she'd fallen from. She heard a rush of air and tried to *will* herself higher. The wall slapped her. The impact made her skull ring and her tender body hurt in ways she had never before imagined. She felt herself falling again. She screamed and clawed for a handhold. Anything that might save her!

She found it. Her claws became entangled in roots clustered on the side of the earthen wall. Hanging there, she hollered until finally Mike and Bertram arrived. Bertram hung his tail over the edge and Janine carefully transferred herself to it. He hauled her up and she sank to the ground, hugging it dearly.

"So where's Candayce?" Mike asked.

BRRRRRRRR-AHHHHHHHPTTT-PLLLLLUHPPPPHHH!

The noxious smell made Janine cough. "The Leptoceratops…"

"No!" Bertram whispered. They all looked around frantically, but Candayce and the Leptoceratops were gone!

Janine rose and helped Mike scan the ground for tracks. He couldn't use his nose to help find Candayce; the smells Bertram was manufacturing had taken that particular sense out of the equation.

They found a confusion of tracks, new and old, and paths that led off in a half-dozen different directions.

Janine shook her head. "You'd think we'd hear her calling for help."

"You'd think," Bertram said, head down. He looked guilty—and worried. "How far could they have taken her by now? Not so far that we can't find her. We'll find her. I know it."

Bending down, Janine picked up her fallen chain. *Cha-ching!* As she tied it tightly around her left wrist, she considered letting Bertram know that she'd told Candayce about his crush on her. But the club-tail was in such a bad state already she decided not to.

Janine didn't feel very good about the position she'd put Bertram in. Maybe she could still reach Candayce before Mike and Bertram and talk her out of punishing Bertram the way she'd vowed. She owed Bertram that much anyway.

Janine looked back to the cliff. If she could fly, really fly, then finding Candayce—and scouting the locale of the Standing Stones and the best route to them—would be easy. What she needed was some flying lessons.

Again she looked to the sky. But Loki was nowhere to be seen.

"All right," Janine said. "I'll just have to figure it out for myself."

Chapter 12 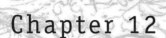 Candayce

Candayce thought she was in a movie. Okay, it wasn't a movie. But it was just as weird. She was being carried. She was on her back, up in the air, a half-dozen Leptoceratops walking in tight formation, shouldering her weight equally among them. She rocked gently, her tail drooping, her view of the world shaky and upside down. She saw trees. A forest. Big surprise. That meant she could be *anywhere*.

She wasn't sure how long it had been since the Leptomaniacs closed in on her near the rise. But it was getting darker. She couldn't tell if that was because the storm Bertram had predicted was coming or because it was getting late.

Think, she commanded herself. *You get sluggish at night. Are you feeling sluggish now?*

Actually, she was, but that might have been a result of having been knocked cold by these lunatics. *Okay, so try something else.*

"MIIIIIIIIIIIIIIIIKE!"

The Leptomaniacs yelped and scattered. Candayce wriggled in midair and fell to the smelly ground with a thud. Before her eyes, a group of white-faced, brown-bodied *ratlike things* scampered off with little squeals. Candayce picked herself up, her heavy feet crunching on a carpet of beetles. Butterflies whipped past her. The air was thick with bees.

Candayce glared at her captors. The whole pack was there. She had no idea why they were doing this. What, had she jumped into the body of the clan's princess or something?

It was possible, she supposed.

"Mike, can you hear me!" she hollered. A strange baying sound left her lips. The other Leptomaniacs imitated the sound. They could hear, but not understand, her mental cries to her friend. This other noise she was making, on the other hand, appeared to have some meaning for them.

Candayce waited. No Mike. Was he asleep? Didn't he care?

Or was he so far away that he couldn't hear her call?

Candayce forced herself to calm down. Mike would come. She knew it. He'd figure out a way and he'd come for her.

She looked around. The Leptomaniacs had taken her to a sparse forest that was lit by the vanishing sun. The light fell upon the vine-covered oaks, dogwoods, magnolias, and ficus, making them shimmer like gold. The shattered remains of tree trunks and withered branches were all around her. The ground was slightly moist.

The body of a large, long-necked plant-eating dinosaur lay dead ahead. Candayce stared at it. She'd never seen so huge a creature in her life, never even imagined she would. It must have been close to seventy feet long. And here it was, lying on its side, the life drained out of it.

She felt saddened in a way she rarely acknowledged. She felt bad not only for herself and her lost opportunity to see this creature in the full of life, but also for the long-neck. Some hidden history deep within her brain told her that the days of the long-necks were drawing to a close, at least in this part of the world. Staring at the creature, she wondered if it had died of loneliness.

A chuffing came from behind her. Candayce realized that the baying had ceased. She turned to the Leptomaniacs. They were closer now. And very attentive.

"All right," she said. "I don't care if you can't understand me exactly or not. I'm gonna talk and you're gonna listen. And you're gonna do what I say. Understood?"

The plain-skinned Leptomaniacs hung on her every word. They were the males. Suitors. Candayce was somehow sure of that. The colorful ones, the females, stared at her angrily, but made no move to stop her.

"Now," Candayce said, "I want you to take me back the exact way we came. My friend Mike will be looking for me. He'll be angry if it takes too long to find me. You don't want that." The Leptomaniacs stared at her. "Mike. The T. rex." They looked at her adoringly. Candayce flushed inwardly. *All right,* she thought, *charades. That'll work.*

She started mimicking Mike's tyrannosaur movements, trying to get her point across that way. The Leptomaniacs imitated her imitation. It made her realize it wasn't a very good imitation to start with. It was no wonder they had no idea what she was talking about.

"Okay," she said. "That's not going to work. We'll go to plan B. I'm walking out of here and no one's stopping me."

She took a few steps before the Leptomaniacs crowded in on her. She couldn't believe this!

"Leave—me—*alone!*" she bellowed. Finally, a reaction! The Leptomaniacs looked around, confused, trying to understand where her voice was really coming from, or so Candayce imagined. It gave her an idea. She thought of a sound. A car horn honking. She played the memory of it in her head at a deafening volume. The Leptoceratops darted about, panicked.

"Oh!" Candayce cried. "Didn't like that one, huh? How about this?" She sent a bullhorn and a police siren into their minds. The Leptos started mashing into one another. Jumping every time she recalled a new sound.

"Don't like it much when you're not in control, do you?" Candayce said. She looked to the females. They were worried, too, but they weren't coming quite as unglued as the males.

Candayce would have to do something about that. She considered Mike's T. rex roar. That would make them show her some respect.

GRRRRRRRR-ROOOOWWWWRRAHRRRRHHHH!

Candayce shuddered. She hadn't made that sound. The roar came again. Closer this time!

Relief spread its wings inside her. "Mike!"

Thunderous footfalls came from the trees behind the Leptomaniacs. The ground shook.

"Mike, just a little farther, here I am!"

GRR-AWWWWWHHHHRRRR!

Weird how he wasn't answering her calls. She looked at the Leptomaniacs. They were coming for her now. "You think I'm going anywhere with you people, well, you're crazy!"

The brightly colored females huddled near Candayce while the males surrounded them in a circular formation, each facing the direction of the threat. They weren't running. They were making a stand.

A tree shattered into a rain of splinters, and a wobbly T. rex appeared. His flesh was sallow. There was a madness in his eyes. It wasn't Mike.

"Oh, no," Candayce whispered. Terror gripped her and she wailed, *"MIKE!"* at the top of her lungs, praying that somehow he would hear her.

The T. rex who was already here grunted in annoyance and came for the small group. The Leptomaniacs held their ground.

Roaring, the T. rex stopped before them. He sniffed the air. Once. Twice. Again.

Candayce was too afraid to fight the instincts of her host. Just by the tyrannosaur's scent, she could tell it was an old T. rex. Two hundred years, maybe. Vision blurred. Senses dulled. And the Leptoceratops, though they might not have looked like much, had it in them to put up a real fight.

The rex looked past the group to the carcass of the long-necked dinosaur. Without a backward glance, he shambled toward it and began his feast.

Candayce stared at the Leptomaniacs in wonder. She thought about the way they had taken her. "It had something to do with Mike, didn't it? It's not natural for plant-eaters to be hanging out with predators. You thought I was being kept for food. Or I was addled or something." She stared at them in shock. "You were trying to protect me!"

The Leptoceratops, of course, did not reply. At least, not in a way Candayce could or would allow herself to understand. One of the females nuzzled her. A male brushed against her. She felt a tail resting on hers. It seemed they sensed a change in her. This time when they walked on, they didn't force her to come with them. They left the decision to her.

Candayce considered remaining on her own. Then she looked back to the old T. rex, who was savaging the long-neck's remains. She'd be safer with the group. And easier to find by Mike and the others.

Hours drifted by as she followed the Leptoceratops. They passed through dense forests, only occasionally glimpsing the waning sun above.

Ahead was a clearing, and Candayce believed they would stop there for the night. Instead, the pack pushed on, and soon a lush valley presented itself. She was startled by the sight of *hundreds* of Leptoceratops like herself. They milled about, separated into small groups.

I wonder which are the popular ones, Candayce thought.

She navigated a fern-covered hill with the others, anxious to find out.

Chapter 13

Janine

The earthen wall rushed toward her. With a sigh, Janine pulled up with her wings, knowing full well that she was going to hit it, and hit it *hard*.

The impact rattled her. Janine fell back, wings spread, and tumbled to the flat ground. She landed staring up at the purple streaks of twilight peeking through the dense black clouds overhead. The dwindling sun was a blinding streak on the horizon. A rumbling came. Mike and Bertram made their way over to her.

"Hey, that was good!" Mike said.

"You think so?" Janine asked. Her voice was almost flat, though it held an undercurrent inching toward sarcasm.

Bertram's head poked into view. "You flew for thirty seconds that time."

"I managed *not to fall* for thirty seconds," Janine corrected.

"There's a difference?"

Janine knew that there was. She climbed up the small rise they'd found hours ago, determined to try again. Her chain was coming loose. *Cha-ching, cha-ching.* For some reason, it was annoying her. But rather than leave it on the ground, she tied it more securely around her wrist. The shells stopped clacking.

"It's not gonna help, your pushing yourself," Mike said. "Why don't you rest?"

"We're losing time," Janine said. "We should have covered another thirty miles today."

"It's not your fault," Bertram called, a slight tremor in his voice. "You couldn't have stopped what happened."

She hated the way Bertram sounded. He was blaming himself for what happened to Candayce.

Janine trudged up the incline. She'd sent herself off from thirty feet last time. She reached the special mark she'd made in the dirt— her tag from her graffiti days. Sighing, she climbed another ten feet, then turned around and unfurled her wings.

"I'm not worried about whose fault it is," Janine said. "I'm…never mind."

Janine didn't want to explain herself to Mike and Bertram. They might not understand. This whole flying thing had become about more than trying to rescue Candayce. In fact, if it weren't for Bertram's feelings of guilt, Janine wouldn't have minded *never* finding that little witch.

Each time she'd soared today, Janine had felt special. A freedom and a sense of peace unlike any she'd ever known had flooded through her. Her refusal to give up had nothing to do with guilt or her natural stubborn resolve not to let anything beat her. She was doing this for herself.

"Can't give up," Janine said. It was true. She couldn't. She felt as if she was close to a breakthrough. If only the Quetzalcoatlus within her would cooperate more. This body *knew* how to fly. But it wouldn't give up its secrets.

Janine launched herself off the flat earthen wall, her wings straight, her stomach again leaping into her long throat.

Rrrrrrrr-crrrrrrwwwwwhhhhhrrrrrr?

Janine fought the urge to look up sharply at the sound. She'd found that the position of her head made a difference in her flying. Besides, she knew who it was. She'd been expecting him for some time. Her heart thundered with excitement. It was Loki. The Trickster.

"Nice one with Candayce's shells," she said.

Her fellow Quetzalcoatlus soared before her. Janine's eyes widened. For an instant, his wings were so close, they obscured her view. She saw a flash of gold, with hints of azure and crimson, then the colors streaked beyond her field of vision. It was like staring into the sun and quickly looking away, the image burning in your vision for a few seconds before fading. Incredible.

Keeping her head straight, she looked down and saw Loki soaring toward Mike and Bertram.

"Hey!" the T. rex yelled. It came out as a terrible roar.

The Quetzalcoatlus turned sharply and dropped his feet downward. For a split second he hung there, wings unfurled, appearing suspended in midair. Then he was driven up and back. He looked like a parachute that had just opened suddenly, catching an updraft.

Janine watched, fascinated, completely unaware of her own actions. Reaching out with her right claw and drawing back an equal distance with her left, she described a lazy circle over her friends.

Loki wasn't finished with the others. He flipped over backward, then gracefully regained his dive-bomber pose. He arced slightly, caught another breeze, and zoomed toward Bertram. He came within a foot of the club-tail and—

BRRRRR-AHHHHHPT!

Loki burped right in Bertram's face! Bertram's head was swaying slightly. He didn't seem to like the smell.

Janine giggled. She couldn't help herself. She giggled like a little kid. Man, she couldn't remember the last time she'd felt like that! "Go get him, fish-breath!" she called to Loki. And without thinking, she sailed in a wide arc, floating effortlessly above the earth. She felt something. A wind. A strange undercurrent. A *thermal.*

Completely relaxed, she closed her eyes and allowed her body to drift into it. There was a moment of turbulence, and it frightened her, but only a little. She held on and her body twisted to one side and rose up, and up...

She opened her eyes and gasped. She was a hundred feet over the land.

Whoa, what was I thinking! she screamed in her head.

She heard a rustle of wings. Looking over, she saw Loki beside her. His head wiggled a little and he made a sharp little *caw!* that made her smile. Her fear receded and he stared at her, his dark eyes instantly arresting.

This is what you wanted, his gaze seemed to say, *so why are you afraid? Don't back down now. Let it go.*

Janine thought of the times late at night when she'd sneak away from the bed-and-breakfast her mother ran. She'd be alone in the streets with her gear stashed in her backpack. Her gaze would search the clean, smooth surfaces of buildings that hadn't yet been graced with her artistic prowess. And she'd feel a near-mystical sensation as she looked at the side of a wall and pictured it as a canvas, ripe and calling out to her for adornment.

That same feeling was with her now—only it was different somehow. Better. Because the thrill that came to her in the middle of the night was gone—the thrill of knowing you were doing something wrong, that you could get busted and be in for a world of trouble. It had been replaced by another, greater feeling. The thrill of knowing she was right where she belonged, and what she was doing was the most natural thing in the whole wide world.

Janine let out her anxiety in a single shuddering breath. A wave of calmness settled over her.

She never took her gaze off Loki.

Her companion arced a little to one side. She followed. He moved his head and wings just a touch and rose a few more yards. She did that, too.

He dove abruptly, racing away from her, becoming tiny so *suddenly* that it took her breath away.

She didn't follow. It was too much. Too fast. Instead, she tried to lower her head and wings a few degrees, then a few more, but she was keeping herself too rigid, trying too hard. A surge of wind came at her, and she wasn't ready for it. Her body was tight and hard. The wind hit her like a balled-up fist and she tumbled backward, spinning, falling—

A caw brought her back. She closed her eyes, found the currents, and righted herself. Then she drifted slowly, awkwardly, in ever-tightening circles back down to the ground.

She smashed into the earthen wall for another hard landing. Pain rippled through her, and she flopped down to the ground. Looking up quickly, she saw Loki soar into the skies. She studied his expression. He seemed annoyed at her for coming down, but this time he was willing to wait.

"I'm going up again," Janine said as Mike and Bertram came over. "Did you see me? Did you see? I'm going up—"

A tiny, far-off voice interrupted. *"—Miiike!"*

Candayce's voice. Then it was gone.

"Did you hear that?" Mike asked.

Janine and Bertram nodded.

Mike turned. "I felt the direction it was coming from. I think I've got an idea which way we need to go."

"I'm with you," Bertram said.

Janine shook her head. "I'm not ready yet."

Mike appeared startled. "But you—"

"I'm not *ready,*" she said firmly. "I need to practice more. Just go on ahead, I'll catch up before too long."

Bertram hesitated. "You were really something up there."

She nodded, feeling something she honestly couldn't put into words. A strangeness about herself, about her companions.

"Okay," Mike said. He turned and started stomping off. "See you soon."

"Not if I see you first," Janine said coolly.

Mike stopped. He looked at her with concern.

"Just kidding," Janine said, though she really wasn't sure why she'd said that—or, more to the point, why she'd said it *that way.*

Nodding, Mike turned and walked on, Bertram rushing in beside him.

"You should go ahead," Bertram said anxiously. "You can get there faster. I'll—"

"We go together. It's getting dark. We stay together."

Janine looked to the sky. Loki was still circling overhead. It occurred to her that she had never seen him on the ground. He couldn't stay in the air all the time. Where did he sleep? What did he like to eat?

She had more of a curiosity about these things than about where Candayce had been taken. A part of her felt this was wrong, while another part felt it couldn't have been more natural.

She climbed up the rise, reaching a hundred feet this time before she turned and launched herself into the blazing sunset without once looking down.

Chapter 14

Candayce

"You've made a mistake," Candayce said. She stood before a collection of brilliantly colored Leptoceratops who stared at her with cool, unblinking eyes. Behind her was a group of very old, very sick, and very young Leptoceratops. Candayce had no idea why she'd been lumped in with them—unless they thought she was crazy.

"Look, I have good reason for being with Mike," Candayce explained. "He might be a T. rex, but he's also the cutest guy in the eighth grade, and I'm by *far* the cutest girl in the eighth grade. It's like a karma thing, you know? Our chakras are meant to merge, y'dig?"

Candayce realized she was blathering. She was mixing together things she'd read in a New Age book with a lesson from her sensei.

It occurred to her that maybe she should have been listening a little more closely to what her sensei had actually said in class. Maybe she should have been paying more attention to a whole lot of things.

Candayce looked around. The Leptoceratops' "village" amounted to flatlands with a half-dozen small mounds bearing who knows what. That was it. Candayce figured that the mounds were important, because the "in" Leptos congregated around them. She'd tried to get close enough to take a look inside one of them, but she'd been shoved away, and pretty roughly, too, for her trouble.

"Okay, here's the thing," Candayce said. "You've seen the way all those guys were drooling over me, right? That makes me a hot property. Like visiting royalty. You don't dump visiting royalty in with the lame-os and the old farts." She looked over her shoulder. "Nothing personal."

The conglomerate of Leptomaniacs conferred among themselves. They gestured toward the group with whom Candayce had been shooed and started making chomping noises.

"It's dinnertime and..." Candayce began, trying to get their drift. "It's dinnertime and you want me to eat with them. No, this is what I'm telling you, I—"

One of the Leptomaniacs charged Candayce, who was totally unprepared for the attack. All she saw was a flash of purple and gold before being slammed onto her backside.

As she lay there, catching her breath, it occurred to her that she'd spent a lot of time like this lately. Knocked down onto her butt.

She didn't like it, but decided to mask her displeasure. She slowly got up. Behind the females, some males were drifting over to see what was going on.

This is more like it, Candayce thought. *These guys will straighten out these stupid-looking cows.*

Two of the females turned sharply and stamped their feet and their tails. The males lowered their heads and retreated.

So much for that. Candayce gave up. "All right. I'll eat with the dweebs or whatever. What's for dinner? No, wait, lemme guess— leaves! Right? We'll eat some leaves! And if we're really lucky, something gross and slimy will be crawling on them first! Hey, can I call 'em or what?"

The female Leptoceratops stared at her. They made chomping noises again.

"Fine," Candayce said. "You're all a bunch of vegetarians. Well, I'll tell you, where I come from, it's not easy staying on a veggie diet. And it's expensive, too. You people have it made. Except for all the carnivores."

The female Leptoceratops gestured at the weak group behind Candayce, next at the forest in the distance, then made chomping sounds. Candayce took a long, hard look at the Leptoceratops behind her. They looked at her pitifully, the young with wide, teary eyes, the old with resignation and need, the sick with envy. They were *all* hungry. She could feel it.

"Well, what?" Candayce asked. "You can't expect them to get food for themselves. What are you waiting for?"

She looked back and found the gathering staring at *her.*

"Oh," she whispered. "You want *me* to get dinner for them. Oh, I get it…like, I've got to prove myself worthy of joining the group or something. Like when some new girl wants to hang with Tanya and me. Okay, I can do that."

A trio of male Leptoceratops pushed their way forward, through the gathering. Candayce recognized them. Han, Brad, and Bluto—the portly one. Candayce went to them, head held high. "Okay, guys. Don't get any ideas."

The females let her by. Candayce saw a healthy-looking grove of trees on the outskirts of the Leptomaniacs' "camp" and pointed. One of the females butted her.

"Thanks," Candayce said.

Another moved in to do the same. Candayce raised one hooflike paw. "Ahhhhhh!" she cried in warning. The second female stopped in her tracks. "One to a customer." The female looked to the others, who appeared equally clueless.

"Whatever. Come on, guys," Candayce said. She led her little entourage toward the outskirts of the valley, passing the well-guarded and mysterious mounds. A sudden memory of the giant turtles laying their eggs on the beach seized her, and she finally had an idea of what was going on here.

Tiny, vibrating chirping sounds came from the mounds. Candayce saw a little Leptoceratops poke his head over one side.

"Oh, how *cute!*" Candayce cooed. Then she caught herself. "In a ridiculous kind of way, of course. They're still a bunch of losers."

She walked with her posse to the grove of six-foot-high drooping horsetails and ferns with four-foot rigid featherlike branches. It occurred to her that if she was back in her own time, and at a party, she wouldn't wander off with three guys she barely knew. Her nervousness instantly subsided when she saw their lovesick expressions.

"Okay, so time to get some," Candayce said.

The trio of Leptomaniacs came a little closer.

"Grub. Get some grub. *Jeez*."

At the grove, Candayce used her beak to tear off low branches covered with leaves. She dropped them to the ground beside her, starting a collection. The male Leptoceratops just watched. They were her escorts, Candayce presumed. Charged with the task of making sure she didn't run off. At least they weren't knocking down any trees in her honor. She could be grateful for that much, anyway.

Soon she had a pile of leaves so big she wanted to take a running leap and dive headlong into it. She hated to admit it, but this was actually fun. And those other Leptoceratops really *were* hungry—the old and sick ones and the little guys.

She wondered what it must be like, not being able to fend for yourself. What if something happened to her and she had to depend on someone else for every little thing? The thought frightened her.

From behind, she heard a munching sound. Spinning, she saw Bluto and the others noshing on her spoils.

"What are you guys doing!" she yelled. She drove them off, hissing and spitting. They backed away sheepishly, huge mouthfuls of branches and leaves hanging from their beaks. "No wonder they send the women to go get food. Men are babies, even back here. Helpless, pathetic. Nothing ever changes, does it? Jeez, why do we girls ever think we need anything from you guys?"

Bluto, Han, and Brad exchanged worried glances. Lowering their heads and moaning, they opened their maws wide and spit out the leaves. Candayce couldn't help but notice that the leaves hadn't been chewed. There was no reason for it—a typical Leptoceratops had fifteen rows of teeth! But these guys had only held the leaves in their mouths, as if preparing to move them, not consume them.

Candayce looked at the pile she'd created, and wondered how *she'd* thought she'd move them. There really was only one way. "Oh," she said. "Sorry, guys. I get it now. You were trying to help."

The Leptoceratops stared at her blankly. Candayce knew she had to find a way to let the guys know it was okay to start hauling the leaves back to the hungry ones. Hmmmmm.

She leaned down, picked up a mouthful of the leaves, and stepped gingerly to her companions. An expectant fire exploded in their eyes. Candayce realized the mistake she was about to make. She dropped the mouthful of leaves as if it was covered in thorns. The guys looked at her, sad and disappointed. Candayce sighed. If she had passed the leaves to any one of the three, that one would have been convinced that she was choosing among them.

Suddenly, all three surged forward, butting heads and shoving at one another to gather up the mouthful of leaves Candayce left on the ground. Candayce turned away from their snorts and grunts. Her suitors would work it out.

She went back to gathering leaves. Her jaws clamped over a heavy branch and accidentally closed on a dark, bumpy sphere sitting nearby. A loud *squish* came from somewhere. Fruitopia!

A rush of flavor filled her mouth. Berries! They were delicious! Then she felt something on her face. Dripping down. She looked at her paws in the dwindling light. They were covered in the crimson goo from the squashed berries.

Her thoughts flashed crazily on Tanya's henna tattoos. And on oddities like Janine, who made being rejected by one's peers an art form. Hmm. She took in her surroundings as if she was seeing them for the first time. The wealth of flowering plants. A rainbow of colors, of possibilities.

"Boys," she whispered, "it's time I got dressed for the party."

Twenty minutes later, Candayce emerged from the grove. Her three stooges followed a considerable distance behind.

At once, all activity among the Leptoceratops came to an end. All gazes were fixed on Candayce. Every head was turned.

Candayce had never looked worse in her entire life—and she was loving it. She'd squashed berries to paint her scales red and purple. She'd mashed up a collection of bright yellow, pink, turquoise, and emerald flowers into a kaleidoscopic paste that she'd mixed with sap and streaked all over herself. She'd glued flowers on her forehead and vines to her head. The vines dangled like dreadlocks

and flopped into her face as she walked. She didn't care. She was, without a doubt, the biggest eyesore ever to walk the Late Cretaceous. It was an honor she cherished.

In her mouth was a collection of leaves. She danced through the valley, shaking her backside, as she let the memory of a song from her time ripple outward from her mind. She swayed. She sashayed. She spun around like a little kid. She pictured spotlights. A dance floor. If this didn't make her suitors go running for the hills, nothing would!

Finally, Candayce reached the little collection of helpless Leptoceratops. She dropped her leaves near them. Brad, Han, and Bluto did the same. Candayce danced around all three of them, throwing her head back, wiggling her hips, and shaking her dumpy, bumpy booty.

Suddenly, a thundering was heard. Candayce felt the earth tremble. She looked around just in time to catch two incredibly alarming facts. The males—every male—had come close, and they were bobbing their heads, swaying a little with her dance, staring at Candayce with wonder—and with powerful interest.

And one of the females, the largest, and most gaudily colored of the herd, was charging her.

Candayce yelped. She saw a blur of pastel green, sky blue, and banana yellow. Then she felt the impact! "Oww!" she yelped as she was knocked on her butt yet again.

Staring up at the sky, she saw the first faint hint of stars. She heard the female turning and coming around again. Then a low growl and a chuffing sounded, and the female halted. Candayce got up slowly, achingly, and saw a male approaching. All the other males parted for this one. Candayce could guess why.

Behind her, another growl. Candayce looked down at her crazily colored form and understood the terrible error she'd made. What was ugly to her wasn't necessarily ugly to these guys. Just look at *them,* she reminded herself.

She awkwardly yanked off the vines, then dropped to the ground and rolled around as if she was having an attack. Dirt and herbs stuck to her, but she didn't care. In fact, the more, the better. When she was done, a small rainbow-colored dent had been left in the earth, and Candayce was back—pretty much—to her old self.

The female who'd charged her and the male who'd displayed momentary interest were now wandering away together, occasionally glancing back. She looked back to the old, the sick, the young ones…and sat down with them.

They stared at her, obviously grateful for the food she'd brought, which they noisily, disgustingly, gobbled up. Burps, snapping twigs, bugs buzzing around, chewing, swallowing, saliva dripping like water from a faucet. Candayce had some, too.

She noticed Brad and Bluto still hanging around. Han had taken off. Candayce thought perhaps the whole thing had just gotten too weird for him. Or maybe he was hungry. Or tired.

The sky darkened completely, and soon only the moon and the stars provided any light. Candayce could still see her companions.

At this point, she didn't care what clique she'd been tossed in with. Mike would come. She was certain of that. Then this craziness would end.

She looked over at Bluto and Brad, and couldn't help but think of Bertram. Had he looked at her with that same kind of puppy-dog affection? Why hadn't she noticed? Of course, if she had noticed, she'd have just made it worse for him. A part of her wondered why.

Staring at the boys, she decided it was habit. Whether it was a good habit or not, well...*whatever.*

A tiny warbling came from off to her left. Candayce saw a very small Leptoceratops sitting alone, shaking. A few leaves lay next to the little guy, but he wasn't eating them. The others were looking at him, not at Candayce, and that much was a relief.

"What's the matter?" Candayce barked. The small Leptoceratops jumped. He looked over his shoulder with wide eyes, then averted his gaze quickly. He was afraid of her. Too afraid to eat. And he needed to eat.

Candayce felt like a complete creep. No one—absolutely no one in her entire life—had made her feel quite as bad as this little *creature* had with that one fleeting look. She knew she had to do something.

She went to him, on all fours. It was gross and humiliating, but something deep inside told her it was the right thing to do. The little guy looked up. His eyes were moist. They glistened in the moonlight.

"Don't be scared," Candayce said in her most soothing voice. She heard a coo from somewhere, a deep, lovely, warbling coo, and was stunned to find that it was drifting from her own beak. The little guy trembled, his flank rising and falling quickly. Candayce was next to him. She gently pushed a leaf close to him, then looked away.

Something tickled her side. She glanced down to see the little guy licking at the sap and flowers still stuck to her. His tongue looked black in the moonlight. Berry juice.

"Ugh," Candayce whispered, "this is taking bonding a little too far." The little guy didn't seem to notice. Candayce picked up the leaves with her beak and dropped them onto her legs. The little guy went for them greedily, biting and chomping, but never hurting her.

"Was it the dancing?" Candayce asked. "Is that what scared you so much? Or was it the music?"

The munching Lepto didn't look up. He just gobbled away, and Candayce felt a warmth spreading through her.

"Did you know I played the piano?" Candayce asked. She looked at her malformed claws. In her time, in her *body,* she had long, slender, perfect fingers. But here—she couldn't play a note with these monstrosities. Or could she?

Candayce closed her eyes and concentrated. A piece of music she'd never quite been able to master flowed from her memory. It was Chopin's *Raindrop* Prelude. She'd struggled so hard to learn the piece because she knew it was one of her mother's favorites, but she could never play it well enough.

It was a beautiful, luscious piece, moving, soft, like the raindrops for which it had been named, but she had never been able to get it right. She'd never managed the emotions, the richness of it, never done it well enough to make her mom smile the way she had when she heard the piece on CD or in concert when someone else, anyone else, played it.

This time, it was different. Candayce felt the music changing. She wasn't just playing back a recording in her head. She was giving it voice with her imagination. She was playing the *Raindrop* Prelude, and playing it very well. Exquisitely, in fact. It was everything she'd dreamed it could be, everything she'd ever imagined.

The music drifted up from her soul. It blanketed the night. And for the first time since she'd fallen out of her body, out of her time, Candayce felt truly happy.

Chapter 15

Mike

Mike and Bertram stumbled through the darkness, desperate to find their way. It had been a long time since they'd heard Candayce's cry. Mike wondered what had made her scream like that—and why they'd heard nothing since.

Sniffing, Mike tried to pick up her scent.

Nothing. Of course, his nose wasn't good for much right now. Beside him, Bertram gasped as another blast of exhaust fumes left his rear compartment. The stink was overwhelming. Mike kept telling himself that he'd get used to it, but he hadn't so far and feared that he never would.

"Bertram, stop eating," Mike said.

"I haven't eaten since earlier today."

"Then stop—"

"I can't help it!"

Mike shook his head. He knew Bertram was telling the truth. He also knew that riding his friend over his indelicate condition wasn't going to help either of them.

His *friend*?

"I don't know if we're going in the right direction anymore," Bertram said at last.

"I haven't known that for the last three hours," Mike said. "Make that four."

Bertram's fat elephantlike foot splashed and water rose up around him. "Puddle," Bertram said morosely.

Mike took a step forward and splashed as well. "Big puddle."

They stepped back. The ground was soft and muddy. Mike turned, took another step, and walked straight into a tree. "I can't see where I'm going. This is hopeless."

"It's not hopeless."

"All right—*we're* hopeless," said Mike.

"No we're not."

"All right, *I* am." Mike waited for a reply. Kept waiting. "Feel free to contradict—"

"Listen!" Bertram whispered.

A light vibrato came to Mike. The sound was unnatural. Hollow. A few tinny notes bouncing off one another, shuddering, shaking, echoing in the darkness.

"Do you think it's Mr. London?" Mike asked anxiously. "Do you think maybe he found a way to send us another message, or maybe a way to get us back without—"

"I don't know. Shh. Just listen."

Mike strained to hear more. The odd trilling sound increased. Two more nearly identical trills joined the first.

"We must be near the river," Bertram said as they moved slowly forward.

"I think this *is* the river."

"Maybe. Dunno."

Mike heard the gentle gurgling of water flowing around stones. Bugs buzzing. Frogs. And that trilling. Mike looked around. "What's making that strange noise? That's what I want to know."

"Let's see if we can get past all these trees," Bertram said. "Maybe if we can see the moon and the stars…"

"Right."

As quietly as they could, Mike and Bertram made their way around a half-dozen trees. Beyond them, they found—more trees.

"Oh, *man*," Mike growled in frustration and threw himself at one of the trees, snapping it. There was a crackling, then a whoosh of air, as the splintered upper portion of the tree fell away and splashed into the water, where it triggered an eruption of movement. Thrashing. Strange calls. Scurrying. Then silence.

Bertram poked his head over the stump. "Hey, Mike?"

"What?"

"Clearing. Three trees down."

Mike's shoulders sagged. He followed Bertram to the clearing. They reached it and Mike took in the stars shimmering on the surface of the rushing river. The water went right up to the tree line. Mike looked at the sky. Beyond the heavy veil of clouds, he could see the stars and the three-quarter moon. The trilling came again.

"There," Bertram said. "Look!"

Floating on the surface of the river was a pair of eyes sparkling with moonlight. Mike saw them blink. One pair of eyelids moved up and down, in a normal fashion, while a second pair closed side to side. Above the eyes was a bumpy, lumpy forehead and a craggy crest that smoothed down into the water.

"Some kind of amphibian," Bertram said.

Mike nodded. The little head rose up a little more, revealing a long, recognizable snout. A long, smooth back and a gently whipping tail emerged. The creature was only three feet in length.

"Crocodile," Mike said. "Just a baby."

The little croc trilled. Somewhere close, his call was joined. Mike relaxed. He studied the water. It was brimming with life. Lowering his snout, he said, "Think I could go for a midnight snack."

"Hey!" Bertram cried.

Mike shook his head. "Not the croc. Look around." He pointed to the water. A school of fish two-thirds the size of the baby croc swam around him. They were golden and looked like eels with fins.

"Ceratodus," Bertram whispered.

Suddenly, the baby croc darted at one of the eel fish and snatched it from the water. The fish struggled, slapping back and forth. Frantically, it whapped the baby croc on the head with its body. The baby croc's jaws opened slightly and the captive fish flew free.

"Here," Mike said to the baby croc, "I'll shove some your way." He dipped his head into the water, his maw open wide. He was beginning to enjoy trawling. He would savor this meal.

His snout bounced off something in the water. He pulled out, only a handful of fish squirming in his mouth. Perplexed, he chewed, crunched, swallowed. He wondered what he'd hit. The water *looked* deep.

Suddenly, Bertram gasped. Mike tensed. The last time Bertram had gasped, it turned out to be a prelude to one of his prehistoric killer gas attacks. Mike really was in no mood for that.

The water rippled, and the baby croc started to rise. Mike blinked. For a moment, he wasn't sure what he was witnessing. The baby croc seemed to be resting on something. Was it a sunken log or piece of flotsam? As he watched, a half-dozen more baby crocs came into view, wriggling and crawling over the rising thing. Mike stared at the "log." It had scales. An immense pair of glaring eyes. A snout. And teeth.

"Big mother—" Mike began.

"Yeah," Bertram finished.

The crocodile rising from the river was—for a moment—as long and as wide as the river itself. Mike couldn't see the other bank. He couldn't see the end of the monster croc's body. It just stretched on and on.

"It's bigger than us!" Bertram said in a high, almost hysterical voice. "A lot bigger."

Mike didn't need to be told that. He saw its tail whip out of the water, and judged that it was at least fifty feet long. The croc was big enough to eat *him*.

"Run," Mike whispered. "Run—"

There was no time for Mike to issue the warning again. The crocodile leaped from the water, her offspring flying from her back, her jaws opened wide. Then she was on him! Her hot, fetid breath filled his snout with a complex mix of horrid stenches. Her jaws closed over Mike's head. Everything went black as he felt her teeth biting into the tough scales of his neck. Mike's little claws trembled. Yet he was still awake. Still *aware*.

Then he was lurching forward, falling headlong into the river. The mighty grip of the crocodile's jaws tightened and pulled, straining to haul him downward.

Mike tried to open his jaws and bite as the water splashed around him. But there was no room inside the pressing depths of the croc's mouth. He couldn't open his jaws. Nor could he breathe. And water was coming in fast, one second a chilling trickle, the next, a freezing torrent.

Holding his breath, he clawed and struggled and kicked. He whipped his tail. He sank.

Suddenly, explosions shook the river. One of the depth charges connected with the crocodile's body, and her hold loosened. Mike's claws found the soft underbelly of the croc. He dug in, hard.

Whipping, fighting, the croc opened her jaws. Mike yanked his head out. He was free!

But water still surrounded him. He couldn't hold his breath much longer. His heavy body struck the gnarled roots of a gigantic tree. Beside it he saw something that sent slivers of cold steel into his brain.

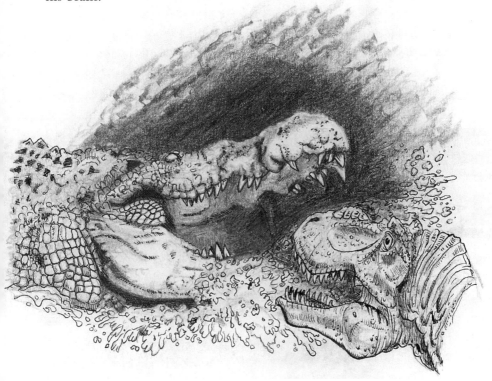

A skeleton sat next to the roots. A *tyrannosaur* skeleton.

He climbed onto the lowest and nearest leg in the tangle of roots. It looked to him like a ladder. He pushed with his powerful legs and drifted upward, his chest burning, straining. Then the moonlit surface came for him. His head broke free! Water poured from his snout. He climbed up the network of roots and thrust himself halfway out of the river.

Ten feet away, standing on the riverbank, was Bertram. The Ankylosaurus yelled and cheered, his tail hanging over the surface of the water. Bertram's club-tail had provided the depth charges!

Suddenly, just beneath Bertram's overhanging tail, the water churned. The trilling rose to a fever pitch.

"Bertram!" Mike screamed.

The croc broke from the water, leaping high, her massive jaws clamping down on Bertram's tail. She sank back and Bertram slid toward the river's edge.

"Dig in, don't let her drag you down!" Mike hollered.

Bertram lowered himself to the ground, shoving with his full weight. The croc's jaws remained fixed on his tail, and her form stilled.

Mike stared at the distance separating him from the mother crocodile. If he leaped fully into the river once more, the current and his momentum would take him to the croc. He tensed his muscles, prepared to spring—

"No—don't!" Bertram hollered.

"Bertram, it'll—"

"I said don't!"

"But, Bertram!" Mike cried anxiously, wondering whether the croc would close her jaws completely and bite his friend's tail off. The croc shuddered. It twisted a few times.

Above, on solid earth, Bertram trembled. And nearby, Mike waited, prepared to go into battle—to drag this monster into the depths and hold it there, to make sure Bertram could get away.

Mike's swollen belly was heaving, his row after row of teeth were grinding, his breath was coming in little snorts and gasps. He stared at the frozen battle before him, aware of the night sounds.

The buzzing flies. The gentle flow of the river. The trilling of the baby crocs.

There were at least a dozen babies floating near their mother. Suddenly, one climbed onto her, his little back foot stepping onto her eye. Both her eyelids closed and the eyeball was poked inward, like a half-deflated beach ball; then the foot was removed and the eye popped back to its normal shape and blinked open.

The mother crocodile shook herself and loosened her maw. Bertram quickly yanked his tail free, slapping it upward and to one side hard enough to make the ground shudder as it connected. There was a slight splash. Mike looked back to the water. He couldn't see the—

"It's still there," Bertram said. "Flat. Its body's so flat, you can't see it."

Mike looked at the ripples in the water, the ones fighting the current. The croc was coming back for him! He scrambled up along the tangled network of roots, anxious to get himself out of the way before it was too late.

"Mike, no!" Bertram wailed.

Mike planted one leg on the firm ledge of solid earth, then heard a snapping of teeth behind him. He vaulted the rest of the way, tripping and falling facedown on the ground, rolling to one side.

He heard a frantic pawing, and he turned over in time to see a blur of movement—something huge, unbelievably big, breaking from the surface with a spray of icy water. A head so big it blotted out the stars, erased reason. Glittering teeth and hungry, insane eyes. The croc was almost on him!

He rolled to his belly, brought his feet up under himself. He heard a scurrying of movement, felt the ground shudder, but he was dizzy and cold and couldn't get his bearings.

"Bertram?" For a split second, he couldn't see the crocodile. "Where—"

"Mike!"

A biting, flashing, roaring pain ripped into Mike's backside as the croc sank her teeth into him. He rose, shaking his tail, desperately trying to dislodge his attacker. He saw a tree ten feet ahead and thought about spinning himself around and smashing the croc into it. He tried to take a step, but the croc's incredible weight—ten times the size of crocodiles in his era—held him fast.

"Don't move!" Bertram cried. "Be submissive!"

"Be—?"

"Pretend it's your coach! Just do what it says, don't worry if it makes sense or not!"

What it says? Mike thought. *It's not saying anything, it's just—it's just telling me…to hold still.*

Mike held still. He lowered his head and waited. The croc wriggled her head a little. She shook her jaws, bringing little needlelike stings of pain to Mike's backside and left flank. He didn't move—and suddenly the croc let go. She slammed him with her snout, knocking him over, then scrambled back to the river. There was a splash, then a flick of her tail, and she settled onto the surface, nearly invisible. The trilling came again, and her young gathered on her.

Mike looked over to Bertram. "Why didn't you use your tail, the way you did before?"

"She didn't like it. She didn't like us being so close to her babies, and she just plain didn't like *you.*"

"Huh," Mike said. "You got all that—how?"

"She could've eaten you, Mike. She could've cut you in half before you hit the water. She didn't. She wasn't hungry. You were lucky. *We* were lucky. How about we move our lucky backsides out of here, okay? We know from before, when you could still scent okay, that the river runs east another twenty miles. So, now that we've got our bearings—"

A brilliant light filled Mike's vision. Thunder sounded from somewhere close.

"Oh, *now* what?" Bertram asked. Mike turned. A curtain of rain struck hard. It came from nowhere. It was as if he'd been under a tent in a thunderstorm and someone had taken a knife to the roof, letting in all the water. The moon, which had been bright a moment before, was now half-buried behind thick dark clouds.

Bertram looked anxiously toward the river. "Oh, no. I was worried about this."

"What?" Mike said. He suddenly realized that all the mucking about in the water had at least cleared his nasal passages. His sense of smell was sharper than ever. He detected a bitter, acrid odor. Smoke? And a crackling electricity, similar to when Mr. London had sent his message. Similar—but not quite the same.

Lightning tore across the sky with skeletal fingers, two strikes from opposite directions that came down and interlocked like joined hands. They faded.

"Whoa," Mike said. He looked to Bertram, who was waddling away as fast as he could. He caught up in seconds. "What was it you worried about?"

"Flash floods," Bertram said, moving swiftly now, as swiftly as he could. "They were common in this time period. The rains made the rivers overflow and—"

Lightning came again. It struck somewhere close.

The rain stopped as suddenly as it had begun.

"Freaky," Mike said. He took another step and nearly tripped. Looking down, he noted a deep depression in the earth. It was a track. A tyrannosaur track. Only—this one was larger than any other Mike had come across. It was so big that it could only have come from one source.

"Moriarty," Mike said breathlessly.

"What?" Bertram asked.

"Nothing," Mike said. But that wasn't true. He'd had nightmares since the day the giant T. rex was taken out to sea by the Elasmosaurus. Dreams that Moriarty had escaped and was stalking him. These are old tracks, he tried to tell himself. Of course, he couldn't really tell old tracks from new. And he wasn't about to wake his sleeping host for a second opinion. It was just a sense he had.

"Mike, what's the matter?" Bertram asked.

"Nothing. Everything's fine," Mike said, doing his best to mask the tremor in his voice. He looked around, half-expecting to see Moriarty nearby, watching, waiting…For a moment, he wondered if he was just imagining all this stuff about Moriarty to give him something else to think about other than Lowell and Sean.

"So much for flash floods," Mike said quickly.

"Believe me, I'm glad to be wrong."

Mike turned to Bertram. "You know, back there, with the crocodile, I was scared out of my mind. Weren't you?"

Bertram looked up. He appeared deep in thought. Finally, he said, "Well, I didn't really have the time. Just trying to deal, that's all."

Mike laughed. "You're pretty amazing, you know that?"

Bertram's head bobbed happily. "You mean that?"

"You've got more guts than I—"

A brilliant, blinding flash of light made Mike freeze in his tracks. He saw lightning strike a tree a hundred yards to his right. The bolt had come from the sky, a zigzag of pure destructive energy. A heavy branch toppled from above and fell in front of them. It was still smoking.

"Lucky it was wet. It didn't catch fire," Bertram said as thunder rumbled ominously around them.

Mike sniffed. "It did catch fire," he said. "Just not here. Look!"

In the distance, a reddish orange glow rose above the treetops.

"The Leptoceratops," Mike said. "I can smell them now." He nodded in the direction of the flames. "Bertram! They're right in the middle of the fire!"

Chapter 16

Candayce

Candayce had been one of the first to realize what was happening. Lightning had struck the dry, brittle trees a mile or so away, setting off a furious blaze. The Leptoceratops were panicking, fleeing the valley and racing into the woods, taking their chances with the fire that had all but ringed them in.

"There's nowhere to go!" Candayce yelled. "We have to stay here, we—!"

A searing bolt of lightning tore from the sky and struck the ground a half-dozen yards behind her. She felt its electric caress, its heat and curiosity. The light flared, then faded, and she understood why the Leptoceratops were abandoning the valley.

She turned to the collection of helpless Leptoceratops she'd been forced to look after. "Okay," she whispered, "I can admit I'm wrong. Come on, guys. Maybe we can find a stream or something to hide in."

They weren't moving. A few looked as if they were injured and *couldn't* move. The others were paralyzed with fear. Candayce screamed for help, projecting sirens into the minds of the Leptomaniacs to get their attention. Nothing.

"Jeez," she muttered. One minute she was *all that*, no matter what she did; the next, she couldn't get arrested by these guys. She

129

saw Brad and Bluto and decided to try one of the oldest routines on record. She placed her hooflike claws to her lower jaw, sighed, and swooned.

She hit the ground hard just as thunder shook the ground and the blackened sky turned white again. Lightning struck the far side of the valley. Brad and Bluto ran her way.

"It's about time," she said. Brad went around her. Bluto tripped over her, then picked himself up and scrambled away.

Candayce sat up. "You—you—"

She couldn't find the words. Lightning came again. One of the fleeing Leptoceratops screamed. Brad. He toppled over, smoking and twitching.

"No," Candayce cried. "No!"

But her screams did nothing to stop nature's fury.

She started to weep, then the words of her sensei emerged from her memory: *Pitying one's self is a form of theft. It robs you of action, and when you are in danger, action is oftentimes all that can save you.*

"Think," she growled. She looked to the helpless Leptos. Counted heads. Nine in all. If she had time, she could find vines, maybe fashion some kind of a litter to carry one or two of the sick. But there was no time. And her claws really weren't dexterous enough for the task.

Lightning flashed. Closer this time. Candayce heard a shrill cry. Another Leptoceratops fell!

Options, she said firmly in her head. *Options, blast it!*

She could maybe nudge and shove one or two of the helpless Leptos ahead of her, using her music to calm the little one and get him to come along. That would save a few, anyway.

Or she could just run and save herself. She didn't know why, but that *wasn't* an option, despite all the Leptomaniacs had done to her.

All they've done to you? And what is that? the voice of her sensei asked in his deceptively serene tone. *Made you face a certain aspect of your being? One that cares about the feelings and the lives of others? If you were to ask me, that side has driven you all your life. But in all the wrong ways.*

"Hush," Candayce said. She had to think. Lightning struck nearby. Blinding, terrifying. Another cry!

Think! she demanded. *You're an A student. You know about lightning. You're not stupid. Think!*

Lightning always struck the tallest object. In the valley, the tallest objects were the Leptoceratops that were fleeing. Candayce scrambled toward the leftover Leptos. A few were sitting up.

"Get down!" she screamed. "Lie flat!"

When they only stared at her, she shoved them, butted them, flattened them one at a time, then held them down. Lightning strikes and screams merged with the raging thunder. Every second felt like an eternity.

After a time, the lightning flashes became fewer, and finally the space between the lightning and the thunder grew long enough to convince her that the danger had passed.

A soft crackling rose up around her. She was about to lift her head when the thunder returned. Only it wasn't alone. And *this* thunder was making the ground shudder.

Her heart sank as she realized it wasn't thunder she was hearing. It was footsteps. Tyrannosaur footsteps.

She scanned the valley. That old T. rex was wandering around, scavenging on the Leptoceratops felled by the lightning. All the other Leptoceratops appeared to be gone.

Candayce remained perfectly still as she gauged the direction of the wind drifting through the valley. It settled on her from up near the rex. That meant he couldn't have smelled her or her little group. Good. So now what?

A sound came from behind her. A shuddering wail. The old T. rex raised his head.

Candayce looked back. The cries weren't coming from any of her Leptoceratops. Candayce didn't understand. Suddenly, a hundred feet back, from one of the mounds where the young were raised, a few tiny heads poked out. A larger shape appeared behind the hatchlings and forced them down.

Fear knotted within her. Some of the Leptoceratops had stayed behind to protect the young, to shield them from the lightning with their own bodies, if necessary. Candayce looked at the old rex. His head was down—he wasn't paying attention. The cries came again, this time from a mound a few yards to the old guy's left, then from one way off to his right. The wailing rose ahead of him, behind him.

"No!" Candayce growled. "Stop it!"

The old rex lifted his head and roared, his dark eyes reflecting the blazing crimsons and ambers of the forest fire beyond the valley. He turned and looked right at Candayce. She wondered, calmly— more calmly than she had any right to—if she could outrun him. It was worth a try.

He came for her. She willed herself into motion—but didn't move, couldn't move. Fear had been poured like cement into her bones and she'd become a statue.

Just pretend it's Mike, she told herself. *This is just a game with Mike. A race.*

But this monster wasn't Mike.

Mike was kind and decent; he had honor, compassion. What was coming at her was hunger. Hunger incarnate. The old rex's jaws opened wide. An aura of flame rose up around his swollen, silhouetted body. It was darkness with gleaming teeth. And it was coming for her.

"Great," she whispered. "*Now* I get some attention."

In just a few seconds, a few precious instants, the rex would snatch her from the thundering, wildly shaking ground and devour her—her, or one of the defenseless Leptoceratops behind her.

"You know what?" Candayce suddenly yelled at the T. rex. "I'm sick of this. The bugs. The stuff crawling on you, like, constantly. You guys roaming around like the biggest, baddest things that ever walked the face of the earth. I got one thing to say to you."

The rex was six feet away. His head reared up. There was madness in his eyes. Bloody anticipation.

Candayce loosed a sound from her memories, one she'd heard a hundred times before. A sound from the movies. A sound that her mind made as loud as it possibly could: *"SSSKREEEONKG!"*

Candayce watched breathlessly as the rex nearly tripped over himself, jamming his feet in the ground. He stopped, squinting, looking around, sniffing the air desperately for some sign of the monstrosity that made the near-deafening roar in his mind.

Godzilla rules, thought Candayce. Then she ran!

In a few seconds, the rex's curiosity was forgotten. He chased after Candayce as she raced across the valley. As she zigzagged, she heard the snapping jaws of the old rex. She smelled his rotten breath and thought, *Pal, you don't have anything on Bertram!*

Her plan was to lead the old rex away from the young and the vulnerable Leptoceratops, and then—

And then—

She knew she'd forgotten something.

"Miiike!" she screamed.

No reply. The ground shook. The old rex was gaining on her. She studied the flaming curtain of the woods before her. It wasn't *all* on fire. At least a third of it hadn't yet been consumed. She aimed herself at a blazing grove.

The old rex fell back a step or two. Candayce wondered if he might break off the chase altogether.

"Oh, no, you don't," she hissed. She had a plan now. A crazy, stupid, probably suicidal plan, but it was *hers* and she wasn't going to let this cretin mess it up for her.

Candayce remembered the sound of the Leptoceratops' hooves crashing en masse upon the ground. It was like a stampede from some old Western. She amplified the sound in her mind. Made it echo and shake. And sent it back at the old rex. He roared in delight! He thought there were dozens of Leptoceratops before him. Sure, with his poor vision he couldn't see them, but he could hear them well enough.

Candayce nearly yelped with glee. She looked back. The rex chomped and snapped at thin air. Head down, he barreled forward, his hunger driving him. Candayce reasoned that he was dimly aware but too overwhelmed by his lust for food to care about the flames. But *she* cared.

The fires were before her now. Their heat reached out and shoved at her. She almost stumbled, her resolve and her legs weakening in unison.

Come on, now, Candayce told herself. *Mummy's always saying how thick-skinned you are, how nothing gets through to you. Let's see if it's true!*

She leaped into the blazing breach. Fiery branches crunched underfoot. The fern-covered ground was smoking, the path before her choked with roiling black clouds. She felt the flames. Felt them burn and sting. And heard her pursuer.

Tripping on a tangled root, Candayce hit the ground hard. She looked up and saw the old rex charging through the blaze. He slammed into a burning tree, shattering it. The heavy, severed upper half of the trunk spun and fell. It nearly struck the old rex on the back but missed by inches. He charged toward her, the phantom sounds of the other Leptoceratops now gone.

Candayce turned and scrambled low on all fours. Dignity didn't mean squat when you were being chased by a five-ton eating machine, she told herself. And she needed to keep herself low to the ground. Needed to see the obstacles—and stay beneath the nightmarish clouds of black smoke.

Flame seared her shoulder. She plunged deeper into the burning woods. Something smashed into her face, a cluster of fiery leaves, some brush, she wasn't sure what. She felt heat licking her cheek. She'd never been so frightened in her life. She ran faster.

Ahead, the forest was *melting*. Low-hanging branches were aflame like the twisting, sagging yellow-white remains of logs on a roaring fire. Shapes wavered. Blurred. The world was yellow, red, and white. She never believed anything could be so hot. She ran.

Smoldering embers fell onto her back. She hollered in pain but didn't stop. The thundering footfalls of her enemy rang in her ears, along with poppings and cracklings from all around. The flames were so intense, so all-consuming, that their steady roar was like the flow of water in a stream.

A stream. Water, cool fresh water, if only—

Crack! Snap! Candayce shuddered as a rain of branches and twigs struck her. The old rex was still coming. The ground shook and thundered. Candayce looked back to see debris bounce off his thick skull and shower down upon her. Candayce coughed. Her breath was coming thick and labored. She slowed. So did the rex. But not by much. *Crack!* Candayce drove herself forward. She heard a loud crash behind her and turned back to see the old rex *dancing* with a tree. He'd slammed into it, and was trying not to fall. His momentum was all but gone now. He stumbled back, turned, and growled at Candayce.

He was injured, she realized. But still coming. She turned and ran.

Before her was an inferno. Impassable. She couldn't see ten feet. Flames ringed her at every possible juncture, but she didn't stop moving.

The rex's thunderous footfalls sounded: *Thud, thump, thud, thump...*

Then the ground quaked violently as the rex fell. The shuddering impact pulled the ground out from under her, and her head struck a smoldering branch with a sharp crack. She rolled onto her side and saw the rex lying like a fallen tree, black smoke billowing from his mouth and nostrils.

Nearby, sounds rose above the licking and crackling of the flames—a series of high chatterings.

She heard a crunching of brush. Saw shadows, dark shapes coming for her.

"What?" she said hoarsely, the smoke clogging her lungs. She didn't think it fair that she was about to be consumed by some *other* predator after winning her race with the rex, not fair at all. But she knew all too well that life was seldom fair, and in this primitive age, that was especially true.

Bluto came into view. Candayce tensed for an instant—then laughed! She laughed until she cried. Several other Leptoceratops crowded in, calling to her, nudging her to follow them. She felt something cool, a breeze.

Craning her neck, she saw a curtain of steam behind the other Leptoceratops. Water. *Of course.* They were in swampland. The flood plains.

She started to rise, and a growl came from behind her. She saw the blackened husk of the old rex picking itself up, opening its maw—and falling again.

Bluto squealed as the rex's wide maw sailed toward him. Candayce tried to move but couldn't. A shape pushed forward through the wall of mist. It barreled into Bluto, knocking him out of the way just in time. The purple female!

Bluto and the female fell in a tangle as the rex's jaws slammed down to the ground. The rex slumped, the energy drained from him. A tree trunk fell on him, pinning him unnecessarily but comfortingly where he lay.

Candayce stared at the rex. He wasn't getting up again.

She frowned inwardly at how, even for a moment, she'd once mistaken this creature for Mike. She missed him so much. Weird as it sounded, she missed all of them. Even Bertram and Janine.

Candayce followed the other Leptoceratops. They made their way toward a steaming lagoon. The waters were hot near the firmer ground, then cooler as she moved to join the other Leptoceratops in the center.

She collapsed, nuzzling another Leptoceratops.

The fire raged until morning.

Chapter 17   Mike

Pale sunlight filtered through the skeletal husk of the forest. A soft, welcome breeze wandered through the wreckage, stirring the thick, foul breath of destruction.

Mike and Bertram crashed and thumped through what was left of the woods. Smoke rose in lazy wisps from the remains of towering trees. Mike looked up as a sound came from above. Bertram looked up, too.

Cawwwwwwwwwwwwwwww!

Janine soared above them, Loki at her side. Mike was amazed at the ease Janine displayed as she lazily performed a figure eight in perfect formation with her partner.

"Looking good!" Mike yelled.

"Up ahead," Janine called. "About a mile, straight on."

With that, she flew off. The second Quetzalcoatlus lingered a moment, staring at Mike and Bertram with the slightly bemused expression that seemed permanently fixed on his face. With a rustle of wings, he departed.

"That was weird," Mike said. "Did you hear how cold she sounded?"

Bertram nodded. "What do you think she's mad about?"

"She might not be mad at all. Maybe she's just tired."

"Yeah, maybe…"

They trudged on. Since the previous night, Mike's sharp sense of smell had been corrupted by the heavy smoke that hung in the air. After losing the scent of the Leptoceratops, he'd gotten himself and Bertram lost. They'd stayed outside the worst of the forest fire but had been unable to sleep because of their concern for Candayce.

Janine's words had given him hope. Bertram, too. Mike could see it burning in his eyes. Mike knew how Bertram felt about Candayce, no matter how badly she treated him. His friend would be devastated if anything happened to her.

Though exhausted, Bertram pushed on, moving faster than ever. Mike still had to stroll so that he didn't pass him.

Soon, they came to a valley that was alive with Leptoceratops. Many were gathered around small mounds.

"You'd better stay here," Bertram suggested. "These guys aren't going to understand that you're not just a typical T. rex."

Mike didn't like it, but he knew Bertram had a point. He waited while the club-tail waddled ahead.

Bertram didn't get very far before Candayce came running.

Mike was shocked at her appearance. She had traces of some colorful mess plastered to her scales, and she'd been burned in several places. It wasn't until she reached them that he could see her wincing a little with every movement.

A few Leptoceratops followed her at a distance. One was a little portly. Another was very young. The last one was a deep purple.

Candayce stopped and looked at them. She shook her head sadly, raised one claw, and waved. The Leptoceratops stared for a long time. The little one gave a heartrending cry, and ran back to the group. The purple Leptoceratops reluctantly joined him. Finally, even the portly one hung his head and slowly made his way back to the others on all fours.

"Hi," Candayce said.

Mike noticed that her shells were gone. She no longer seemed self-conscious without them.

"Candayce," Bertram began, "your—"

"You're looking good," Mike said, whacking Bertram with his tail. If they made too much of the shells, Candayce might begin to miss them again.

Bertram looked at him and appeared to catch on. "Right. Yes, you are."

"Yeah, well, I feel like crap," Candayce said. She looked at the soft pastel blue of the sky and the pale streaks of lavender and crimson. The sun burned high and steady above the horizon. "But it sure is nice to see daylight again."

Bertram's tail sagged. His head bobbed in what Mike realized was blissful relief.

"We've lost some time," Candayce said. "We're going to have to make it up. At least thirty miles a day, for starters."

Mike was stunned. "Um, right. That's right."

Candayce looked back at the other Leptoceratops mulling around. A strange fire played in her eyes. Mike wondered what it meant. Then it came to him. She actually appeared sad that she was going to have to leave the others behind. But not so sad that she wouldn't have traded it in a second for a return ticket home and a shopping spree at the mall.

"So what happened?" Mike said.

"They thought they were rescuing me from you guys," Candayce said. "I think now they've got the idea that I don't need to be rescued by anyone."

"That's it?" Bertram asked.

Candayce nodded.

Mike was thoroughly amazed. He couldn't think of a time when Candayce wouldn't jump at the chance to talk about herself and her trials.

"Let's get going," Candayce said.

"Sure," Mike said, "but—where's Janine?"

Candayce looked around. "She's not with you guys?"

Suddenly, a sharp *caw!* came from above. Mike looked up, relieved. Then something fell from the sky as two blurs passed overhead. Janine's "key chain" fell at Mike's feet.

"Janine?"

A pair of *caws* answered him. Mike swiveled his huge head in time to see Janine and Loki soar over the trees and quickly disappear from view.

"What just happened?" Candayce asked.

Bertram looked at the collection of shells lying on the ground. "There's something written on them!"

Candayce dropped down to all fours to inspect the shells more closely. "One of them says, 'Good luck.'"

Mike felt chilled. "What about the other one?"

Candayce looked away. "I don't believe this."

"What?" Bertram asked.

Stepping forward, Mike picked up the shells. "The other one says, 'Good-bye.'"

Mike looked to the skies once more, but there was nothing to see except a few soft clouds and the glaring light of morning.

Janine was gone.

P
A
R
T

T
H
R
E
E

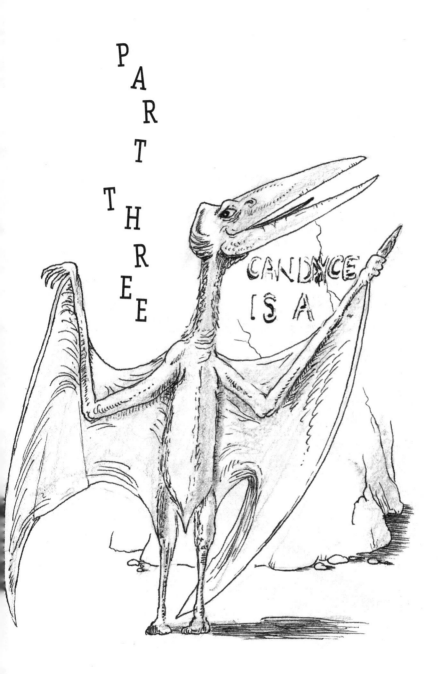

CANDYCE
IS A

Quetzalcoatlus Quiz

Chapter 18

Janine

Clouds reached out and engulfed her with fine white tendrils of mist. Brilliant light flashed before her. The wind caressed her wings. She moved in an elegant ballet, the currents lifting her and turning her in their gentle, invisible hands.

Janine flew—and it was glorious. She'd never known anything like this, not even in dreams. Loki was beside her. His golden body was magnificent.

As they pierced the clouds and dropped below them, she studied his rippling muscles. The streaks of gray, blue, and scarlet adorning his body suddenly became blurs as he dived. Slicing through the air, Loki grew smaller, barreling down, twisting and flying toward the greenish mass that was a copse of trees far below. Then he leveled off, caught by a draft of air that gave him speed enough to disappear from view in seconds.

Janine was gripped by a sudden panic. She had to follow him. She *needed* him. He was all she had in this strange world! Raising her head in alarm, Janine chided herself: *Are you kidding me? Just listen to yourself!*

She waited, resisting the urge to chase after him. *He'll come back,* she told herself. *You watch…*

Janine gradually flew lower. She saw a group of Triceratops

feeding on low-lying shrubs and playing near a pond. A few miles down, she saw a pair of Tyrannosaurus eyeing each other warily, their wounded prey, an Ankylosaurus, attempting to crawl away. The club-tail looked a little like Bertram, but she knew it wasn't him. Two days had passed since she left the group. They'd be a good fifty or sixty miles west by now. More, considering how far *she'd* traveled.

Below, she saw a herd of hadrosaurs with three-foot-long tube-like crests on their skulls marching across a field. Beautiful, yet mournful, sounds rose up from them. Janine briefly wondered if something was wrong—then reminded herself that she had to stop judging all she saw and heard by human standards. These Parasaurolophus weren't human and neither was she. Not anymore.

Ten miles ahead, she encountered a smaller group of hadrosaurs. The sounds from the first herd came and they answered.

Janine got it. This was how they communicated over long distances. Like elephants. She rose higher. Shapes appeared in the distance. Other flyers. She wondered how they would take to her. Only one way to find out…

Janine glided unhurriedly until she came to a great ravine. Three fellow Quetzalcoatlus soared near a waterfall, one going close enough to refresh himself in the chill, frothing spray. Loki wasn't with them.

Janine cawed and waited. They responded with sharp, friendly cries of their own. Janine flew closer.

The flyers were older than she, with greater wingspans. She lowered her head and flew toward the waterfall, careful to allow only the spray to reach her. She sensed that if she flew into the falls themselves, she would be slapped down by the heavy force of the water to the jagged rocks below.

The spray was cool. It sighed and tickled. Janine laughed as she let it wash over her, then she quickly sailed away. Turning in a wide arc, she searched for the trio of flyers but couldn't spot them. Had they fled? Were they frightened of her because they sensed she was different?

A shrill caw sounded, mingled with the roar of the waterfall. Janine saw the flyers. They had taken up stations on either side of the waterfall, their bodies upside down, their wings tucked close, their claws clutching holds on the rocky crags. Their heads bobbed as they watched her.

"Cool," she said, wondering if she could do that. She imagined she could, but this ravine, with its terrible drop, was not the place to practice. She cawed again and allowed the thermals to take hold. She rose steadily, flying out of the ravine, beyond the roar and crash of the waterfall, and into a peaceful stretch of flood plains. She rose higher, and higher still, the clouds again her destination, when a familiar cry burst from behind her.

Cawwwwwwwwwwrrrrraaaaaagggggggghhhhh!

Loki was back. He'd tried to make her jump by falling out of the clouds at her back and yelling practically in her ear, but it hadn't worked. Janine angled herself and flew in lazy circles until her companion caught up. He joined her, small chirping sounds bubbling in his throat.

"What's the matter?" Janine asked. "Annoyed I didn't follow? Hmm?"

Loki looked away.

"Oh, what a face. You look like my Aunt Liz after she tried a cheap perm at home and all her hair fell out."

Loki cawed.

"That would have been bad enough for anyone else, but Aunt Liz was in the record books for tying one end of a rope to her hair and the other end to the bumper of a car and hauling it down Main Street. You should see the family I come from. Her and my Cousin Joey, who won't go on an airplane without her own parachute. The flight attendants just love her..."

Loki cawed again.

"Yes, you are a font of conversation, now, aren't you?"

Smiling to herself, Janine plunged into a nosedive. The ground rushed up, spinning wildly. She corrected her flight effortlessly, catching a pocket of thermals, leveling out, and using the momentum to bullet herself forward. She aimed low, flying only fifty feet above the ground, and pierced the tangled reaches of a dense patch of woods. The two-hundred-foot-tall Sequoiadendrons hid her nicely. She navigated the rising threats of the thick-trunked sentinels and their raking, snaking branches with ease.

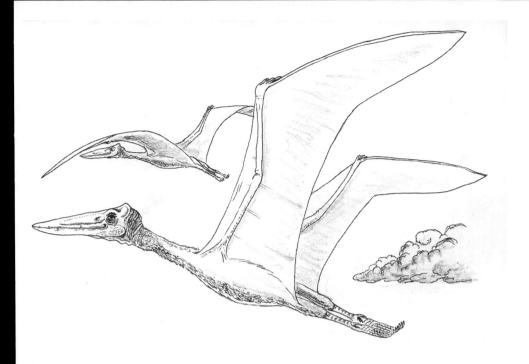

Loki was right on her tail. She led him on a terrific chase, then burst from the trees and took to the air once more. They cruised together until Janine's stomach began to growl. It was that time again. Her body required so much energy that food was a constant concern. That didn't bother her. It now seemed the natural way of things.

They soared out over the river, heading east, to the inland sea. Loki's chosen territory. There were dangers. There were *always* dangers. But somehow, Janine didn't mind. The problems that had seemed insurmountable just days ago were behind her now.

No, they were *beneath* her now. She was rising above them in a way she never thought possible.

Janine shrieked in absolute bliss. Loki joined her cries.

Below loomed the alien world that, after only a handful of days, had become more like home to her than Montana and her mother's bed-and-breakfast ever had. Janine heard the rush of water over rocks, the churning, twisting howl of the river, the chirps and growls and howls of the region's inhabitants. Closing her eyes, smiling to herself, she felt a warmth inside her, a glow that was brighter than the light of a summer sun. She was at home. She was at peace.

She was happy.

Chapter 19

Mike

"We can't go back," Mike growled. He was tired, he was hungry, and he was in no mood to be argued with. Bertram, his spiky, armored Ankylosaurus body emitting a steady stream of noxious fumes, strained to keep up as Mike increased his strides. Candayce walked a good hundred yards ahead.

The river had curved sharply, and following it would have taken them days out of their way. So they were cutting across the flatlands, hoping to meet up with the river farther west when it snaked back.

The view was monotonously flat. Occasionally, a hundred-foot-high gingko or conifer would crop up on the stark horizon. Or maybe they'd see moss-covered rocks, small berry bushes, or generous patches of herbs, along with wandering herbivores made skittish by the sight of the T. rex and his plant-eating companions. But that was it.

"We're never gonna find the Standing Stones without Janine," Bertram complained. "We've lost so much time, so much distance—"

"All the more reason to keep going west. We *are* going west, right?"

"I think so. But if we had Janine, we'd know for sure, we'd—"

Mike roared. He turned on his companion, his eyes burning

148

with frustration, his maw wide, his tiny Tyrannosaurus claws twitching.

"We *are* going west, right?" Mike hollered. "You're the one with the map buried in your head. If you don't know—"

"Yes! We're going west! All right? Are you satisfied? Can I *go* now?" Bertram's tail whipped back and forth. His entire body tensed.

"Excuse me," Candayce called.

Mike glared at Bertram. There were so many things he wanted to say. It *was* Bertram's fault, after all. If it hadn't been for him and his stupid machine, they wouldn't be back in the Late Cretaceous, and they wouldn't be facing the ever-increasing likelihood that they were never going to get back to their own time, their own bodies.

They needed to cover close to 250 *miles*. Mike could do that in two or three days. So could Candayce. So could Janine, for that matter. It was Bertram who was slowing them down! Plodding, methodical, pain-in-the-butt *Bertram!*

But without *him,* they wouldn't know where they were going. Mike just wanted to—

"*Guys!*" Candayce hollered.

Mike looked away from Bertram. Candayce was right in front of them now.

"We're not *moving,*" Candayce said sharply. "We're not getting anywhere."

Mike felt his anger seep out of him. He looked to the club-tail. *And if it hadn't been for Bertram, Moriarty would have torn you apart and that croc would have had you for a midnight snack!*

"I'm sorry," Mike said. He looked ahead. Before him was a mind-numbing stretch of flatlands. It seemed endless—as if no matter how far they traveled, they would never really get anywhere. "I guess it's just getting to me."

Mike considered the way he'd been acting and felt completely ashamed. He hadn't slept well in days. Not since the night of the fire, when he'd seen the footprint that he was certain belonged to Moriarty. There'd been plenty of others since. And just last night he'd glimpsed...something. A burst of heat lightning had lit up the sky, and Mike saw a shape a few dozen yards off. He tried to scent it, but his nose was still unreliable. So he stared and stared at that shape, waiting for it to move, but it never did. Mike considered rising up and challenging the shape, but he was afraid of what might follow.

Somehow, he'd drifted off to sleep. He hadn't meant to. He'd been trying to keep himself alert, to not allow the shape to leave his field of vision for even a second. But for whatever reason—the strain of the day, the stress of their situation, his body's absolute exhaustion—he'd slept.

When he woke, the shape was gone. He searched for footprints, but couldn't find any. The ground had been recently disturbed, but the only prints were those of an Ankylosaurus like Bertram.

"Mike?" Candayce yelled. "Are you listening to me?"

"Sure, right," Mike said, shaking himself out of his reverie. "We should get going."

Candayce walked off. Mike was about to follow when he noticed Bertram's massive club-tail. It was covered in dirt.

"Last night," Mike whispered. "Last night, I saw—"

Bertram lowered his head. "I cleared away the tracks," he said in a low voice. "I didn't want Candayce to get scared."

Mike's mind reeled. Moriarty *had* been near! He was stalking them. Mike had challenged and shattered Moriarty's authority among the rexes and Moriarty wouldn't stop until—

"Mike?"

Shuddering, Mike looked down. Candayce was doubling back.

"It's Gigantor, isn't it?" Candayce asked.

Mike stared at her. "Huh?"

"The big rex. The one you fought. Nessie must have spit him back."

Mike and Bertram exchanged stunned glances.

"Hey," she said, "I've been the one taking point. You think I don't know what's going on? I mean, I've been doing it to get away from the stench—no offense, Bertram—"

"It could be some other big Tyrannosaurus," Mike said quickly.

"Maybe," Candayce admitted.

"That *is* possible," Bertram said. "Predators hunt those who are weak or strange. Outcasts. That we're banding together—plant- and meat-eaters, defying the rules of nature—makes us objects of curiosity and suspicion. To some, prey."

It wasn't any other rex, it was him, Mike wanted to say. *I can feel it.* But could he? Really? Or was his imagination running away with him?

From somewhere far off, a rumbling came. Bertram looked up in alarm. Then he sighed with relief. "No storm clouds. Good. A flash flood is the last thing we need right now."

Mike nodded. Bertram had brought up the possibility of flash floods every time there was even a vague threat of rain. And from the way he'd described them, Mike had decided that he didn't want to be caught in the middle of one.

The rumbling came again.

"What is that?" Mike asked, scanning the horizon but seeing nothing the least bit unusual.

Candayce came up to him and kicked his leg. "Hello?"

Mike looked down at her. "What was that for?"

"I had to get your attention somehow. We have to make a decision. About Janine."

"I thought we already—"

"No," Candayce said. "*You* decided. In case you didn't notice, there are three of us. I say we put it to a vote."

Mike couldn't believe what he was hearing. "Janine left. She didn't want to be with us anymore. What makes you think we can talk her into coming back?"

"I don't think *you* could," Candayce said. "You don't know her the way I do. But I could."

Mike shook his head. "This is crazy."

"I vote we go back for Janine," Candayce said.

"I think we should keep going west," Mike said. "We'll never make it unless we keep going!"

Candayce looked to Bertram. "It's up to you."

Bertram's head wobbled. "I—I shouldn't go. I'm too slow."

"That's it," Candayce said. "I'm going to find her—"

"But," Bertram said firmly, "Candayce shouldn't go *alone.* Mike, you have to go with her."

"Me? But—"

"She's going," Bertram said. "And I can't go with her. Do you want her going alone?"

"Of course not," Mike muttered.

"Besides, there's something I've been thinking about lately: The M.I.N.D. Machine took the four of us as a group. It's probably going to be searching for the same pattern for the trip back. If we give it three, instead of four—"

"You mean...if we don't go back together, none of us may be going back at all?"

Bertram nodded. "That might be what Mr. London was—"

The earth suddenly shuddered.

"Moriarty!" Mike screamed, though he knew it was impossible. The land was flat in every direction—there was nowhere for the giant T. rex to be hiding.

The ground ahead of Mike suddenly *split*. He stared mutely, unable to comprehend what he was seeing. A fissure ran along the ground, scurrying wildly like a wagging finger. The entire world began to come apart.

"Run!" Candayce hollered, speeding past him.

"Earthquake!" Bertram cried. He turned and scrambled in Mike's direction, but even at a scramble, he couldn't move fast enough. None of them could.

Mike saw cracks racing outward throughout the land. Entire shelves of earth tipped and sank into the ground like ships capsizing and sinking beneath the ocean. Ten-story-high trees were knocked down and swallowed. It was incredible.

Mike knew he should run, but he was transfixed. He felt as if he had a ringside seat at creation. Besides, a part of him understood that there was no place he could really run to.

He watched as a section of earth trembled and wavered like a cake in an oven: it rose, then fell as if it had been deflated. Elsewhere, the ground was shimmering, disappearing. And the *sounds*—

A part of Mike wished he could be struck deaf rather than listen to those sounds. It was the earth screaming. Being pulled apart. It was the growl of the world dying and being born, dying and being born...

The landscape was changing. Rock was being thrown up, the

sky was filling with clouds of dirt and geysers of stone. Yet his little piece of ground was safe. It shuddered, it trembled, but it didn't fall.

Bertram had already warned him that this was the time when the Rocky Mountains were being created. He said there'd be massive earthquakes as the land reformed itself. Was that what was happening now?

"Mike!" Candayce screamed.

He started to turn, but something ripped out of the earth beneath him, tossing him from his feet. He fell—and kept falling. The strange calm he'd known was replaced by panic. He wouldn't close his eyes, refused to miss a moment of this, though his heart raced and he was certain it would stop—or be stopped—at any moment.

His body struck solid rock. Pain cut through him. He bounced and spun and fell. He saw blurs of gray rock, *things* of unimaginable size rising out of the earth as he fell, stone walls springing up all around, and he fell, and fell, and fell, turning, twisting, roaring...

He was slapped by hard unyielding stone and his fall ended, but he still felt as if he was moving, the world had become a dizzying, blurring plane of madness. Then came a sharp crackle and a final deafening, shuddering shift of earth and stone, and he witnessed a *thing* rising upward before him, a wall that rose higher than any skyscraper, taller than anything he'd ever imagined.

Mike didn't want to see this, didn't know if his mind could take it. Then a shovelful of darkness slapped down on him, choking him, crushing him. There was pain, then the great shifting ceased, replaced with mild, timid tremors.

He heard a slow, churning growl, a last testament to all that had preceded it. The sound vibrated through the walls around him, the debris pressed in on him, and suddenly, he was blanketed in silence.

Mike's first thought was, *Buried alive—I'm buried alive.*

But he hadn't been. He quickly cleared the thin layer of blackened earth and stone from his face and climbed to his feet. The flatlands were gone. In their place was a jagged, incredibly deep, and shadowy valley walled in by huge flat earthen surfaces that jammed themselves defiantly toward the heavens. The air was golden with dirt. Mike was trapped deep down in this hollow.

Bertram? Candayce?

"Mike!" came a familiar holler. Mike turned to see Bertram shambling his way. But what about—

"Up here!" Mike and Bertram looked up to see Candayce standing on a ledge far above.

"I guess that settles which of us goes hunting for Janine!" Candayce called.

Mike dropped to his knees, hurt, exhausted, but grateful to be alive. He looked around, praying there would be no aftershocks. He could picture these walls tumbling in on them. Bertram came and rested his head on Mike's shoulder.

"Are you guys okay?" Candayce asked.

Mike looked to Bertram. The Ankylosaurus nodded. "We're okay."

"Great. I'm outta here!"

Mike eased away from Bertram and stood. "Candayce, it's too dangerous, you can't—"

"Gotta run," she said with a wave. "See ya!"

"Candayce, no!" Bertram cried.

He watched helplessly as the pudgy Leptoceratops waved, then vanished over the rim.

"So what do we do?" Bertram asked. "We've got to get out of here. We've got to help her!"

Mike stared at Bertram. His companion looked frantic with concern. "She'll be all right," Mike said, knowing his words were little comfort.

But it was good to talk, good to say *something,* even if he didn't really believe what he was saying, because there was something else on his mind, something he had to hide from his companion: He hadn't eaten much this morning. They were now cut off from the river. And he was starting to feel hungry again.

Chapter 20

Janine

Janine and Loki flew with a collection of Quetzalcoatlus. Many were twice their size. They circled over the inland sea, diving for small fish.

"Come on, I'll race ya!" Janine called to a smaller Quetzalcoatlus. This one had a bright yellow body with streaks of crimson and midnight blue. Every time he descended to snatch a fish from the waters, a larger Quetzalcoatlus dove past him and stole his prize. Janine was determined to help see this little guy get something to eat.

The small Quetzalcoatlus stared at her blankly.

"Okay, Bobo," Janine said to him. "I'll have to work on my non-verbal communication." She looked over and saw Loki buzz a larger flyer. Annoyed, the bigger Quetzalcoatlus snapped at Loki, then gave chase. With ease, Loki outmaneuvered the unfortunate victim of his prank—and sent him crashing into the flank of a third Quetzalcoatlus!

Janine soared close to the small flyer she'd named Bobo and bit him on the backside. The flyer's head came up in alarm. She sailed in again and gently whacked him on the head. His eyes became slits. She went after him a third time, prepared to caw right in his ear, but he spun out of her way and arced around, nearly biting her! Janine fled and Bobo soared after her.

A part of her was afraid of the little guy's wrath—but within moments, she felt so exhilarated in her flight that her anxieties melted away. She heard an inquisitive cawing behind her and had the sense that her pursuer had already forgotten why he was supposed to be upset.

"This might be why you don't get the fish, Bobo," she said. She still felt for the guy, even if he wasn't all that smart. She responded with a bright shrill cry of abandon and led the yellow-and-red flyer toward a school of radiant orange fish she saw just below the surface of the water.

Another flyer was coming near, this one with a wingspan a good eight feet longer than Janine's. He was going to snatch up Bobo's food! She gave a yell of warning, and suddenly Loki was there, distracting and annoying the incoming flyer.

With the field clear, Janine dove for the fish. As she allowed the breeze to carry her up and away from the school, she turned to see Bobo snatching a mouthful of fish, too. Mission accomplished!

She felt wonderful—until she noticed a great vibrating *ring* appear on the surface of the water. It shimmered, and at its center, the water dipped for just an instant.

Suddenly, a giant green shape propelled itself out of the water. Janine shrieked at the muscular, camouflage-striped hide and the wide-open mouth filled with razor-sharp teeth. It was a Mosasaurus, the largest and most deadly lizard in history!

Janine watched helplessly as its thirty-foot torso thrust out of the water and its snout brushed the wings of Bobo. It raged higher, its jaws closing on another flyer. She heard a sharp crackling and a strangled cry. The flyer's eyes rolled back. The fins lining the Mosasaurus's back wriggled. Its flippers pushed at the air as if the creature was attempting to applaud its own graceful, skilled, and deadly performance.

The Mosasaurus jerked back into the water as if an anchor had suddenly been thrown around its tail. It took the unconscious Quetzalcoatlus with it. Then it was gone.

The flyers circled the slowly quieting surface of the water.

Other fish appeared. Janine watched as a few brave—or stupid—flyers snatched at them.

Loki flew to Janine's side. Together, they broke from the group and glided to shore. Even after a few miles, Janine was still shuddering. She looked to her companion. He appeared as unruffled as ever.

This is the way of things, Janine reminded herself. *This is the decision you made.*

Despite herself, she thought of Mike, Bertram, and Candayce. She laughed as she recalled the prank Loki had played on Candayce when she'd been asleep—stealing her "bikini" top. It'd been classic.

It'd *also* been nearly impossible, now that she considered things. Loki couldn't have just swooped down from the sky, severed the vine holding the shells in place, and made off with them in a single movement. True, he might have cut the vine on one trip and snatched the shells on another, but the precision necessary would have been incredible. And somehow, he'd done all this without waking Candayce? How?

Janine could see Loki pulling it off if he'd been on the ground. But there was no "launch point" nearby that particular locale—and he'd been back in the air very quickly after committing his crime. So…did he have a way of actually flying, not just gliding, as Janine had been doing all this time? Of taking off from a landing strip instead of vaulting off a cliff and riding the thermals?

"What about it?" Janine asked.

Loki didn't even look at her. So she cawed.

He cawed back.

Janine knew she wasn't going to get any answers this way. She wasn't really certain why she'd even tried. Habit, she supposed. Thinking human thoughts, seeing things the human way, using human language—those were the things natural to her.

Janine wondered if a time would come when she would forget what speech was like. Forget the written word altogether. Forget her family, her world…It was possible. She had no use for them anymore. And honestly, at least as far as her family had been concerned, *they'd* never had much use for *her.*

So why couldn't she stop thinking about them?

Janine and Loki glided past the shore, topped the forest beyond, and ended up on the ledge of a cliff ten miles inland. There was a deep cave burrowed into the side of the cliff. There Janine had built a kind of nest.

Her first act had been to decorate. She'd learned how to crush the garish-colored flowers that were plentiful in this area into a kind of paste and use it as paint. Now the walls were covered with graffiti and proudly bearing her tag. She'd even carved an inscription above the mouth of the cave:

FREEDOM

Janine stared at the word. She considered what it meant. All she'd be giving up: No more books. No more movies. No more *chocolate.* No more games. No more music. And what about all the conversations she'd never have?

Yeah, like the ones with Mom? "Janine, is 3A ready yet? I don't want to hear your excuses, it's five in the morning and you haven't done a blasted thing—"

Yeah. Like those. Her mom had no idea what she did at night—sneaking out, getting up the whole town with her graffiti, and all her other mischief, like the Long Dark Night of the Soap Bubbles in the fountain near Town Hall…heh. Her mother didn't have a clue. No one did.

Janine didn't need to brag to anyone. She kept to herself and liked it that way. Other people had always been a source of amusement, or obstacles to get around, but nothing more.

No, the decision she'd made was the right one. So why did she feel so down? Cawing in frustration, she bolted past Loki and leaped off the cliff, into the air. She spread her wings and waited for the invisible hands of the thermals to carry her up. They did not disappoint.

Janine heard a cry behind her and opened her eyes. There was no danger. Loki was just calling to her. She glided in a sharp figure eight, and saw her companion—her first boyfriend, really—sailing toward the flood plains below. A low, mournful sound, like a lonely tuba, echoed from that direction. Janine followed him.

In minutes, she found Loki circling over a small group of

Parasaurolophus traveling through a grove of what looked like oak and poplar trees. She'd seen these particular duckbills before. Their crests were unusual—long, curved affairs that bent back and away from their skulls for several feet. With them, they made the tubalike sounds.

She counted three adult Parasaurolophus, each around thirty feet long, and four youngsters, the biggest twelve feet long. Their fat, round bodies were green, with pale yellow stripes down their backs and tails. At a glance, they melted into their surroundings.

Two of the adults walked on all fours, their thick, heavy tails held straight in the air. The third one stood on his hind legs and bayed at Loki.

Janine recalled that these dinosaurs were almost constantly wearing out their sharp, grinding teeth. They went through up to twenty thousand teeth in a lifetime. She'd be grumpy if she was teething all the time, but these folks seemed to be in a pretty good mood, despite the depressing sounds they made.

Stop trying to humanize them—they're not human, and neither are you!

They were plant-eaters, no threat. Janine wondered what Loki wanted with them. He cawed and cried, circling above them, subtly altering his course so that he was heading west.

The tuba-heads followed. Janine had seen a herd of Parasaurolophus earlier and now came upon other lost members who were using their deep bassy calls to signal their location. But all of *those* tuba-heads were in the other direction!

Loki let out a yelp of triumph as the lost group followed him. Janine understood what he was doing. He was leading them *away* from the herd. Not toward it. He was playing another prank, like the one he'd played on Candayce with her shells.

Well, messing with Candayce was one thing. *She* had it coming. But these guys were another matter. Leading them astray was cruel.

Janine recalled the terrain to the east. Vast earthen walls would separate the herd from its lost members. The Parasaurolophus had an acute sense of smell, but those earthen walls must have cut off their scent and their calls. Janine knew a path around the earthen walls. *She* could lead these dinosaurs to their friends. The only thing standing in her way was Loki. He was circling, leading them astray, and cackling about it in a way they couldn't recognize.

"All right, *you*," Janine said. She flew toward her companion, came up alongside of him—and bit his wing!

Loki was startled. Janine hadn't bit hard. It had just been a warning. But his distress was evident. Janine flew from him, recalling the sounds the herd had made. If only she could broadcast those sounds...

She closed her eyes and drifted in a lazy circle, trying to be still, trying hard to make silence fill her mind so she could replace it with the sounds she wanted there.

A sudden stinging pain in her left wing snapped her out of it. Her eyes opened and she saw Loki drifting off, his head bobbing happily. She chased him, driving him east. Every time he tried to head the other direction she cut him off, cawing and spitting.

It took her a while to realize that the tuba-heads were following them. And this time, they were going the right way. Janine heard their cries in her head. She recalled the sounds of the herd she'd seen earlier, even their scent, and *pushed* the memories into the heads of the Parasaurolophus. She also laid out a "map" of the terrain they'd be facing and showed them how to travel it to get to their friends.

The tuba-heads eagerly trod east as Janine held Loki at bay. Once she was certain the tuba-heads would follow her instructions, Janine broke off from them. Loki flew with her.

She soared with him happily, and he seemed to sense the change in her mood. His attitude improved as they raced to the clouds.

"We're a lot alike," Janine said. "You just need some training. Tell you what, let's go find some T. rexes and see if we can't give them some grief. Those guys *always* have it coming!"

Loki, clearly not understanding her words but picking up some smidgen of her intent, cawed happily.

Janine dove to the valley just ahead, any doubts that she'd made the right decision falling away from her like the morning mist.

Chapter 21

Bertram

"We've blown it," Bertram declared. "It's over."

"What are you talking about?"

Bertram waddled beside Mike and came to a stop. He sat down hard, drawing his stubby legs under him. The walls of the mazelike chasm into which they'd been dropped were sheer, rising up a hundred feet on either side of them. There was no water. No vegetation. Nothing.

"We have to keep moving," Mike said. "We're hitting higher ground now. I'm certain of it."

"You keep moving. Scout ahead. I'll wait here."

Mike shook his head. "When was the last time you had something to eat?"

"I can't help it!"

"I'm not talking about the exhaust fumes," Mike said. "Well, actually, I guess I am. In a way. My nose is better than before. I can scent pretty good right now. And that means your stomach isn't digesting anything. You haven't eaten. And when you don't eat, you get grumpy."

"I ate *light* this morning."

Mike nodded gravely. His stomach growled.

Bertram looked up sharply in alarm. "You, too?"

161

"Sorry. Didn't expect something like this." Mike turned away. "The truth is, I was so worried about Moriarty, I didn't have much appetite. Umm…what did you mean, we blew it?"

"The Standing Stones. There's no way we can reach them in time. No way *I* can, anyway," he moaned. "And Mr. London said that I was the one who has to figure out that last thing we have to do to get home. How can I do that if I'm nowhere near the stones?"

"We're not going to abandon you," Mike said.

"But that's what you *should* do!" Bertram cried. "If you can find a way out of this place, then you should take it!" He snuffled. Bobbed his head morosely. "Of course, there probably is *no way*…"

"That's it," Mike said, "I'm not letting you go back into Eeyore mode. What we need to do is get our minds focused on things we can actually do something about. Now, until Candayce comes back with Janine—"

"Never gonna happen. You're dreaming."

"Until then, we're going to find some roots or *something* for you to eat." Mike sniffed. The customary explosion of aromas and sensations entered his mind and he sifted through them with practiced ease. "I think there's some shrubs and stuff that are uncovered about three miles from here. Come on."

"But if I eat, I'll pass gas, and your nose—"

"I'll survive. In fact, I smell some other stuff a few miles past the shrubs and the greens that I can eat."

"Fish? Did the river connect with all this? If it did, we could be flooded! It would be like a flash—"

"No flash floods," Mike said. "Just…stuff. Stuff I can eat. If I have to."

"Oh," Bertram said, deciding not to push it. Besides, he and his dad had made up their minds on the "T. rex—scavenger or predator" issue. It made the most sense to them that a normal T. rex would prefer fresh meat, but would scavenge when there was none available. The latter was probably what Mike was going to have to do to survive, and he clearly wasn't happy about it. Bertram lifted himself up and plodded beside Mike. "Sorry I got so down."

"You're human," Mike said, tapping his tail to Bertram's flank.

They walked together for ten minutes before either spoke. Mike broke the silence. "Bertram...did you ever think about, um, this is going to sound weird..."

"You can tell me anything."

Mike nodded. "Did you ever think about your place in things? I mean, back here, I'm a T. rex. A predator. While we've been walking, we've come across what's left of other T. rexes' meals. They kill to survive. When I eat fish, I'm—"

"You can't torture yourself about that," Bertram said.

"No, it's just...I know what I did with Moriarty and the turtles was the right thing. I know it. But now he's after us. And what did I really change, anyway? Another day and there'd be other turtles, other rexes. It's the nature of things. Survival of the fittest. I know what I did was right, but sometimes I feel like it was wrong. Like it didn't mean anything. Like it wasn't for anything."

The maze before them twisted and turned and clouds drew over them from above. "Well," Bertram said, "if you look at it that way, you're probably right."

Mike stopped dead. "What?"

"Mr. London and I talked about this kind of thing all the time. It's the Tree of Life. Everyone has their place. Being a predator is a natural—"

Mike looked away and walked on quickly. "Never mind."

"Wait, you don't understand—"

The Tyrannosaurus turned on Bertram with a lightning-quick twist of his thick neck. His eyes were reckless and wild. His lips pulled back. His maw opened.

"Mike?"

"I'm gonna scout up ahead," Mike roared. "Do you have any problem with that? Do you want to make any comments?"

"I'm sorry, I—"

"Save it." Mike stomped off, growling and roaring. He turned a corner and was gone.

Bertram stood perfectly still, his belly quavering, his heart thundering, his mind racing. He wanted to yell something to Mike, something that would explain what he really meant and make it all better. But, when it came to communicating, he'd always been too slow. Always come up with just the right thing to say just after—or long after—the fact.

He didn't know how to react to Mike's flare-up. All he wanted to do was dig in and cry.

A terrible roar came from somewhere up ahead. It was louder and more savage than any Bertram had heard from Mike in a long time.

Bertram got to his feet and ran as fast as he could. He turned one corner, hurried down another long corridor of stone, made a left, kept moving, turned one last time—

And saw Mike standing at a dead end. A mound of stone and earth blocked the way to the food he had smelled earlier.

"What are we gonna do?" Bertram asked, feeling the first vague tremors of fear as he looked at the tyrannosaur who housed his friend. The *hungry* tyrannosaur.

Mike turned, but before he could answer, a sound came from above. Bertram and Mike looked up just in time to see another Tyrannosaurus bellowing from a ledge fifty feet up.

Moriarty. The twenty-foot-tall giant T. rex was beaten and bruised, but all too recognizable as the shadow that had been stalking them for days.

"Get away from us!" Mike screamed. "Sean, go back, all right?"

Moriarty's head swiveled, as if in confusion.

Bertram stared at his friend. "Sean? Mike, that's—"

Mike spun. "What are you talking about?"

"You called him Sean, you—"

"I didn't say that."

Suddenly, a huge rock fell before them, smashing and cracking at their feet. Bertram and Mike looked up. Moriarty was hard at work, ripping down chunks from the loose wall of stone behind him.

"We have to get out of here," Mike said. "We have to go—now!"

Bertram turned just as he heard a rumbling from above, followed by the skittering dance of stone skipping along the sleek wall next to them.

"Bertram, look out!" Mike yelled.

Bertram saw a shadow descending. A huge shadow. *Several* huge shadows. A rockslide.

There was no time to think, no time to prepare, the boulders and stones were upon him—

Chapter 22

Candayce

Candayce Chambers was running for her life. Unlike several other instances since she'd been taken to the Late Cretaceous, however, there were no carnivores chasing her now.

She was running to find Janine. Running to have a chance, however slim, of reclaiming the life that had been stolen from her.

Candayce charged through a shallow stream. Fallen Metasequoias, thick as drainage pipes, stretched across the stream, leaving gaps she could duck beneath.

She wasn't sure how long it had been since she left Bertram and Mike. During her travels, she had come across cracks in the earth of various sizes and widths—some only a few feet long and an inch wide, others hundreds of feet long and twenty or thirty feet wide. She didn't even want to think about how deep they were.

She pressed on, vines slapping against her shoulders and parrot-like face as she splashed through the waters. Her injured shoulder still ached, the burned areas were sore, but she ignored her discomfort. She felt the first terrible pangs of hunger and knew she'd have to stop to "gas up" soon. Something fell on her, and she screamed, convinced it was a snake. It was just a vine.

Heart racing, Candayce drove her dinosaur body onward, her

thick, round, stubby legs getting a terrific workout. She laughed inwardly. It would take a lot more than diet and exercise to do much for this body.

Still, she had to admit that being a dinosaur had some advantages. Sure, the bugs were terrible. And the smells. And all the things that wanted nothing more than to chew her up and spit her out. Actually, *that* part seemed a lot like being home. But she *loved* to run. And in this body, she was as fast as the breeze and a whole lot stronger than she'd ever been before. It was also kind of nice having all her typical pressures removed. Nice not having all her "friends" being sweet to her face while whispering behind her back, hoping she'd fail, hoping she'd do something rotten with her hair, wear clothes that were out of style, or do *something* that would give one of them the chance to be queen for a day. It got her nowhere. Kind of like this run.

Soon, the stream she was following widened out and merged with the river. The banks stretched out in a wide V shape, and even the current changed, becoming stronger. She thought she saw something floating nearby. Probably just a log, but why take chances?

She climbed onto the bank and watched as the five-foot "log" she'd just avoided lazily opened its maw, exposing rows of jagged teeth. Some kind of croc.

Chomp, chomp, in the swamp... An old children's song came to her. She tuned it out and went exploring. A few hundred yards into the woods, she found a berry tree. She leaned up against it, nibbling happily, unaware for several moments that she wasn't alone.

High chirping sounds came from somewhere close. Cracking noises accompanied them. A shrill tittering. Thumps.

Screams.

Candayce abandoned her meal and plunged through the woods. Maple and beech trees blurred past. She stopped at the crest of a small rise and peered down into a deep depression. What she saw horrified her.

Twelve-foot-long, seven-foot-tall ostrichlike dinosaurs swarmed around a nest that lay at the bottom of a crater. Their gray-and-gold scales glistened as they crawled over one another, bits of shattered eggs scattered about. She recalled Bertram droning on about these predators. Ornithomimus. Egg stealers.

Bertram said that many paleontologists didn't believe these long-necked, sharp-beaked creatures really plundered nests at all. Well, Candayce had news for them!

"Get away from there!" she screamed.

All five ostrich dinos looked up. One held a squirming baby dino in his beak. Candayce screamed as she barreled forward, head down, and launched herself at the egg thief.

Candayce was smaller than the ostrich dino, but her weight was enough to drive the wailing, screeching Ornithomimus back. As she slammed him against the hard earthen walls, the baby dino popped from his beak and scampered away. Before Candayce could do anything, another Ornithomimus snatched the baby up—and swallowed it.

Candayce attacked that dino. She knocked him to the ground, staring at the lump moving down his throat. She had to get him to dislodge it somehow. She'd seen the Heimlich maneuver performed on TV enough times. Maybe she could—

The other egg stealers were on her before she could even try. They clawed at her, opening cuts and scrapes, bit her with their beaks, drove themselves at her. Suddenly, the ground began to shake. Candayce wondered if it was another quake.

A roar sounded from above. The egg stealers froze, looked at each other, and scrambled out of the nest. Candayce got to her feet and kicked one of them in the backside. It looked over its shoulder and yelped, but it kept running.

Candayce emerged from the nest, took a few wobbly steps, and saw seven *tanks* looming before her. Triceratops. Looking back into the nest, she saw the little crests on the foreheads of the babies. The Ornithomimus clan stood on one side of her. The Triceratops—their gray-and-green scales glistening, their enormous curved horns reaching out with their razor-sharp tips—stood on the other.

Candayce moved to one side, and one of the Triceratops rushed forward, then lurched to a stop. She froze.

Behind her, the egg stealers anxiously gazed at the prizes below.

To Candayce it seemed that a few were entertaining thoughts of running back down there at any moment. She could picture it in her mind *so* easily.

"Don't you even *think* about it!" Candayce yelled, turning her back on the Triceratops. She realized her mistake instantly. She had broadcast her thoughts, and with them the images of the egg stealers at work!

Behind her came a deafening series of roars. She looked back at the Triceratops. Fury was in their eyes. They'd seen the images from Candayce's mind!

"Wait!" Candayce said. "It was a mistake, I—"

The Triceratops charged. The egg stealers ran from the nest, Candayce at their heels. The Triceratops raced after them all. The ground thundered, and Candayce looked desperately for a way out. There was none. As the egg stealers tried to escape, they spread themselves out, running in different directions. The Triceratops kept a steady line. Stampede!

Candayce ran faster than ever before, but the Triceratops were gaining. They knocked down trees, trampled the ground, and roared in anger. This wasn't fair! She'd tried to *stop* the Ornithomimus from hurting the Triceratops young! Now—

Cawwwwwwwwww! Candayce looked up and saw a pair of Quetzalcoatlus soaring down over the horizon. "Janine!"

"Candayce! What are you doing?" Janine cried.

"Find me a way out! Maybe there's a ditch I can hide in—"

"There's nothing!"

Candayce heard the thunder of the stampede becoming louder. The earth was trembling. This was it.

"Turn around!" Janine yelled.

Candayce couldn't believe what she was hearing. "What?"

"Do it! Turn around and stop!"

It took Candayce no time at all to calculate exactly how much she trusted Janine. She turned around and stopped.

The Triceratops were nearly a dozen strong. They looked like a surging, shimmering line of muscle and sharp, deadly bone.

"Get ready!" Janine yelled.

"Get ready?" Candayce called. "Get ready for what?"

Janine swooped down from the air, cutting in front of a Triceratops. She whipped around, pulling her wing down over its eyes. Candayce couldn't see what Janine was doing, but somehow the flyer coaxed, coerced, tickled, threatened, and bit—and managed to get the Triceratops to turn right and smash into the side of another member of the stampeding herd. With a shriek, Janine was hurled high into the air as they collided. Candayce lost sight of her in the cloud of earth that mushroomed up.

A break appeared in the line and Candayce ran for it. Two more Triceratops aimed themselves her way. She saw their horns shining in the amber sunlight, smelled their breath—and she knew this time it was up to her. She thought of her studies. The music she'd learned so that she could play at her mother's parties, those dainty little piano pieces—then she quickly chose what she'd always preferred.

Forcing herself to stare into the eyes of the oncoming rippling masses of scales and muscle, Candayce concentrated. Suddenly, a booming orchestra exploded all around her. It was as if the heavens had parted and all the fire and fury of the cosmos were raining down.

"Wagner," she hissed. "*Ride of the Valkyries*. Like it?"

A gap appeared between the unnerved Triceratops. Candayce ran between them. She felt their shuddering flanks. Nearly screamed as they pressed against her—

And she was free! She stumbled to the ground, panting for breath. In seconds, Candayce heard the deafening roar of the Triceratops ebb. She turned to look over her shoulder and saw the backsides of the herd as they raced after the egg stealers. Then something slapped into her, something hard and unyielding, and she whipped back and tumbled to the ground, her feet caught in a twisting fistful of gnarled roots.

"Owwwwwww," she moaned, reaching for her head.

A rustling of wings came from above. Candayce looked up and saw a tall palm tree, its sheltering branches reaching out in all directions. She'd run into a tree. A definite Smooth Move Award contender. Circling above the tree was a Quetzalcoatlus. It wasn't Janine. The colors were all wrong.

"Janine!" Candayce yelled, looking at the savaged field the stampede had left. She saw a figure lying on the ground, a dark crimson body with bright blue wings. *"Janine!"*

The fallen figure did not answer.

Chapter 23

Mike

Before the heavy rock could flatten Bertram, his tail whipped around and *smashed* it to pieces. Mike watched a few smaller stones hit the club-tail's spiky, armored form, but Bertram appeared unhurt.

Mike was stunned—and impressed.

A few more stones tumbled down. Mike looked up and saw Moriarty struggling to free more debris.

"Bertram, come on!" Mike called. "It won't be so easy if he's got a moving target!"

Head bobbing, Bertram looked over. "I got it, didn't I?"

"You sure did."

Bertram moved as fast as he could. They backtracked along the deep channel. Above, Moriarty roared in frustration and rage. He followed them, showering them with rocks whenever he could. Bertram, unable to move swiftly enough, took the worst of it.

Mike decided he had to do something about that.

"Hey, butt-crack breath!" Mike yelled, waving his little arms and hopping in place. "It's me you want, stupid. I'm right here! Come on!"

Moriarty turned his full attention on Mike, sending rocks down

172

upon the teenage T. rex. Mike darted and danced, only occasionally getting struck—and struck hard—by the falling debris.

"You really think what I did was good?" Bertram asked timidly. "Smashing the rock with my tail?"

"It was incredible!" Mike wheezed. "If it was baseball season, I'd put you on my team any day!"

"You'd be the first."

"I mean it!" Mike dodged another oncoming rock. It exploded beside him. He kept hoping Moriarty would run out of ledge up there and would no longer be able to follow them, but it didn't seem to be happening.

Mike looked at Bertram's raised and swinging tail. Then he saw all the rocks lying about at their feet. "Hey, Bertram, how about a little batting practice?"

Bertram looked at him strangely. Mike grinned to himself. He knelt with his legs and bent forward, pressing his head against the wall to keep himself from pitching forward and falling flat. His small but immensely powerful arms picked up a boulder. It was a good two feet around.

"Mike, what are you doing? Moriarty's still gathering ammo!"

"I'm the pitcher, you're at the plate."

"What?"

Mike gently tossed the boulder at Bertram's tail. Bertram looked over his shoulder and whacked the rock so hard it shattered. Mike had to duck to avoid the explosion of smaller stones!

"This could work," Mike said, grabbing another rock. "Once more, just lighten up a little. You want to make the ball go on a little trip for you, you don't want to pulverize it. Okay?"

"Mike—"

He tossed the "ball."

Bertram swung! There was a sharp crack, and the rock became a blur. It smacked into the wall, leaving a small crater. But at least it stayed in one piece.

"Not bad!" Mike said. He looked up and saw Moriarty watching them uncomprehendingly. Good. At least the monster had forgotten his own little game.

Mike found another rock. "You're a natural, Bertram. When we get back—"

"If we get back—"

"*When* we get back, you and me are gonna do some serious practicing, you got that?"

"*Really?*" Bertram asked.

"Darned straight. Here comes the pitch!"

Bertram whacked the boulder. It sailed straight up and landed a few inches to Mike's right. "Fly ball. It happens."

Mike grabbed another rock and tossed it. Bertram's tail whipped around.

This is the one, Mike thought. *I can feel it…*

Bertram's tail snapped forward and smacked into the rock at just the right angle. It flew up at Moriarty as if it'd been launched by a catapult!

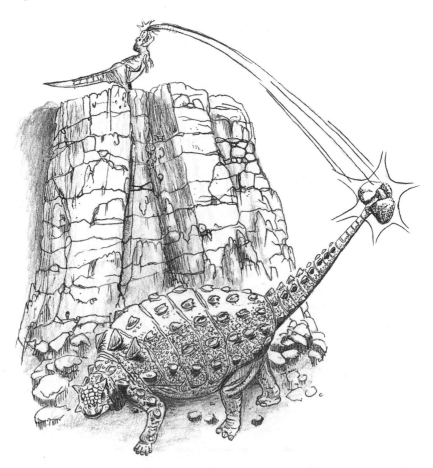

The giant T. rex had enough time to issue a slight grunt of confusion—and then the rock hit him square in the forehead! He rocked back, legs buckling.

"Again, again, again!" Mike howled. He tossed another stone. *Whack!* It was good! Mike laughed as it struck Moriarty in the stomach. Another—and it struck his knee. Moriarty roared and fell onto one side, his tail hanging over the cliff. Another pitch—and Moriarty, who'd gotten to his wobbly feet once more, took it squarely on the jaw. He snapped back and fell with a thunderclap that caused an entire shelf of rock to rain down on Mike and Bertram.

Once the dust had cleared and Mike knew that Bertram was okay, he looked up. He couldn't see Moriarty.

"We did it!" Mike yelled. "Home run!"

"Oh, yes! Oh, yes!" Bertram bellowed.

Mike looked over at Bertram, who was happily bouncing from side to side and bobbing his head.

"You're a heckuva guy!" Mike hollered.

"Me?" Bertram asked.

"You tha man!"

"*Who* tha man?"

"You tha man! It's you, Bertram!" Mike shook his head. "I wouldn't want to be here with anyone else."

Bertram looked up at Mike with wide, vulnerable eyes. "You mean it?"

"Sure." Mike's stomach growled and Bertram turned back to the path leading to the food.

"Mike, look!"

Mike did, and he saw that a kind of ramp had been formed by the last round of falling rock. It led up the wall of debris that had blocked them from the food Mike smelled earlier.

"I'll race ya," Mike said, but he saw that Bertram looked troubled. "What?"

"I'm sorry about before. I didn't mean it the way you took it. About being a predator, and that what you did on the beach didn't mean anything."

Mike hung his head. "Bertram, there's something I should probably tell you. It's something I'm not really proud of. And once you hear it, you might not think of me the same—"

Bertram shook his head. He didn't look as if he was listening. His eyes were tearing. "All I was trying to say is that to a predator, a real predator, what you did wouldn't mean anything. But that's not what you are. Just because you're in that body, just because *it* wants to do things sometimes, or not do things, doesn't make any difference as far as who *you* really are. What you did was right for you. It was the most incredible thing I've ever seen. If you had to do it again, you would. When it comes right down to it, you would. That's who you are. That's what makes you better than Moriarty."

"But the killer instinct," Mike said.

"You do what you have to do to survive. Moriarty was hurting those turtles because he liked it. Because it made him feel good. Like he was better than everybody else. Believe me, Mike, I've been dealing with predators all my life, and you're not one of them. You're better than that. You are."

Mike didn't know what to say.

"What—what'd you want to tell me?" Bertram asked.

Mike shook his head. "Not now." He needed time to think about everything Bertram had said. And what he would do *if* and *when* they got back. "Bertram—"

But the Ankylosaurus was already waddling happily ahead.

Mike looked up at the cliff where he'd last seen Moriarty. He wanted to believe this was the end of it, that Moriarty would leave them alone. Somehow, though, he knew that wouldn't be the case.

Then he looked at Bertram and thought, *We'll be ready for you.*

And for the first time since he'd glimpsed the giant T. rex on the beach, Mike was no longer afraid.

Chapter 24

Janine

Janine was shaking her head, trying to get the sound of the thundering herd out of her ears, when Candayce descended on her. The other girl was all flashing hooves and licking tongue, snapping beak and comically rolling eyes. "Are you okay? Are you all right? Are you—"

"Get, get, *get!*" Janine snapped.

"I'm just—I'm so glad you're all right," Candayce said as she scrambled back. "That was *amazing!*"

Janine stretched out her wings and stood. "Do you know how close that thing came to ripping my wing open?"

"Never seen anything like it," Candayce said. Her eyes looked teary. Maybe it was sweat.

Janine couldn't handle this. "Is there a *reason* why I'm looking at your ugly…little…*face?*"

Candayce drew back, as if she'd been slapped. For a moment it looked as if she might crumble, then her eyes became hard. "Okay, I had that coming."

A lot more than that, Janine thought.

"We need you," Candayce said. "We're not gonna make it if you don't come back."

"Give me a break."

"It's true! There was an earthquake. Didn't you feel it?"

Janine nodded reluctantly. She'd seen the earth tremble.

"The ground—it, like, opened up and swallowed Mike and Bertram. They're trapped. It's a maze down there. When I was standing above it, I couldn't see the end of it. It went on for miles. We have to help them!"

"You're serious."

"You can fly above it, help guide them out."

Janine was silent. "You *are* serious…"

"Please," Candayce whispered. "Bertram's your friend. So's Mike. You can't just—"

"Don't tell me what I can and cannot do!" Janine screeched. Above, Loki wailed and circled, agitated.

"You're right, okay? I'm sorry. I'm just…"

"You're just *what?*"

Candayce didn't answer.

"I asked you a question."

Candayce turned away. She shuddered and hugged herself. "I hadn't even…I didn't consider that you might say no."

Janine was stung. She hadn't said no. She hadn't said anything yet. She was too busy trying to take it all in. Mike and Bertram in some chasm…but she'd *made* her choice. This wasn't fair. Janine asked, "Are they hurt?"

Candayce shook her head.

"Thank goodness for that much, anyway."

"Janine—"

"Let me think!"

Candayce fell onto all fours and waddled a few feet on wobbly legs. She dropped onto her side and looked as if she might start sobbing at any moment.

Don't be so pathetic, Janine thought. She knew she was being cruel, but all she could think about was the last time she'd really spoken to Candayce, when she'd begged her to be nicer to Bertram—and Candayce swore to torture the poor guy for caring about her.

Janine heard Loki caw in summons. The tone tipped her off. "Give me a minute, I'm thinking."

"I didn't *say* anything!" Candayce wailed.

"Not you."

Candayce looked up at the Quetzalcoatlus circling above. "Oh. You can understand him."

Better than I can understand someone like you. Janine shook her long head. "It just had to be *you,* didn't it?"

Candayce rolled over and looked to Janine. "What?"

"It couldn't have been Mike. No, it had to be *you* asking."

"Mike's—"

"I know." It came to Janine suddenly. "Now I get it! Without them, you can't get back. That's why you're worried!"

Candayce's little beak trembled. Her eyes narrowed. For a moment, her shoulders tensed, then the fight drained out of her and she said, "Okay...okay, if that's what you want."

"I don't see where it's a matter of what I want," Janine said. "I was just trying to figure out why you looked so concerned. For a minute there, I was actually wondering if it was because you had it in you to be worried about someone else. But now it makes sense."

"Janine," Candayce said softly, "will you..."

"Of course I'll do it."

Candayce's eyes widened. "You will?"

"Yes."

"Good. Wonderful. Thank God." Candayce tromped her way excitedly.

"Stop!" Janine hollered.

Candayce froze.

"Get that smug look off your stupid little face. Don't gloat. Don't even—I swear—"

"Gloat? I—"

"One more word, *one more word* out of you and I'll stay here and that's the end of it. I mean it."

Candayce got to her feet and tensed up like a new recruit at boot camp. Janine waited for nearly a minute, and Candayce remained still and mercifully, eerily, silent.

"I can't believe this. I've finally shut you up."

Candayce looked away. Janine could sense the anger within her companion, but that was all right.

"You know what?" Janine asked. "This'll be worth it. Just to have the chance to say all the things I've wanted to say to you. Yeah, this'll be worth it."

They walked together until they found a hillock a quarter mile off. Janine launched herself into the air. Candayce ran below her. They traveled through an open area, with only a few trees and shrubs. Janine wanted to be able to keep an eye on Candayce.

Soon, the sky was darkening. Rumbling sounded from far off, in the distance. Was it thunder? Or another earthquake?

Fear twisted Janine's insides into a knot. She thought of aftershocks, of Mike and Bertram being buried beneath the rocks—no, she had to think about something else! Anything else. Janine cried, "So, Chambers! Remember the day we met? *Don't answer that!*"

Candayce ran, glancing up to check Janine's position. She didn't say a word.

"I remember. My mother had made a brand-new dress for me. I was on the bus. Fourth grade. We'd just inherited the bed-and-breakfast and come back to town, and my mom wanted me to make a good impression. I guess you picked up on that. I remember you and your friends coming over, acting so nice…I thought, wow, this really isn't as bad as I thought, and that was when I looked down and saw that you'd just opened your pen and let it spill all over my dress. Everyone got a good laugh at that one."

Candayce ran, head down. Janine soared triumphantly above, wondering why this wasn't more fun…

"Then there was Sherilyn. Remember her? My best friend until sixth grade. Then you guys started being nice to her, and the next thing I knew, it was a Monday morning and I was about to go into class, when Sherilyn started hitting me. I didn't know what was going on, I couldn't believe it was happening. I went down *hard,* and I saw you and your thugs just standing around, laughing, making jokes. Sherilyn told me to stop hanging around her, stop bugging her, she didn't have time for a loser like me.

"But I bet you don't know about the best part. About what she did later? I'll tell you. She came over after school that day. She said it didn't mean anything. Her beating me up. Isn't that something? She said it was just to impress you. But we could still be friends. Just not at school, or at the mall, or anything. We could still be friends, so long as we didn't go anywhere where anyone'd see us. Isn't that *classic?*"

The rumbling Janine had heard earlier came again. The day was deepening and clouds were moving in. Loki sailed close. His wings nearly grazed Janine's. "Hey!" she yelled, with a piercing shriek. He veered off, straining in the direction of the clouds. He flew toward them, then back at Janine several times. The rumbling came again.

"What're you, scared of a little rain or something?" Janine asked. "You fuzzbutt!"

Janine liked being out in the rain. When she was still human, she'd looked forward to rainy days the most. Everyone at school was too busy being miserable over the weather to get on *her*. She heard the rumbling again. It was still so distant, yet...

"Hey, Chambers, you're off the hook for a while. I wanna be able to listen. We've got some weather up ahead."

Below, Candayce loped on, nodding upward at Janine.

Janine shook out her wings. "This wasn't any fun, anyway. You probably didn't listen to a word I said..."

Candayce was no longer looking Janine's way.

They traveled for hours. The sky remained bleak, the thunder a threatening phantom they appeared to be chasing. Janine had been tempted several times to pick up her little tirade, but recounting all the hurts Candayce had caused her when they were both human wasn't doing her any good.

She could have cursed and screamed and called Candayce Chambers every name she could think of, and it wouldn't have mattered. This was just—old tapes. Old tapes that needed to be erased. And once she made sure Mike and Bertram were all right, and safely on their way, that's just what she would do. She'd erase those tapes. Forget the life she'd led...

If only the silence hadn't been so terrible.

She hadn't noticed it before. Not when she was talking *at* Loki—because, of course, that was all she really could do, talk at him, not to him. She had really felt it only in the last few hours as she'd silently flown above and Candayce had followed her below.

She *missed* talking. She couldn't help but think of all the conversations she would never have once Mike and the others were gone.

"Candayce," Janine called.

The running Leptoceratops didn't answer.

"Chambers, hey!"

Still, no reply, just an upward glance.

"You can talk now. It's all right."

Candayce nodded, then looked down and away. The thunder sounded again. It was louder now. Closer. Janine didn't notice. "Look, all that stuff before…it just doesn't matter, all right?"

Silence. Gathering. Rolling in. Beating on her.

"Didn't you hear me? I said—"

The silence was shattered by a savage crackling and a brilliant flash of blinding white fire. Janine felt the air around her become supercharged, fired with electricity and agonizing little lances of vibrating terror that held her and ripped through her.

She smelled something beginning to burn and her head went numb. She could still remember how to fly, but instead she was falling, even as the light and the pain were subsiding. She was falling, and an image came to her, a moment from that other life, that nightmare life, that dream of flesh.

It was a moment of touch and laughter and her father's smiling face. It was the day he'd helped her fly her first kite. She saw the kite whipping around in the sky, then it fell, and she thought for a silly moment of what it must have looked like from the kite's view as it sailed downward and the green earth rose up. The kite struck, crackled, and broke.

Then she didn't have to imagine. The ground pummeled her and her arm twisted beneath her. She heard Loki screeching and Candayce wailing and the storm coming in. Little drops of rain tapped her face as she tumbled to a jarring, nasty stop.

"Janine!" Candayce shouted. *"Janine!"*

Shaking, Janine tried to clear her head, tried to force herself up, but something was wrong. Her right claw grasped the earth, yet when she put pressure on it nothing happened, there was just a wobbling, and she didn't understand…

"Lightning—the lightning hit you, Janine!"

Then Candayce was on her, helping her, and Janine was sitting up, and her arm and her wing lay at an odd angle, folded in a way that was impossible, that was wrong. Then, as words from a children's rhyme came into her head, she knew.

Little wing, broken wing…

She knew.

Chapter 25

Candayce

It was over. Candayce stared at Janine's twisted wing and knew there was no hope of helping Mike and Bertram, no hope of getting home. They were trapped here.

Yet these thoughts were quickly replaced by more urgent concerns. Candayce knew they could not stay here. It was too dangerous. There was no protection from the storm. No tall trees to draw the lightning, only some small shrubs. They were out in the open.

"You've gotta get up," she said.

Janine stared off in the opposite direction.

"It's your wing. You don't need your wing to walk."

A clicking came from Janine. Her beak.

"I can't drag you." Candayce held out her hooflike claws. "See? I can't do it. I would if I could."

"Go away."

"It's not safe."

"Not safe anywhere," Janine muttered. "Stupid."

"It doesn't look that bad!"

Janine's long beak tilted toward Candayce. "It doesn't?"

"Look."

Staring at her bent wing, Janine shuddered. "Bad enough."

184

"Listen to me. I don't know *anything* about first aid. I don't know how to recognize if someone's in shock. I—"

Janine snapped her beak, almost biting her. Candayce drew back, trembling. "So you're just gonna wallow in it," accused Candayce.

"Stuffed," Janine whispered, hugging her bent wing to her like it was a sick child as the rain poured down. "Get stuffed, you selfish little—"

Candayce backed off. "Drop dead. I don't need this. I don't have to listen to this. I don't have to listen to you."

"Good. Go."

"I am." Candayce went a few yards, and stopped. She was waiting for Janine to call her back. She didn't.

Candayce went back anyway. She dropped to all fours, then knelt before Janine. She waited. Janine finally looked up. Candayce snagged her beak in her claws.

"What are you doing?" Janine cried.

Candayce leaned in close, staring into Janine's frantic eyes. "You know what I'm doing. You've done it to me enough times." Candayce didn't have the first clue as to how to actually *look inside* someone, but she was counting on Janine being too upset to consider that. Janine struggled and raked at Candayce with her good claw, but the Leptoceratops ignored the weak blows.

"Oh, I see what your problem is," Candayce said, which was true enough. Only she'd known it before she even returned for the wounded flyer. Janine stopped struggling. She opened her mouth— and exhaled. A foul smell drifted over and attacked Candayce. It stung her nose. "Fish breath, gah!"

Candayce released Janine. The Quetzalcoatlus sprang up on her back legs, and eyed Candayce warily. A caw drifted down from the hissing rain and moaning winds. Janine looked up. Loki stared down at her. Lightning bruised the clouds and lit his face. He looked different, somehow. His gaze was as imperious as ever, but he appeared stony, removed.

Candayce knew that look. She knew it all too well.

"Loki?" Janine said. Her voice almost broke.

With a flash of his wings, Loki flew off. He sailed north, disappearing into the darkness in seconds.

"Don't!" Janine called. "Don't go…"

Candayce felt horrible. She hadn't expected any of this. "He's not coming back," she told Janine.

"What are you *babbling* about?"

"Guys. I know what it means when they give you that look."

"He's a Quetzalcoatlus, you imbecile! Not some *guy*."

"That look means you're damaged goods. You're not desirable anymore."

"Yeah. I'm sure *you've* had guys look at you like that. Yeah, right."

Candayce shrugged. "This is me you're talking to. If they gave away prizes for every time you steal someone's boyfriend just because it's a really horrible thing to do, just 'cause you can, how many do you think I'd have?"

Janine waited. "You're scum. I know that."

"That's the look. That's the look they give the one they're leaving behind."

"No."

"No?"

"He'll be back," insisted Janine.

"Okay. So, until then, come on, let's go."

"Get *away* from me! This is all your fault!"

"You bet."

"I wouldn't have been flying this way, wouldn't have been out in this if—"

"Right. I'm the bad guy. That's fine, I'm used to that. I know all about it. Now can we leave here?"

"You leave."

Candayce looked up. The rain was getting worse, and in a way, that was a comfort. Her summers in Cocoa Beach had taught her that the most dangerous time to be out in a storm was just before it really opened up—and just after. The times when it looked calm were the most threatening. The lightning was more likely to get you then.

"I'm not going anywhere," Candayce said.

"The lightning."

She thought of the Leptoceratops she'd seen struck down by lightning several nights earlier. It'd been a horrible sight. "It gets both of us or it doesn't get either of us."

"Bull."

"Hey, I'm here, aren't I?"

Janine's beak darted about crazily as she searched for a reply. "I hate you!"

"I hate you, too, but I'm still not going anywhere."

Janine fell back on her tailbone. "Haven't you done enough?"

"No. I want you to understand that you don't know every-thing."

"What?"

The torrent was freezing. Lightning flashed and Candayce saw it rip apart a solitary tree in the distance. "That was *close*."

"So go."

"No. Like I said, I want you to understand—"

"I wish you were dead."

"Sure."

Janine shook. *"Stop agreeing with me!"*

"No. Well, maybe. One condition."

"What?"

"You and I, we play the Quiz. We play, then I go. You follow or you don't." Candayce hesitated. "You know what the Quiz is, don't you?"

Slowly, Janine nodded.

"Playing is simple. All you have to do is tell the truth. You remember what that's like, right?"

"Ask your question."

"Do you have any idea why I'm so afraid of you?"

Janine looked startled. Her wide eyes sparkled in the dim light of the storm. "What?"

"That's not an answer."

Janine thought. "Because I don't want to be like you. Because I don't care what you think of me anymore. You can't control me. You can't get to me like you could before."

"That's part of it."

Janine took a faltering step forward. Her back straightened. She loomed over Candayce, which seemed to make her feel better. "So what's the rest?"

Candayce wanted to keep her mouth shut. She'd driven herself into this trap, laid herself out, and *knew* the whole time where it was heading. And she did it anyway.

Janine was right. She was an imbecile.

"I admire you," Candayce said in a small, strangled voice.

"What?"

"It's true. I wish I was more like you."

"I am gonna kick your—"

"You've got integrity." Candayce spoke so softly the hard rain nearly swallowed up her words.

"Say that again. I'm not sure I heard you right."

"You wouldn't stab a friend in the back just to get a date to the dance." Candayce's chest heaved. Her words faltered. She choked. "I was scared, always scared…that you really *could* look inside people. Scared you'd look deep enough, you'd see—"

"Shut up!"

Candayce drew back. "I can't be like you. You don't know what it's like. What they expect out of me. My mom, I mean. Everyone. It's like, I don't even sleep at night, not really. It's why I'm in therapy. It's why I have to punch things, the tae kwon do, the kickboxing, why I can't ever do anything right on the piano, 'cause I'm too busy slamming the keys, why I can't ever tell anyone—"

"You selfish little *witch!*"

"I'm telling you the truth! It's the rules. Ask me—"

"It's always got to be about you, doesn't it? You expect me to feel sorry for you? To like you? *You made my life hell!*"

Candayce hugged herself. "I know."

"You just can't stand it, can you? You can't stand that I'm out here, and everything I want is here, and I'm happy, and you can't stand it!"

"I—"

"You just have to take! You have to take and take and—I hate you, you selfish little—you don't know anything about me!"

Lightning tore across the sky. "You don't know everything. You only think you do. That's your problem."

"I know what you are."

"I know what you are, too!" Candayce screamed. The downpour lessened, the thunder fell away, and suddenly, there was only a thin wall of drizzle separating her from Janine. Candayce wanted the rain to keep going. To never stop. She knew she was crying, even though she couldn't tell if tears were really falling or not. She could feel a sharp, biting cloud of regret and sorrow easing from her. She didn't want Janine to be able to hurt her again.

"You know what I am. What am I?" asked Janine.

"Your mother knows."

Janine stiffened. "She knows what?"

"Your mother knows, I know, everyone knows."

"What are you talking about?"

"What you do at night. Your mother knows you go out and deface property. Your graffiti. She *knows*."

Janine cradled her wounded wing. "No…"

"Who do you think has to pay for it every time they go around and paint over what you've done? Why do you think your mother never has any money? It's because she's spending it cleaning up after you. Those days when she's not around, and you have to stay home from school and work, where you do think she is? She's trying to keep you from getting busted, she's trying to keep you from getting in trouble, she's—"

"You shut up! You don't know! You don't!"

Candayce sat down wearily. "You call *me* selfish. You're out there every night, because—what? Your mom doesn't pay you any attention? I should have your problems. Your mom doesn't talk to you because she doesn't know what to say. She's afraid you'll run off if she confronts you. She's afraid you will anyway. And, hey, look around! I guess she had pretty good cause for feeling that way, *don't you?*"

Janine trembled. She folded herself up and sat down across from Candayce. Her body was quaking. "Y-y-you're…she knows?"

Candayce nodded.

"How can you say you *admire* me, then say all *that?*"

Candayce didn't answer. Not right away. "I don't know. Maybe it's because you always do what you want, no matter what, and I just do what people tell me. You do the things I'd be too afraid of doing."

Janine stared at her with unblinking eyes.

Candayce felt tired. So very tired. She hung her head. "Not everybody knows. I shouldn't have said that. My mom, she knows because of the bank. 'Cause she's one of the officers. She doesn't *want* it getting out. And I won't say anything. Not to anyone."

"Sure you won't."

"I *haven't*. And I've known for a long time."

Janine stared at the ground. "My mom really knows?"

"Yeah."

"Everything."

"Uh-huh."

Janine looked into Candayce's eyes. "Even about the fountain?"

"The fountain?"

"That time I put all that pink bubble bath in the fountain across from Town Hall. It was in the papers. You should've heard my mom going on about it, she was so mad. I never understood it, why that would make her so mad, but—"

"That was *you?*" Candayce yelped.

Janine leaned forward, excited. "You didn't know?"

"No. But…that was funny."

"So she doesn't know."

"No. I don't think so." Candayce hesitated. "Why'd you do it? Why'd you do any of it?"

"Why'd you make Sherilyn hate me?"

Candayce looked at Janine. Small, chirping, bubbling sounds were rising from inside her. Sobs. She didn't want to cry. She wouldn't cry. She wouldn't.

As the rains finally stopped, Candayce found herself moving. On all fours, moving, until Janine rose up before her, her left wing spreading, enfolding her. Candayce hid herself in the welcoming darkness and cried until she ran out of tears.

She wasn't alone.

Chapter 26

Janine

They walked for hours, exhausted, wet, cold, desperately in need of sleep, and terrified of what each of them might say to the other. Janine refused to stop, refused to sleep, refused to even consider all that Candayce had told her. They ate, stuffing themselves, then trudged on.

"I'm worried about Mike," Candayce said finally.

"Me, too."

"And Bertram. I mean, what if Mike loses it? If he can't find anything to eat? I should've stayed. I should've brought them food. I didn't think."

Guess not, Janine considered. But she didn't say it. "Not gonna do any good now. Don't beat yourself up."

They walked on, until pale slivers of silver and blue appeared on the horizon. Janine saw treetops—beech and maple. Heard the rushing sounds of the river. Smelled herbs.

"We should be close to where Mike and Bertram fell," Candayce said. "I mean, relatively."

For some reason, Janine didn't think so. This was more like the flood plains—

Suddenly, the ground rumbled. Janine and Candayce fell

together as the darkness tossed them from their feet. Trees toppled in the distance. The earth moaned and crashed and—

It was over.

"That was it?" Candayce asked.

"I think so."

Candayce's body was wracked with tremors. "We're so close to Mike and Bertram. That was another earthquake. It might have buried them!"

Janine placed the claw of her good wing on Candayce's back and guided her forward. Soon, a dim gray light washed over the woods ahead. Sounds rose up and shapes scurried about in the near darkness. Two of the shapes were enormous.

"Not T. rexes," Candayce whined. "Please, anything but that."

"Shhhhhhhh!"

The shapes moved off in the other direction. A shaft of sunlight leaped between the thick covering of maple leaves above and struck them. Janine saw pairs of curving horns and elephantlike bodies.

"Triceratops," Janine whispered.

Candayce sank onto all fours in relief. She hugged the ground. "No rexes. Thank you, thank you…"

Janine fought back the urge to remind Candayce of what had happened the last time she'd faced Triceratops. She won the fight.

Lifting herself up again, Candayce said, "The river's off to the right of us. I can hear it."

"The right?" Janine felt vaguely disturbed. It should have been off to their *left*. Had the minor quake they'd just experienced opened a ford to the other side of them? Were they trapped?

"I was thinking, we should keep to the shallows, the way I did when I was looking for you. That way it'll throw off our scent and we won't leave tracks and—"

"Yeah, maybe." Janine was too busy looking ahead and studying the terrain to really listen.

They walked farther on, passing between a pair of towering Metasequoias, and Janine saw the river. It wasn't some newly made ford. It was the river she'd flown over for days.

She sat down hard. "We're lost."

"What?" Candayce asked.

"We got lost. We went around in a big circle. Look." Janine pointed away from the river, toward a group of Triceratops gathered around a host of fallen trees. They were a good distance off, but enough of the forest had been leveled to reveal them. "Look familiar?"

"The Triceratops?"

"Not just Triceratops. The *same* Triceratops."

Candayce was very quiet for a time. She looked to the river, then said, "I'm tired."

Janine felt herself becoming very calm, just as she had when she'd first entered this world, falling to what should have been her death. "We need to sleep. You go first, I'll watch. Then we'll switch. After that, we'll get something to eat, and we'll start over."

"Yeah. Yeah, okay." Candayce looked toward the Triceratops. A strange expression came over her parrotlike face. *"The nests."*

Candayce lifted herself up and started off in the Triceratops' direction. Janine gaped at her and said, "Are you crazy? What are you doing?"

"The nests." It was all Candayce would say. "The nests..."

Janine followed her. "They won't let you *near* the nests."

Candayce kept going. Janine realized that she hadn't even questioned how or why Candayce had ended up between the Triceratops and the egg stealers the first time.

"They won't hurt us," Candayce said as she drew closer to the herd.

"Really?" Janine stared at the massive bodies of the Triceratops and wished she could believe that. A dull, throbbing pain appeared in her wounded arm, which had been numb until now.

"They won't," Candayce said. To Janine's ears, her voice was dreamy. A singsong. "They won't, they won't, they..."

Little wing, broken wing...

Janine shook herself. It was all catching up with her. She stopped a hundred yards behind the meandering group of Triceratops. Candayce kept going.

"You can't do anything!" Janine called. "You don't even know there's anything wrong!"

"The nests," Candayce said. *"The nests, the nests…"*

Janine looked around. She saw cracks in the earth. Small fissures radiating from some point far beyond the spot the Triceratops had chosen to lay their eggs. The nests.

Little wing, broken wing, fly in your heart, soar in your soul, believe that all things are possible, and you will be made whole…

Janine saw Candayce bend low and awkwardly pick up something in her claws. She cradled it close and kept walking.

Was that an egg? Janine wondered. An egg that had rolled from the nest during the tremor? How could Candayce have spotted it from so far away? How could she have known?

You will be made whole…

Janine went after Candayce. She stopped thinking, stopped questioning.

Candayce walked between a pair of Triceratops. They regarded her with dark, mournful eyes. Candayce nodded, then lowered her gaze. She walked past them.

Janine approached the Triceratops slowly. Fear was within her, a twisting, inquisitive flame threatening to burst into full frantic life at the first sign of danger. Like a sleepwalker on the edge of consciousness, she walked on anyway.

One of the Triceratops glared.

She nodded toward Candayce. "I'm with stupid."

The Triceratops grunted and turned his attention back to the Leptoceratops ahead.

Sure, Janine thought. *Why should they be afraid of me? I'm wounded. I'm sick. If I get out of line, they can just stomp me.* Somehow, it wasn't a really comforting thought.

She caught up with Candayce at the rim of the nest she'd seen earlier. Only the ground had torn itself open at the lowest reaches of the nest. It now looked more like a well, with one side carved out unevenly. Branches and bits of rock led down into the darkness, and a handful of eggs lay perched on a small ledge a good dozen feet straight down. Beyond that lay a heavy darkness, a shimmering pool of river water.

Janine thought it was possible that if the rain came again, the water level in the "well" might rise and carry the eggs to the surface. Peering again into the depths, Janine saw that the eggs were caught in a netting of tangled roots. No, the eggs didn't have a chance after all.

She turned and saw Candayce gently laying the egg she'd found before one of the Triceratops. She backed away from the treasure she'd delivered. The egg had a small crack on one side, but was otherwise perfect.

The Triceratops gathered around the egg, transfixed.

"We have to get the others," Candayce said.

Janine glanced down into the darkness of the chasm. "I don't see how."

Candayce walked over to a Triceratops whose back was to the wall. She rubbed the side of her face against his neck. Then she drew back behind him and tugged gently on his tail. He took a lumbering step backward.

Janine heard a sound from the pit. She looked down to see the eggs rattling together in their cradle. Each time a Triceratops moved, the vibrations shook the eggs. "I don't think this is a good idea…"

Candayce kept the Triceratops moving in reverse.

Janine watched the eggs tremble as the Triceratops approached. A single egg nearly rolled from the cradle. It sat perched on the edge of the abyss for a few horrible seconds, then rolled back to the others with a slap. Looking up again, Janine saw Candayce motioning for the Triceratops to stop. Again, it didn't appear to understand. Candayce sat down behind it, near the edge of the well.

Janine couldn't believe it. "This is nuts. *Candayce*—"

"He won't hurt me."

The Triceratops took a few more steps back. It lifted its leg, brought it down inches above Candayce—and stopped. Looking over its shoulder, the Triceratops squinted at Candayce. The leg moved forward a little, then came down with a thunderous *bang*.

Janine checked the eggs. They were fine, for now.

Candayce turned over onto her bloated belly. She braced her pudgy but powerful legs around the Triceratops's leg and awkwardly climbed, face first, into the pit. She stretched out her arms, dislodging earth and stone. A few rocks hit either side of the eggs, then skipped down to the water with a slight splash. Candayce couldn't reach the eggs. Not on her own.

"Your turn!" Candayce called.

"Wait a minute," Janine said. "My arm, it's—"

"You're hollow-boned. Light. I'll hold your leg with my mouth. You scoop the eggs up with your beak, one at a time."

Janine thought of all the ways this could go wrong. She strained to foresee at least one scenario in which she and Candayce wouldn't end up trapped at the bottom of the well. She couldn't.

Believe…

She bent down next to Candayce, eyeing the Triceratops. It was one thing for the Triceratops to trust Candayce. She was a plant-eater, and she had brought one of their eggs. But Janine was a predator. And she was hungry. They'd probably scented her hunger already. Being here was crazy! Yet, when she glanced back at the eggs, she knew it was right.

"Okay," Janine said. "I'm going to lower my leg to you. *Don't bite down.*"

"Right."

Janine pushed the image of an idea into Candayce's thoughts. Candayce, who'd been mountain climbing half her life, parried with a few ideas of her own.

"Yeah, cool," Janine said, amazed that she and Candayce had actually been able to agree on something.

Janine then turned to face the Triceratops who was acting as Candayce's brace. Her back was to the abyss.

"All right, McGurk," she said. "Don't move. Get it? If you move, bad things could happen. Okay? So *don't move.*"

The Triceratops didn't even look her way. Janine sighed. "Good McGurk."

Janine drew a deep breath, and slowly unfurled both of her wings. Her wounded arm exploded with pain as she tried to straighten it. She pulled it back, keeping it slightly bent. Taking another deep breath, she hugged the earthen wall and lowered her feet down to Candayce. She struck something hard. A rock maybe.

"Ow!" came a cry from below.

"What?"

"That was my head."

"Sorry," Janine said. *Mostly. Okay, focus, focus, focus,* Janine chided herself. She lowered her feet a little more. Candayce chomped down on her left ankle.

"Hey!" Janine wailed.

Candayce eased up on the pressure.

"Better," Janine said. She dug her claws into the earthen wall, grateful that it was firm and not sodden. Not so far, anyway. She tried to beat back images of falling into the well and never getting out again, images of thrashing wildly in the dark water. Tension wound itself tight in her stomach. Janine told herself, *Try not to think about anything. Pretend you're flying!*

Slowly, Janine tested, then secured, her left claw three feet down and to the side. Then she brought her right over and found a hold with it. Her ankle moved just a little in Candayce's mouth, and she used her other foot to dig a foothold. She thought of geometry classes in which she had used protractors and wondered what possible use any of these lessons could be in the real world. Now she knew. *She* was the protractor.

Candayce held Janine's ankle firmly, but with just the right amount of give. Janine crawled along the earthen wall as if she was the hand of a clock moving backward. Soon her long beak and her spine faced eleven o'clock. Ten. Then she was at a parallel with the horizon. She kept crawling. Eight o'clock. Seven…

The eggs came into view. Janine had to strain to reach, but her beak closed over one of them. She lifted it gingerly, but it was stuck! Tenderly, with the utmost care, she released the egg. It clicked against its companions. The whole cradle of eggs trembled.

Janine studied the network of vines and roots holding the eggs in place. She had to snap a few of those vines so that she could free the eggs and lift them out. If she chose the wrong ones, all the eggs could topple into the darkness.

Thunder sounded from above. Candayce sagged and Janine was wrenched from her claw- and footholds. She screamed as she plummeted, her beak thrusting down at the eggs like a sword. Then a sharp jerk and a small biting pain in her leg stopped her descent.

Candayce had caught her. Dangling, Janine dug new holds, securing herself.

The thundering above ceased. Janine wondered what had happened. An aftershock? Or had McGurk faltered?

Looking at the vines from her new vantage, she had a better idea of which ones to cut to release the eggs. Using the tip of her beak, she snapped and pulled back a trio of vines that were keeping her from her prize.

Then she opened her beak carefully, closed it over one of the eggs, tested for just the right amount of pressure, and lifted it out. The egg was heavier than she'd expected, and she nearly dropped it, but somehow she held on. She started the long climb back to the surface. Eight o'clock. Nine. Ten...

As the rim of the pit came into view, Janine saw a conference of Triceratops gazing down at her like scientists observing an experiment. Their horns glinted in the harsh sunlight. McGurk, on the other hand, was holding still. He'd only moved back a few feet— apparently to make room for the newcomers.

Janine raised the egg over the top of the rim, her beak poking out and away from the pit. She opened it and the egg rolled to the foot of a Triceratops and stopped. All the Triceratops stared at the egg. Fortunately, none of them moved.

Janine's muscles ached. Her right wing was killing her.

Five to go.

Janine worked for close to thirty minutes and managed to retrieve the next three eggs without much difficulty. She desperately wanted a break. She needed food. But she couldn't stop.

"You doin' okay?" she asked Candayce.

The Leptoceratops grunted.

Janine went back for the last two eggs. She was at ten o'clock when a flaring pain ripped through her right arm. Her whole wing twitched and straightened involuntarily. It whipped outward and caught a slight breeze wafting in from above. Janine gasped as suddenly she was torn free of the earthen wall. She spun back, certain that the ankle Candayce was holding would be ground to dust in the Leptoceratops's startled grasp.

Instead, Candayce held on, tight enough to keep her from

falling, but loose enough so that as Janine fell back and spun around, her ankle moved in Candayce's mouth like a ball in a socket. Janine cried out as she saw the opposite wall, then flipped again and *slapped* into the earthen wall she'd been climbing. She grasped hard with both claws, dug in her other foot, and heard a crackling, the whisper of earth shifting, and—

A sigh as one of the eggs fell. Janine looked down into the darkness. She saw the egg plunge toward the murky water. Shuddering, she looked away as she heard it splash. Something made her look back.

The egg was bobbing on the surface.

Janine thought of the Quetzalcoatlus she'd seen near the waterfall. The way they clung to the rocks upside down. Could she climb without the "safety line" Candayce provided?

Maybe…if it hadn't been for her injured wing.

Janine tried putting more weight on her right wing. For a moment, it held—then it sagged.

There was still one more egg in the nest. She had to concentrate on that one.

Janine turned to look at it when there was a sudden thundering and Candayce fell! Janine was flung forward and down, toward the water. A moment later, her fall was stopped with a yanking pressure on her leg. Janine gasped. She saw the fallen egg bobbing nearby in the water, and she scooped it up in her mouth.

Chest heaving, she called, "Okay, haul me out of here!"

Nothing happened.

So Janine climbed. She had a longer way to go now and the earthen wall was muddier, harder to navigate. But she didn't have much choice. She was hanging directly upside down. That now made the water twelve o'clock.

Favoring her wounded wing, she found holds off to her left and scrambled. Eleven o'clock. Ten…

She couldn't see the nest when she came to nine o'clock. She was still six feet below it. But Candayce could reach it. If she could just scramble up on her own—

The walls shuddered. Dirt showered down on her. She looked up, and saw exactly what she didn't want to see.

McGurk was dangling one tree-trunk leg over the side of the earthen wall. Candayce was still attached to it, her legs clamped around his, her eyes squeezed shut, her body trembling with exertion and, Janine was certain, absolute, flaring agony. But she didn't let go—and she didn't bite down, because that would have meant crushing Janine's leg.

Janine was stunned. This was the reason she'd been thrust down toward the water—the wall was collapsing under McGurk's weight!

Janine reached out with her hurt wing. She stretched it to full length and clawed at the earthen wall. She sent an image into Candayce's mind of the Leptoceratops releasing her. The return mail was a wave of panic. Still, Candayce opened her mouth and Janine yanked her leg free. Trembling with fear, Janine dug both feet into the wall, then extended her bad arm.

Bright, fiery lances of molten pain ripped through her, but she gripped with her right, then hauled up her good arm and clawed a firm hold, then did it again, and again, until the rim of the pit loomed. She whipped her beak over the top and opened it, allowing the egg to roll free. Then she climbed, with shuddering steps, out of the pit.

Janine flopped onto the solid ground, her every muscle vibrating, and she laughed with relief, spreading her wings—

And striking McGurk.

Candayce!

Janine quickly got to her feet. McGurk was leaning back over the edge of the pit, his hind leg dangling over the rim. Janine gazed into the darkness to see Candayce with the final egg gripped firmly in her beak.

"Hold on!" Janine cried. "Just hold on!"

McGurk's other foot was halfway over the rim. The ground beneath it was giving way. Most of his weight and part of his massive rump were centered on the limb dangling over the abyss. His tail flopped around and whacked Candayce's back.

The other Triceratops looked toward Janine with growing uneasiness.

"Okay, okay, okay, what do we do?" Janine said, pacing, trembling, wrenching her claws in frustration.

Janine picked up the egg she'd just saved. The other Triceratops watched her carefully as she moved in front of McGurk. She waved her beak back and forth quickly and acted as if she might drop the egg at any moment.

McGurk snorted. He didn't like this. His head lowered. His sharp, twisting horns came level with Janine.

Around her, other Triceratops gathered.

Janine danced. She hopped, shaking the egg, nearly dropping it twice, then opened her beak just a little.

"Yum, yum, yum, McGurk! I'm hungry. Come on. I'm making you mad, I can see it, come on—*do something!*"

With a cry, McGurk flung himself forward. Janine darted back, tripped, and the egg fell from her beak, rolling free. Janine fell on her rump, her wings outstretched, and nearly howled with laughter as she saw McGurk hauling Candayce away from the collapsing pit.

And he kept coming!

"Oh, no," Janine whispered. She got to her feet, spread her wings, and sensed—a thermal. The current was low. She caught the breeze and was taken back a dozen yards, whipping into the air above the heads of the other Triceratops. She spun, spiraled, danced, felt the freedom she thought lost to her forever, and fell in a heap.

Thundering footsteps chased after her. She looked up and saw McGurk heading her way, along with his newly angered buddies.

"STOP!"

Candayce's command rang in her ears and her mind. It was the most grating, wretched, and insanely beautiful thing she'd ever heard, and it made the Triceratops halt their gallop, dirt flying up around them as they screeched to a stop.

Candayce came around with the last of the eggs. She set it down with the others.

"Enough already," Candayce said.

The Triceratops agreed. As they went back to their young; Candayce walked over to Janine.

"I'm starved," she said. "Let's get something to eat, then find someplace safe to hole up and get some rest."

"I, uh…yeah," Janine said. "Sounds good."

And it was.

Chapter 27

Candayce

Candayce and Janine had spent the day sprinting along riverbanks, then breaking off and following a trail only Candayce could see. Janine, clearly worried about being lost despite Candayce's almost mystical certainty, scratched her tag into every third or fourth tree.

Twilight was upon them now, and they were moving slowly. Candayce noticed that Janine was still nursing her wounded arm, though she'd complained about it less as the day wore on.

Candayce had the feeling Janine had dislocated a bone, then wrenched it back into place during the climb to save the eggs. But she wasn't going to say anything, because even touching on that subject might lead to more yelling and screaming. And when they were just talking, really talking, it was surprisingly nice.

Ahead stretched desolate plains interrupted by rocks, moss, shrubs, fallen trees, and wide, snaking fissures in the earth. Tall shapes loomed on the horizon. Jagged cliffs—perhaps the area where she'd left Mike and Bertram. But Candayce couldn't get excited yet because they'd been *looming* in exactly the same position for a very long time.

"So you think *Keith* is good-looking?" Janine asked, sounding amazed.

"Don't you?"

"I think he's stuck-up."

"The two don't exactly cancel each other out." Candayce shook her head. "Look, 'eighth-grade studs' doesn't seem to be a very safe topic. Why don't we move—"

"Keith is not a stud."

"Fine."

"Mike, maybe, not Keith."

Candayce whirled on Janine. She wasn't sure if Janine was trying to punch her buttons or if she really meant it.

"You're right, let's change the subject," Janine said quickly.

They walked on, and Candayce suggested a game she liked to play with her folks on long trips. "The whole thing is, I'm seeing something, and you have to figure out what I'm seeing."

"Yeah, all right."

Candayce spotted something in the distance. "I spy with my little eye something beginning with the letter I."

Janine looked around. A bug whapped her beak. She ate it.

"You're disgusting."

"At least I don't drag vines around with me for miles and floss with them—"

"Maybe you should!"

Janine's shoulders sagged. "The letter I?"

"I don't know if I'm speaking to you."

"Of course you are. You'd go insane if you couldn't hear the sound of your own voice."

"Still wouldn't need you for that."

"Yes, you do, you have to have an audience—"

"*The letter I!*" Candayce wailed.

Janine looked around. She swallowed. "Insects?"

"Yeah…"

The game went on. Candayce said, "I spy with my little eye—what *is* that thing?"

An eleven-foot-long dinosaur plodded across the plain, heading away from them. It looked like a cross between an egg stealer and an iguana, with a glimmering jade body and rows of bony studs along its back. It kept looking over its shoulder at a tall uprising of rock half a mile off.

"Doesn't count if neither of us knows what it is."

Candayce shook her head. A few pale stars appeared overhead. "We should find some shelter. Someplace to dig in for the night."

Janine stopped suddenly. "Over there."

"What?"

"I spy, with my little eye, something beginning with—"

"Mike!" Candayce exclaimed.

Ahead, a T. rex and an Ankylosaurus came around a large boulder. Candayce dropped to all fours and galloped their way! *"Mike! Bertram!"*

They were out! They were out and they were all right and they were—well, Bertram was the closest, and before Candayce exactly knew what she was doing, she ran up to Bertram and *kissed him!*

For an instant, all of the Cretaceous fell away, and even though Candayce knew she was kissing the rough equivalent of a horned rhino, even though she couldn't even feel that much, it was all right, because Bertram, that great gaseous windbag, smelled and tasted like—

Peppermint. Candayce drew back.

"I found these tiny little plants along the ground," Bertram said, shaking. "I mean, I know this is the age of the flowering plants and flowering herbs, but, boy, they tasted good, and it's kind of like mouthwash, and I wouldn't be surprised if we couldn't find some oregano and some other stuff, and…Hi."

Janine caught up with Candayce. "How?"

Mike came up around Bertram. "The second quake. It filled in the corridor where we'd started and some other places, too. It made shelves, sort of. It was tough going, but we were able to climb out."

"Moriarty was there," Bertram said, looking around nervously.

Mike laughed and tapped his tail on the club-tail's head. "Yeah. Bertram kicked his butt."

"Bertram?" Candayce asked.

"Look at him. He's a tank."

Candayce nodded slowly. She felt her eyes beginning to tear. She opened her arms, and pressed herself between Mike and Bertram, awkwardly managing to hug them both as her legs gave out and she started to sob.

A sharp cry from above startled her. Candayce looked up to see a Quetzalcoatlus soaring above.

"Loki," Janine whispered.

Candayce was stunned. She'd been wrong, and about the one thing she thought she could count on, the one thing she was certain she knew above all others—guys. Yet here Loki was. "I guess I don't know everything after all."

Janine nodded, looking at the circling Quetzalcoatlus. "I guess neither of us does."

Candayce stood back and watched as Loki squawked and Janine ran after him. She spread her wings, flapped a few times, and leaped into the air. She didn't fly long. She didn't fly fast. At best, she rose and fluttered in the air for a few hundred feet before tumbling to the ground.

But she flew. And for some reason, the sight couldn't have made Candayce any happier.

Ankylosaurus
Ambush

Chapter 28

Bertram

The river was calling. It knew him. Bertram glanced away from the bushes he was grazing on and stared at the river's churning rapids, its gray, pounding depths, its long, inviting reaches. Candayce was beside him. Mike and Janine were at the river's edge, fishing for their breakfasts. Loki hadn't been seen since late the night before, but he would show up again. He always did.

"Looks like rain," Candayce said, nodding toward the rapidly darkening sky.

Bertram shrugged. "A little. But I'm not gonna let that get me down."

Candayce nibbled on some peppermint leaves Bertram had uncovered for her. "Bertram, you seem…different."

"I feel different. Everything's a lot clearer than it's been in a *long* time. Ever since you and Janine came back."

Candayce sighed. "Um, Bertram, I don't want you making too much of things. It might not be—"

"You're worried about that kiss you gave me."

Candayce's parrotlike beak opened wide. "Yeah."

"Don't. It wasn't that great."

"Excuse me?"

"Well, in a way it was. It woke me up to a lot of things. I mean,

I know what I *thought* it was going to be like, but…it was actually like being kissed by my sister."

"Your sister! You got a big wet one from *me* and it was like being kissed by your sister? You don't even *have* a sister."

Bertram chomped happily on the smorgasbord of leaves before him. "It's wonderful. I'm *cured*. One minute all I could think about was you, the next I can't believe I was acting so dopey. How embarrassing, you know?"

Candayce's shoulders bunched. "Can we drop this?"

"Sure, I—"

"Thank you."

Bertram looked to the sky again. Despite the threatening clouds and the storm that was already hitting hard in the distance, he felt wonderful today. He had a sense that today would be special. A day that would change his life forever. A song came into his head, and he wiggled his backside, clumsily dancing and singing along with the beat.

"Who taught you how to dance?" Candayce asked.

The song faded. His head low, Bertram looked over to Candayce. "No one."

"I can tell. Come on, crank it up again."

Bertram did and Candayce cried, "Now watch me!" She bumped her hips from side to side, rolled her shoulders, slapped her tail, and started bouncing around from claw to claw. Bertram's head bobbed in time with the beat. His massive feet banged. He kicked up one foot, planted it. Kicked up the other, planted it. Then his head whipped around in a dizzying circle.

"That's it! Let go!" Candayce said, dancing around him as the music swelled. "You got it goin' on!"

For the first time in his young life, Bertram believed it!

Chapter 29

Mike

"Do you believe you're seeing this?" Janine asked. "'Cause I don't."

Mike laughed and shook his head. Candayce and Bertram were rocking out on the shore, dancing and wiggling and thumping and giggling. Unreal. "It *is* great, though," Mike said.

"Yeah…"

"Wanna dance?" Mike started swishing his tail around in the shallows, rolling his shoulders, waving his little arms.

Janine looked at the storm clouds nervously. "Nah. We've got a long way to go, and I don't like the look of things."

"Right." Mike plunged his muzzle into the water and came up with a mouthful of fish. Most were eight inches long, with fat aqua bodies and upturned mouths. Beside him, Janine snagged a few herself. Three-foot-long turtles drifted by. An enormous five-and-a-half-foot flounder with gold plating bumped into Mike's leg.

They stepped out of the water. Janine swallowed the last of her meal, then studied the heavens. Mike felt a little nervous. It had been a day of hard travel after Janine came back to the group, and she'd said very little about why she'd left them in the first place. No one had asked her about it, either. It was as if they were afraid of the answer.

"Bertram's got your key chain," Mike blurted. "It's wrapped

around a couple of his spikes. I thought you might want it. Kept meaning to mention it to you."

"That's okay. Thanks."

Mike noticed that she didn't say whether she would bother retrieving it or not. He wished he had some idea of what was on her mind.

"I'm curious," Janine said suddenly. "Remember the first time we went fishing? I could see something bothering you."

Mike nodded slowly.

"It was something to do with back home, right?"

Mike considered the situation that had been facing him when he'd been yanked out of his body. He was suddenly anxious to talk about it, to finally tell *someone* what was going on. "Janine, I—"

"I mean, it stays with me. Here you are, Mike Peterefsky, for heaven's sake, you've got what anyone who isn't you would probably consider a perfect life, and that world back there was crushing you just like it was crushing all the rest of us. That's the truth, isn't it?"

"Yeah. But some of it...some of it I brought on myself. See, there's this thing that Sean—"

"I don't want the gory details," Janine said. "I just want to know if I was right."

"You were right. Sort of. But that doesn't mean things can't change. Look at us. We're changing history."

"Are we?"

"Mr. London said if we were hearing his message, then we'd already made sure that his future never came to pass."

"Oh, yeah? If that future never happens, how could he have sent the message? That Mr. London would never have existed."

Mike froze at the thought. "I don't—"

Janine shook her head. "Forget it. I woke up feeling really negative."

Mike shrugged. He surveyed the horizon nervously.

"Don't lose sleep over what I just said. I'm sure there's some loophole, some time paradox or something. Maybe sixty years after we get back, Bertram will be sitting there with Mr. London, telling him what message to send. Anything's possible."

"Yeah," Mike said distractedly.

"Wait a minute. You're not worried about what I said, are you? You're thinking about Moriarty."

"That obvious, huh?"

"Yep."

"I know what Coach Garibaldi would tell me. It's mind over matter. If you don't mind, it don't matter." Mike laughed.

A cloudburst overhead made him jump, and a cold biting rain beat down upon them. He almost felt relieved for the distraction. "We'd better find somewhere to wait this out."

Janine was silent. Her back was to him and she was staring at the river.

"What's the matter?"

Strangled cries escaped her. Mike turned and saw a towering curtain of brown mist a few hundred yards downriver, moving their way. In seconds, it swallowed the horizon.

Then there was no more time for thought or speech or even reason. The wall was upon them, and the mist he'd seen was little more than a herald for the raging, towering, all-encompassing flood of rain and rising brown water that came their way, a thick, dark, muddy torrent that snapped trees and swallowed whole anything that waited in its path.

Like them.

Chapter 30 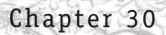Candayce

"Flash flood!" Wailing, Bertram turned and raced toward the trees.

Candayce tried to move but couldn't. There was nowhere to go, and she knew it.

"Bertram! What do we do?"

The Ankylosaurus was falling over his own feet. It was as if he'd forgotten once more how to be a dinosaur, and was trying to run like a thirteen-year-old human boy.

"Bertram!" Candayce screamed. "What do we do?"

The club-tail looked at her, eyes wide, gasping in terror.

For the last day, she'd considered talking with Bertram about how far behind they'd gotten in their journey, how little chance they actually had of finding the Standing Stones in time, and if anyone besides Janine had actually considered what life would be like if they were trapped forever in this era. The prospect of a future in the Late Cretaceous certainly hadn't thrilled her. But now, staring at the rushing wall of mud, she considered that any future, even one in this era, was better than no future at all.

"We need you, Bertram! *I* need you! Tell me what to do!"

Then the tough resolve he'd displayed several times before returned. "Don't fight it. Let it carry you! Whatever you do, don't panic!"

The water slammed into Candayce from behind. It slopped over her, and she was blinded and gagged by the foul-smelling, foul-tasting mud and pulsing, invading water. She sank underwater, her arms and legs pinwheeling, panic taking hold.

Let go. The river grasped her and she felt things knocking into her. Rocks. Bits of tree trunks. Fish. Holding her breath, she prayed as the flood carried her along.

Then she was rising, and she burst to the surface, gasping for air. She looked around for Bertram, Mike, and Janine as the river swept her on, twisting and undulating, but all she could see were blurs.

Lightning crashed and thunder bellowed, competing with the deafening roar of the river. She was dragged farther and farther, her thoughts on the world she was now certain she'd lost, and on Bertram and Mike and even Janine.

The river held her, mud and gunk splashing over her, the steady rain thrumming down on the top of her skull, gigantic boulders bobbing to the surface and dropping again, tree trunks spinning, one of which missed her head by inches.

A swarm of ratlike mammals chittered around her, their furry bodies battering her skull before they were swept into the waters beyond. They were all passengers, all at the mercy of the flood.

Candayce had never felt so small, so insignificant, so helpless.

Twice, she nearly fainted. But the water was cold and bracing. And as the flood whipped her about, Candayce realized that she was in a raging battle, one she'd fought for what seemed like hours.

She was floating, twisting, her eyes squeezed shut, and suddenly, the rain stopped and the water became gentle. Warmth seeped into her, and she opened her eyes.

The sun had come out at last. She was floating in the shallows of the river, in a place she'd seen before. Or had she? Jagged white mountain peaks rose in the distance. Towering 130-foot spruce trees lined the shore. Odd slabs of stone thrust out of the water and stabbed into the shore like questing swords.

She was home. This was the Montana she knew!

She looked down at her hooflike claws. No. This only *looked* like home. Where was she? And where was everyone else?

Shattered trees and other debris floated around her as she swam for shore. She climbed out, shivering, her entire body vibrating as if the current had snaked its way inside her somehow. Her ears popped and she heard the steady hiss of the river. A dinosaur roared.

"Mike?" she called. "Bertram?"

No reply. In the forest she found leaves and berries and ate greedily. Then she settled back and lay in a patch of golden sunlight, soaking up its heat.

She was alone. She had to proceed from that assumption. Mike and Bertram and Janine either hadn't made it through the flood, or they'd been deposited somewhere else along the countless miles of the river's length. If she met up with them, great. But the chances weren't good.

The roar came again. Closer this time. Candayce bolted to her feet. That is, she tried to. Her legs were watery. She fell on all fours. For an instant, she felt a twinge of frustration and embarrassment, but she was a Leptoceratops, she reminded herself, and this stance was perfectly natural.

All right…if I have to try to get along, at least for now, as a dinosaur, then I'd better try thinking like one. So what have I learned? First order of business: eat. Check. Second order of business: survive. That means don't mess with anything that isn't messing with you.

The roar gave way to a mournful cry. An invisible hand closed on Candayce's heart, tugging at her, and she wondered what was making that sound and why.

Leave it alone. Curiosity is not a good thing in the Late Cretaceous. You have to be tough now. You're a dinosaur, get it? Just an average, every-day—

"Hah," Candayce muttered. "I've never been *average* in my life." She didn't care what her inner dino was urging her to do, she was going to see who or what was making the noise. Maybe she could help. She carefully navigated the woods, and suddenly, a familiar, noxious scent came to her. "Bertram?"

Only the moaning answered her. She sniffed again. It was him—she was certain of it!

Candayce broke into a gallop, smashing branches that were in her way, ignoring the rat-thingies and roaches and all the wretched little creatures of the forest. Dead ahead, an opossum hung from a low-hanging branch by his tail. His eyes opened wide and he raced up into the upper reaches of his tree before Candayce could knock him loose in her blind, panicked flight. She yelled, *"Bertram!"*

The gas scent was more overpowering than ever. Ugly and disgusting. But right now, that smell was as welcome as a whiff of Chanel. It was Bertram, all right. It had to be!

Candayce burst through the trees into a wide, lush plain. A jagged tributary of the river cut through the green, and a club-tail stood at the edge of the water, head down, moaning.

"Bertram!" Candayce raced to the club-tail, thinking, *So my kiss didn't do anything for you, huh? Just wait until you get this one, you big, fat, adorable—*

The club-tail turned sharply in Candayce's direction.

She stopped, a half-dozen yards from it. Close enough to know she'd made a mistake. A heavy boulder smashed down on the ground. The Ankylosaurus, eyes burning with rage, roared and raised its tail again. It advanced on Candayce.

Two things were now fearfully obvious: This club-tail wasn't Bertram—and she was in trouble.

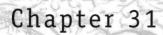

Chapter 31

Bertram

Bertram had known that Triceratops and other large dinosaurs had the ability to swim. It made sense to him that an Ankylosaurus like himself could do it, too.

He had clung to that hypothesis as he allowed the river to carry him to his fate. He'd bounced around like the hapless silver ball in a pinball game, he'd spun like a bottle cap, and he'd taken some scrapes and bruises, but he'd *survived*.

After hours as a prisoner of the flood, Bertram climbed onto the riverbank and dropped to the ground, panting with relief. After a few minutes, he looked around. He knew this mountainous area, although not from his own time. Despite some superficial similarities, sixty-seven million years had wrought many changes in these lands—or would, to be more precise. No, he recognized this land from computer re-creations, from diagrams, from texts he'd studied. And if he was right, they were less than a day's journey from the Standing Stones!

They? Bertram looked around. "Mike? Candayce?"

No answer.

"Janine!"

Silence.

Bertram's greatest concern was over the fragile, hollow-boned Janine. The brutal punishment of the trip downriver had been difficult enough for him to endure. But for her...

Feeling something on his back, Bertram looked over his shoulder and saw part of a tree trunk jammed onto his spikes. Janine's chain of shells was trapped beneath it. Many of the shells had been crushed, but a few remained.

He wiggled a little. *Cha-ching!* The noise gave him comfort—and hope. Now to find the others. He needed a plan. It occurred to him that Mike had the best nose and therefore the greatest chance of reuniting them.

He figured his best bet was to grab some food and let nature—via his digestive system—take its course. Then he would just sit here, where he could easily be smelled—and eventually be found.

There was danger, naturally. Some predator might come across him. But he could handle himself.

Bertram found some low-lying shrubs and went to work on them. He thought of the event he'd just witnessed and miraculously survived. Flash floods were the allies of paleontologists. They served to bury fallen tree trunks and all kinds of life beneath tons of sand and silt, creating the particular conditions necessary for fossilization. Bertram's dad had described flash floods as nature doing a little remodeling. Often, entire mountains were robbed of several layers of soil, and the valleys through which the flood traveled were resurfaced.

Now that he'd seen it firsthand, he was appropriately awed.

A familiar voice interrupted Bertram's thoughts. *"Get away from me, you horny witch!"*

Candayce!

"I'm coming," Bertram called. "I'm coming!"

He stomped off, heading west, following the steady stream of psychic cries and curses. A couple of times, to make a path for himself, he had to knock down baby Araucaria, or monkey-puzzle trees—spiny affairs that were only ten feet tall now but would have easily grown to one hundred. Soon, Candayce's yells stopped.

Bertram heard roars and deep, melancholy bellows that wrenched at the very core of his being. By the time he reached the verdant plain where Candayce had been facing her terrible trial—whatever it had been—all the excitement had faded. Candayce sat across from an Ankylosaurus. They stared at each other warily. Both seemed depressed.

"You know what I would give for a box of Cracker Jacks right now?" Candayce asked. "I mean…I would eat *cafeteria* food. I would eat cafeteria food and I would *like* it."

Bertram barely heard her. His attention was arrested by the sight of the club-tail. *This* was what he looked like to others. He was fascinated. And impressed. It was a female. He could sense it. "Magnificent," he whispered.

The Ankylosaurus looked over at him, grunting inquisitively. Her eyes were dark and curious, filled with an inexpressible longing. She rose, and took a step back to the water. "It's all right," Bertram said. "No one's going to hurt you."

Candayce nodded. "I know she's not going to hurt me. I just spooked her, I guess."

"I wasn't talking to you."

For a moment, Candayce silently sputtered, then she dropped her parrotlike head on her dumpy chest and said, "Of course not."

The second Ankylosaurus stopped backing up. Bertram came a little closer, staring in wonder at the spiky two-ton tank.

Suddenly, a cry sounded from the other side of the creek. *"Bertram! Candayce!"*

Looking up sharply, Bertram saw Mike charging their way. The T. rex splashed into the creek, heedless of the danger. The female Ankylosaurus chuffed and backed up in pure terror.

"Mike, wait!" Bertram yelled to the ecstatic Tyrannosaurus. Mike was beyond listening. He tore through the creek, whooping and hollering. He looked like a quarterback who'd just led his team to the championship.

Behind Bertram, the second Ankylosaurus shuddered and raised her tail. Her head bobbed and darted frantically as she surveyed the flatland. Bertram guessed she was looking for a battlefield with a greater strategic advantage. Finding none, she was preparing to make her stand here.

"He's not going to hurt you," Bertram said, his gaze flickering between the oncoming rex and the fearful newcomer.

Then Mike was upon them, splashing them with fresh cold water. Bertram raised his tail—and *whacked* Mike in the stomach!

Mike grunted, the wind driven out of him. He teetered for an instant, then fell backward. Candayce scrambled out of the way as he hit the ground hard, the impact spewing chunks of dirt and ferns everywhere.

The female Ankylosaurus hurried around Bertram, her tail raised over Mike's skull. She was moving in for the kill.

"Wait! Stop!" Bertram screamed. He scrambled into action, shoving himself against the newcomer just as her tail slammed down, missing Mike's head by inches.

"Hey!" Mike cried. "What is this?"

Mike brought his feet up underneath him and was about to stand when Bertram's tail smashed once more into his belly. Back he went, crashing onto the ground, making the earth shake.

"I don't wanna wrestle!" Mike growled. He sounded a little punchy. Before the female Ankylosaurus could make another move, Bertram put his tail against Mike's neck.

"Play along," Bertram commanded. "Be submissive."

"This I gotta see," Candayce muttered.

Mike sighed and lay back, putting his little claws up in the air and panting like a dog showing his belly. "There. Is this enough?"

Bertram shifted his gaze to the female. She was staring at Bertram in awe. Her tail dropped all the way to the ground, and she averted her gaze.

"I'm taking that as a good sign." Bertram raised his tail. Mike got up slowly. Bertram went to the female. "See? Nothing to worry about."

The female approached him carefully, eyeing Mike the entire time. Then she nuzzled Bertram's neck, and licked the side of his face. Embarrassed, Bertram looked to Mike and Candayce.

"My hero," Candayce said flatly.

Mike nudged her. "Shh."

From above, a shrill cry sounded. *Cahhhwr!*

Bertram drew back from the female and looked up to see Janine circling above. "You made it! But how?"

"It was Mike," Janine called. "He saw the flood coming and he grabbed me with his jaws and tossed me high. I got lucky and caught a current, then I rode out the flood in the air. My arm's pretty sore, but otherwise, I'm okay."

She came in for a graceful landing, her wings spread behind her.

"Wow," Bertram said. Beside him, the female Ankylosaurus tapped her tail against his. Bertram took a few steps away from her and she scrambled after him. He looked her way and she stared right at him, plaintively. When he looked away, she raced around so that he could see her face.

BRRAHHPPTT!

Bertram shuddered as his digestive process kicked in. "Sorry."

The female nuzzled him again. Everyone else backed away until the wind carried off the worst of the fumes. Bertram looked over to see the female staring in fear and distrust at Mike.

"Mike, could you come here?" Bertram asked.

"I don't want to scare your friend."

"Come here. Please."

Mike wandered over. The female bared her teeth and swiped her tail from side to side, smashing it to the ground.

"You're not gonna hit me again, are you?" Mike asked.

"See this log?" Bertram said. "The one on my back? Could you get it off for me?"

Using his tail, Bertram nudged the female away. She cried out, but Bertram stamped his feet. She backed off.

"Bertram—"

"Consider it a show of faith. She needs to know you're not dangerous. Besides, it's itching."

Mike nodded. "Milord." He bowed slightly, opened his maw, and carefully bit into the log. He yanked it off Bertram's spikes and tossed it into the creek. Then he backed away.

The female again looked to Bertram as if he was a god.

"Show-off," Candayce said. "I tamed the mighty T. rex for you, *baby*. Wanna take a spin around the block?"

"It's not like that," Bertram said. Though, in his heart, he wasn't entirely sure. "Oh, Janine! Your chain, it's still on my spikes—"

"I've kinda gotten used to not having it," Janine said nervously. "Why don't you keep it for now?"

Bertram nodded gravely. He didn't like the sound of that, but he wasn't going to start something he wasn't prepared to finish. They needed Janine. Especially now.

"Listen, everyone, I have some news," Bertram said. "We're about twenty-five miles from the Standing Stones. We did it! We're going home!"

Mike, Candayce, and Janine were silent. Then Candayce started to cry and Mike held her as best he could with his stubby little arms. Janine stiffened, stalked to Bertram, and plucked her chain of shells from his spikes. She snapped it forward. *Cha-ching!* And walked off, whipping it hard.

"I don't get it," Bertram said. "I thought everyone would be happy."

"We are," Mike said gently, brushing his snout over the top of Candayce's scaly head. "We are."

Bertram looked to the female. She was wandering away from him now, but still glancing his way, as if she wanted him to follow. He wasn't sure why exactly, but he did. "I'll be back. Just wait there." Bertram followed the female down the length of the creek and through twisting woods—Araucaria and Picea, thirteen-story-high spruce—then back to the riverbank.

They walked together for half an hour until they came to what looked like a boulder that was half-stuck in the sand, silt, and shimmering water. It took Bertram a moment to understand that he was looking at the half-submerged body of another Ankylosaurus. A male.

He looked at the female. "Your mate."

The mournful sound he'd heard before issued from her lips one final time. Then she hung her head and nuzzled Bertram.

"Don't worry," he said. "I won't abandon you. I won't…I mean, not right away. We'll find a place for you, we'll…"

Closing his eyes, he nuzzled the female back.

Chapter 32

Janine

Janine soared over the cliffs as the last few moments of daylight played upon the horizon. Endless bands of rich violet and pale blue had been painted across the sky by a hand infinitely more skilled than her own. The cloud cover was light and the sun was a crimson sphere sinking beyond the end of the world. The air was clean and crisp. Her skin tingled and danced. She cried out in pure heavenly bliss as she soared delightedly over the spectacular rocky vistas below.

She had to see the Standing Stones. Bertram had placed an image of them in her mind, but it wasn't enough. Her curiosity had her, and so she'd ignored the swelling pain in her arm and flown off in search of them. She'd suffered twinges and flares of wrenching hurt as she'd flown, but she told herself it would be worth the discomfort. She had to see, had to *know* if the way back was really there.

Studying the ground below, she saw that it wouldn't be long now. The plateau of stones had to be dead ahead.

She flew, the plateau coming into bold relief. And at its apex stood—nothing at all.

The stones weren't there. Janine circled frantically. She flew off and studied the terrain leading to the plateau, convinced that she must have made an error. But there'd been no mistake. She'd come all this way—they'd all come so far—for nothing.

Janine screamed in rage. She dived, plunging sharply toward the ground as the last pale rays of sunlight faded. Her vision blurring, she finally came to an awkward landing on the plateau and collapsed.

It was too dark to find her way back now. Besides, she needed time. She had to think.

What was she so upset about, anyway? She'd made the decision not to go back. She'd only accompanied Mike and the others to help *them* find this place. They were the ones who wanted to leave, who needed the "comforts" of home. Not her. She was the one who belonged here.

Janine thought about Candayce's revelations. *Mom knows,* Janine thought. *She knows.*

All the more reason to stay here. She wouldn't ever have to worry about causing her mother grief again.

Besides, she didn't have any choice in the matter. Not anymore. Bertram had been wrong. Mr. London had been wrong. She'd trusted them, just as she'd trusted her dad to come home that summer, and they'd all let her down.

A *caw!* interrupted her thoughts. Janine looked up and saw Loki flying above. He'd returned, as she knew he would. It was possible he'd even wait out the long night on the plateau with her. Right now, she wouldn't say no to the company.

Come first light, she'd fly down to her friends and tell them the bad news.

Chapter 33

Bertram

"PAHHHRRR-TEEE!" Mike howled.

Bertram watched as Mike and Candayce danced. Music flooded the pebble-strewn area they'd chosen as their resting place for the night. They'd already shaved a good eight miles off their journey. By dinnertime tomorrow, they'd be home.

Behind Bertram there was a small whimper. He looked back to see the female crouching low, shuddering.

"The music's scaring her," Bertram told Candayce. "Keep it down!"

The tune only got louder.

"You got it! You got it!" Candayce yelped to Mike.

Bertram slammed his tail down with explosive force. Candayce was knocked from her feet. Mike wobbled a little.

The music stopped.

"What's your *problem?*" Candayce snarled.

Bertram looked to the female. "Your *music* was frightening her. I told you. I asked nicely. Now knock it off!"

Mike sat back against a tree. "Yeah, sure, whatever. Oh, man, I can't wait to get out on the field, throw a few passes." He lowered his head. In a small, concerned voice he said, "I wonder if it'll be the same day when we get back?"

"I have to feed the fish," Candayce said. "I forgot to do it before I left! I mean, before…y'know…"

"Yeah, and I have to do everything," Bertram said, thinking about how the entire upkeep of the household, even paying the bills, was in his hands. "What about it?"

Candayce set her claws on her hips and walked over. "All right. Look, I understand some of what you're feeling. The same thing happened to me when I met up with other Leptoceratops. There's all this *stuff* that gets opened up inside you, and it's confusing, I know, but the important thing—"

"Please," Bertram said. "This has nothing to do with Beanie."

"Beanie?"

"Well, she's…brown. And round. Like a bean."

"Beanie. Like…what I wore when I was a Brownie? When you used to follow me all over the place?"

"It's not like that."

Candayce rolled back. "Mike!"

"Um?"

"Bertram's got a girlfriend!"

"Do not!" Bertram kicked at Candayce. She darted back.

"Studly!" Mike called.

"Isn't she so *sweet?*" Candayce burbled in baby talk. "Are we going to take her to the prom?"

Bertram couldn't handle this right now. "Just shut up."

"You shut up," Candayce said. "I'm having fun! I—hey!"

A huge club-tail nearly smashed Candayce into the ground. Bertram looked around in shock and saw Beanie advancing on Candayce.

"Call her off! Call her off!" Candayce yelped. "Tell her I'm sorry, okay!"

Beanie whacked the ground again, making Candayce barrel out of the way and into Mike's stubby arms. Mike roared. It wasn't much of a roar, but it was enough to make Beanie quit. The female Ankylosaurus raised her chin and strutted over to Bertram. She settled down beside him and started licking his jowls.

"Very nice," Mike said.

"She's crazy!" Candayce hollered.

Bertram sank on his haunches. "She's *protective*. She lost her mate. She took me to where he drowned in the river."

Candayce stepped away from Mike. "So she really has, like, adopted you?"

"I think it's more serious than that."

"You mean...she wants you to be her, uh..."

"Glad to know you find that a ridiculous notion."

"No, I—"

"From what I understand, she's lost her mate, and she's grieving, and she doesn't want to be alone. I'm just worried about what happens tomorrow. I don't know if she can handle another loss so soon."

Mike shook his head. "It's possible you're just reading too much into things."

"Yeah," Candayce said, wandering closer. "I mean, I know when guys have gotten crushes on me—"

Beanie surged forward, her tail up, swinging, ready to smash down—

"Yiiiiiee!" Candayce yipped, shaking and racing back to Mike. "Okay, fine! She wants you bad. You're the man!"

"You know," Mike said, "she might like the music if you were the one making it."

"Yeah, that's a good idea!" Candayce said. "Start with something light. Classical."

"I don't know much classical..."

"*1812 Overture*. Everyone knows that. They play it every July Fourth."

"I thought you said *light*."

"It starts soft, then builds up. It's perfect."

Bertram sighed. It *would* be nice to be able to party with his friends. He turned to Beanie. "Now...don't be afraid. This is music. It's nice. Something from my world."

He closed his eyes and concentrated. Nah-nah nah-nah nah-nah nah *nah*...boom boom...

"Grmph?" Beanie asked.

Bertram looked into her dark eyes. He let the music rise up around them. "It's okay..."

Nah-nah nah-nah nah-nah nah-nah nah *nah*...boom—
BHHHRAPHHHPTTT!

"Whoa!" Bertram was enveloped by a noxious cloud. He'd forgotten Beanie had just eaten an hour ago.

"Not this again!" Candayce yelled.

"We're heading upwind!" Mike warned.

"Hey," Bertram said as Mike and Candayce stole away. He drew closer to Beanie. "That was on the beat. Did you do that on purpose?"

He started the music again, and this time, just when the cannons were about to fire—
BHHHRAPHHHPTTT!

She did it again! He kicked up the music, and next time, *he* did it! Beanie started swaying with the music, and they settled into a long, loud, smelly duet of dueling vapors. The whole thing made Bertram laugh and laugh harder than he ever thought he would in his life.

It was a night to remember.

Chapter 34

Mike

Mike Peterefsky walked through the dimly lit corridor of a hospital at night. The entire place seemed to be deserted, except for one room at the end of the hall. A light blazed in that room, and people were sobbing.

Mike didn't have to reach the end of the corridor to know whose room it was.

"No!" Mike screamed. He woke trembling, his thick skin tingling, his every muscle tensed. He looked around and saw that he was alone, lying on his side across the trail they'd found. A shape was moving in the darkness. Coming his way. Mike felt an icy fear overtake him. "Moriarty?"

"I'm afraid not, my dear Holmes," Bertram said.

Mike forced himself to relax. A heavy sigh left him. "I thought Candayce had first watch tonight."

"I couldn't sleep, so I took over. What's wrong? I heard you cry out."

"It's nothing." *Liar,* Mike chided himself.

Bertram ambled close as Mike slowly rose. "Worried about tomorrow?"

"Yeah." *That much is true, anyway,* Mike thought.

Bertram nodded. "In my head, I've been going over every discussion I've ever had with Mr. London. The interconnectedness of all things. The way matter cannot be created or destroyed, and therefore our bodies in the twentieth century are made of much the same stuff as the dinosaurs and what existed before them...theories of Stanislav Grof, and Jung. You name it. But I still have no idea exactly how the M.I.N.D. Machine did what it did, or why."

"What's the difference why, Bertram?" Mike shrugged. "I mean, it just worked, right?"

"I know, but...well, there's a reason for everything, isn't there? That's what my dad always says."

Mike thought about that. "Bertram, can I tell you something? It's something I never thought I'd tell anyone, but...I mean, you're smart."

"So are you."

"Yeah, but...you don't have a problem just opening up about stuff. I've never been really good at saying what's bothering me. I always just try to act like everything's cool. But now, I just..."

"Tell me."

"You might not like what you hear."

Bertram shook his head. "There isn't anything you can say that's going to change the way I think of you. Whatever it is, just tell me."

Mike took a deep, shuddering breath, then let it out. "Sean's planned a hit on one of our own guys. It was gonna happen after school, at practice. The day we got sent here."

"Why?"

Mike rolled his shoulders. "'Cause Sean's crazy. He's not the same guy anymore. He's just come to believe that it doesn't matter how people feel about you, so long as they do what you say. And so long as you end up on top."

"Predators," Bertram murmured. "Boy, do I know the type. The strong survive, the weak perish. Win at all costs."

Mike nodded.

"How long have you known?"

"A while." Mike felt too ashamed to tell him any more than that. "I just don't know what to *do*. I love football. The game's my whole life. If I tell on Sean, if I do anything, that's it for me. The whole team's with him."

"Why?"

"They think this guy Lowell's responsible for us losing the first two games of the season, because he's not as big or strong or fast as some of the others. But Lowell's a good guy. He tries. He gives everything he has, and Coach Garibaldi says if someone, anyone, is willing to make the sacrifices it takes to get on the team and stay there, if he plays with heart, if he gives his all, then he stays on the team."

Bertram was silent for several long moments. "You really don't have any idea how people see you. What you mean to them."

"What?" Mike was totally baffled by Bertram's words.

"There are things you haven't thought of. But it's not going to do any good hearing them from me. You have to figure this out for yourself. And you will. I know you will."

Bertram started to walk away, then he stopped and looked back. "Hey, Mike. Thanks for telling me. I've never had anyone…thanks. I'm gonna wake Candayce, have her take watch. Big day tomorrow. We need our sleep."

Mike watched the Ankylosaurus as he ambled off, the pale moonlight shining in his eyes.

And even though he didn't have any more answers than he did before, Mike felt better than he had in a long time.

Chapter 35

Bertram

Bertram woke to the sound of a Tyrannosaurus rex pacing.

"So…which of us tells him?" came Mike's voice in hushed tones.

"I will, if you want." Janine's voice.

A low growl, then, "I don't know. I'm just not sure how he's gonna take it. Maybe I should talk to him."

"Fine. Just…*someone's* got to."

The voices and Mike's thunderous footfalls receded. Bertram opened his eyes and saw Mike and Janine one hundred yards off still chatting and moving farther away. Beanie stood before him. Bertram had an idea that Mike and Janine were talking about her. They were probably worried about how attached he was becoming to her, and how it might be best to leave her now, before continuing with their journey.

Beanie nudged something at Bertram's feet. He looked down and saw a huge pile of rich green leaves, including peppermint and at least three clusters of berries.

"Breakfast in bed," Candayce said.

Bertram looked sharply to the right. Candayce sat about a dozen feet away. "Did you?"

Candayce shook her head and nodded toward Beanie. "She did

it. You got the royal treatment. She gave me a few twigs caked with muck. I think she's trying to tell me something."

"Maybe," Bertram said, happily munching on the breakfast that had been laid out for him. At home, he would've been the one preparing the grub. In fact, he couldn't remember the last time *anyone* had cooked for him.

Bertram looked to Beanie. "Thank you." A comforting warmth emanated from her. She cooed. Bertram hesitantly shifted his gaze to Candayce. "Go on. Say it."

"I think it's kind of nice, actually."

"Really?" Bertram was stunned.

"Yep."

So did he. The thundering footfalls of the pacing T. rex grew louder. Bertram scanned the area. There were only conifers and a few bushes around now. No flowering plants, no forests, just a scattering of trees. Bertram saw Mike and Janine about five hundred feet down the trail. Well, as far as he was concerned, Beanie was going with them, and that was *it*.

"I'm going to talk with Mike and Janine," Bertram said to Beanie. "You wait here."

Bertram turned, about to depart, and Candayce suddenly broke into hysterical laughter. "What?" Bertram demanded.

"Oh, that's classic!"

"What?"

Candayce rolled on the ground. "Janine. She painted stuff on your butt. Graffiti."

"What's it say?"

"It says WIDE LOAD." She couldn't stop giggling. Beanie approached, tail raised.

"Hey!" Candayce yelped.

"It's all right, it's all right," Bertram said. Beanie backed off.

"And she put red flowers on your tail. Like you would on the back end of a truck!"

Bertram brought his tail around so he could see the flowers. It *was* funny, he had to admit. And, considering their surroundings, Janine must have flown some distance to find the necessary materials. There were no flowers here.

He looked to Beanie, and saw that she'd been untouched. He wondered what had possessed Janine to do such a thing. Shrugging, he walked a few yards, Beanie practically glued to him. He stopped and glared at her. "No. *You* wait *here.*"

Candayce sighed. "It works better if you say 'dear' or 'my little love monkey' or something like that at the end. Makes it sound like more of a request than an order."

"My little love monkey?"

"I've heard 'em all. Pathetic, huh?"

Bertram nodded. He nuzzled Beanie. She trilled. "Wait here, okay…dear?"

Her head bobbed. He turned, and she followed. "So much for your advice," Bertram growled.

"Hey, all I've got to go on are eighth- and ninth-grade boys. What do you want? Besides, I just had to hear you say it. You *stud.*"

Bertram shook his head. He approached Mike and Janine, with Beanie and Candayce, his entourage, right behind him. Mike appeared nervous, Janine resolved.

"Thanks for the redecorating," Bertram said.

Janine looked away. "Sorry. Couldn't resist."

"What are you talking about?" Mike asked.

Bertram turned in a full three-sixty so Mike could see all the graffiti. Mike growled, "*Jeez*, Janine…"

"I couldn't help myself." Janine sighed. She looked back to Bertram. "You're not really mad, are you?"

"Well, I *am* concerned about temporal anomalies. I mean, if this Ankylosaurus's shell were to become fossilized, and the 'paint' you used left some kind of raised surface, it's possible paleontologists could find this writing and freak."

"Oh. So I shouldn't tell you about all the stuff I've been scratching into rocks, huh?"

"You didn't!"

Janine looked around innocently.

Mike cleared his throat. "Bertram, we need to talk."

Bertram was about to make a preemptive strike, to demand that Beanie go with them, and to make it clear he would accept no other course of action—when Janine leaped in.

"The Standing Stones aren't standing," she said.

"*What?*" Bertram asked.

"I found the plateau last night, just before sunset. There were no big rock formations, let alone the seven all clustered together that you described."

"Did you go to the right place?"

"Everything else checked out."

Bertram shuddered. "We have to go there. I have to see this for myself."

Mike lowered his head. "That's what we thought you'd say."

"Wait a minute," Bertram said. "You two have been talking about this?"

"It's not like it's a conspiracy," Janine said. "Don't get paranoid."

The T. rex bobbed his massive head. "Yeah, we didn't say anything to Candayce."

"Thanks," Candayce snipped.

Janine stepped forward. "It's gonna be all right. Really, it is. I was mad at first. I was shocked. Then I figured it out. You were right about most of it, but not *all* of it. There's got to be another plateau where the Standing Stones are. It probably has to do with all the earthquakes and shifting of land masses. That would explain why your info is off. The bottom line is, there's no reason to panic. We've got time. Mike and I can scout the area for a while—"

Bertram slammed his tail on the ground. "I'm not wrong!"

"Bertram..." Mike said, studying his feet.

"I *know* it. I can *feel* it."

Janine spread her wings in annoyance. "You made a mistake, Bertram. You're human. Just admit it and move on."

Candayce stood at Bertram's side. She pointed at Janine. "Why should we listen to you? You don't *want* to go back."

"I—" Janine hung her head. "The *three* of you don't belong here. I want to help you get back. I do."

"Sure," Candayce said. "But Bertram told us it's possible that either all four of us go back at the same time or none of us might make it through. I bet you've figured that out, too."

"I don't think that's true anymore," Bertram said softly.

"If I wanted to abandon the three of you, I could have done it!" Janine cried.

"Like before?" Candayce asked.

"Yes, like before. But I'm here, aren't I? Your *therapist* should have told you the one about judging people by what they do, not by what they say."

"Therapy?" Mike asked.

"Cheap shot," Candayce snarled. She fixed her gaze on Janine. "I want to see this plateau. I want to go there. Like in the plan."

"There's no point!" Janine said. "I've been there. There are no Standing Stones. What part of that can't you grasp?"

"Great," Mike said. "Now we're going to start fighting among ourselves."

Bertram stared at the T. rex. "Mike, come on, you know you can trust me. I've gotten us this far, right?"

"Actually, you haven't," Janine said. "It was fate. Dumb luck."

"Fate and dumb luck aren't the same," Candayce said.

Janine shook her beak. "Whatever. Bertram didn't bring us here intentionally. It was a one-in-a-billion shot, an accident. He even said so."

The Ankylosaurus hung his head. "That's true."

"Don't you get it?" Janine asked. "All life is random. It doesn't go according to *anyone's* plan. I mean, I believed in this *map* Bertram had in his head because I didn't have anything else to believe in. Same goes for the message from Mr. London. But now—"

Mike growled. "Guys, we did it Bertram's way and it just didn't work out. Now we have to try something else."

"No," Candayce said. "I'm with Bertram. We stick to the plan. We go to the plateau."

Bertram did his best to conceal his surprise. His tail lightly touched hers. "Thank you."

She nodded.

Janine shook her head. "Fine. You guys do what you want. Mike and I'll start scouting."

Bertram watched Mike and Janine turn and start on their way. He exchanged a panicked glance with Candayce.

"Wait!" Candayce cried.

They stopped.

"Janine—give me your chain."

"What?" The Quetzalcoatlus looked at her as if she'd completely lost it.

"You can't trust in anything, can you?" Candayce asked. "You just don't have it in you."

Janine unhooked her chain from her wrist and handed it to Candayce. "I don't see the—"

Candayce whipped the chain out. *Cha-ching! Cha-ching!* She let it dangle. "Okay, here's the deal. You say everything's just chance, right?"

Janine nodded.

"So let's make it a coin toss. This shell, the one you scratched *good-bye* into. If it comes up heads, you guys win. I'll go with Bertram and Beanie to the plateau and you two can meet us there later. Tails, we go together."

"Candayce—" Bertram didn't like this.

"Hey, come on. It's a fifty-fifty shot. If we don't try, we'll never know."

"All right," Janine said. "Do it."

Candayce hurled the chain of shells into the air. Bertram tensed as he watched it flip several times and dance in the bright sunlight. Then it came crashing to the ground, scarred side up. Bertram hung his head in defeat.

"Well, that proved nothing," Janine said, snatching her chain from the ground.

"Wait," Mike said. "Maybe they've got a point."

Janine stared at Mike. "Excuse me? We made a deal. The shells landed—"

"It can't just be random," Mike said. "There's got to be a reason for all of this."

"I don't believe it." Janine shook out her wings.

"Bertram didn't make the M.I.N.D. Machine thinking it could send us back in time. Not purposely," Mike said. "But I have to believe that some part of him, deep down, had an idea of what might happen. That he knew where we were all heading and that we needed a time out. A chance to think about what we were doing with our lives."

"Mike—" Janine said impatiently.

"Every time I've trusted Bertram, every time I've put my life in his hands, everything's come out okay. I think maybe I need to believe in that one more time."

"What do you think is going to happen?" Janine asked. "Do you think we'll walk into that valley and the Standing Stones are just going to magically appear?"

"Mr. London did say there was one last thing we had to know, something we had to do," Bertram said quickly. "Maybe it's going to the Standing Stones together. Being there at the same time, whether all four of us decide to come back or not. Maybe that's what it'll take to open the doorway back."

"The rocks aren't just going to materialize!" Janine shrieked.

"Maybe they will," Mike said. "We're sixty-seven million years in the past. We're in the bodies of dinosaurs. We've survived fire, flood, and earthquakes. We've taken everything this world can throw at us and we're still here. If that's possible, then I don't see what's so strange about a couple of rocks popping up out of nowhere. I say we go."

"Mike—" Janine said desperately.

"We go to the plateau. If there's nothing there, Bertram, Candayce, and Beanie can wait and we'll scout the area, just like we planned. All right?"

Janine hung her head. "If that's how you want it."

"It is," Mike said.

Candayce and Bertram agreed.

"Thank you," Bertram said. He could feel deep within him that this last opportunity was all he needed. For an instant, he felt like whooping and dancing—then he looked to Beanie. She stared at him strangely, concern etched plainly upon her face. He nuzzled her. Then the group set out together.

Chapter 36

Mike

"Hey, everyone!" Janine squawked from overhead. "You'll never guess what I just found!"

Mike looked up from the arduous mountain trail. They'd been climbing for five hours and he was beginning to feel irritable. "What?"

"Nothing! I've been to the plateau again and—there're *still* no rocks!"

"Just the ones in your head," Candayce muttered.

Janine fluttered her wings. "You can do better than that."

"You're not worth 'better' today."

"How much longer?" Mike called.

Janine sighed. "You're pretty close. About another twenty minutes."

"You said that an hour ago!" Candayce yelled.

"Well, you're *slow.*"

Mike closed his eyes and drew in a deep breath of cool, crisp mountain air. It was glorious up here. They had walked a good five miles to a range of mountains. Janine had led them to a strange-looking solitary mountain with a winding path around its lower reaches.

The trail had been bumpy and treacherous. Mike had been

obligated to go first, clearing trees and rock to make the journey easier for Bertram and Beanie. The club-tails moved carefully, the way sometimes only slightly wider than their six-foot-wide chassis.

Once, about a hundred feet up, the left-hand side of the ledge had spilled down toward the waiting abyss. Mike couldn't see how the two Ankylosaurus would manage the way without sliding and falling off the mountain. But Bertram had come up with the idea of stomping footholds into the good side of the trail and using his tail for balance. Beanie had mimicked his moves exactly, and they had pulled through.

Now they were close to the plateau. Above, Janine cawed. "I'm going to find something to snack on. Be back soon!"

Mike watched as she flew off, haunted by her words from earlier in the day. *The three of you don't belong here.* Meaning that she did. And looking at her graceful, soaring form twisting over the breathtaking horizon, he wondered if she was right.

"It's odd," Bertram said. "This trail. It looks perfectly natural, and such things do happen. But I have a strange feeling about it."

"Like what?" Mike asked.

"It's been well traveled, possibly by dinos as large as we are. That's why it's so smooth—relatively speaking."

Mike looked down for tracks. He saw some smaller ones, but he had no idea what had made them. They weren't Moriarty's tracks, and that's all that concerned him.

Suddenly, he stopped and looked at the hard ground behind him. *He'd* barely left any tracks, either. So Moriarty *could* already be ahead of them. Lying in wait. Preparing a trap.

No. Janine would have seen him. *Unless he was hiding.*

"Mike?" Bertram asked.

A scrambling sound came from off to Mike's left. He turned to face a darkness that was far deeper than he'd first thought. It was a cave! A few rocks tumbled out of the darkness and struck Mike's feet. There was a skittering, scratching, scraping sound. Mike's heart thundered. If Moriarty was crouching low, he could be hiding in the cave!

No. Crazy thing to think about now. Mike tensed as he saw

something approcahing from the mouth of the cave. Eyes…claws…something was scurrying about.

"Ook!" it cried.

Two more shadows ran beyond it. "Eek!" "Ack!"

Suddenly, a trio of shapes came running from the darkness. Three dinosaurs, each fifteen feet long, but standing only six or seven feet tall. They had thick dome-shaped heads and purple, brown, and white scales. They crowded into the path.

"Pachys!" Bertram cried. "Pachycephalosaurus! Bone-headed dinos! Oh, this is great! I'd so hoped to see some Pachys!"

"Great," Mike said. "Glad you're excited. Now…how do I let them know to get out of our way?"

"Ookeekack!" one of the Pachys cried. Then he put his head down and rammed Mike's leg! He teetered and nearly fell. He saw the edge of the trail, the jagged, grinding rocks, the irregular ledges, the trees far below that looked like stakes. He righted himself. Bending down, he opened his maw wide and snatched up the offending bonehead. He tossed the Pachy at his two pals. They scrambled back into the darkness.

"Ookeekack! Ookeekack!"

Bertram shook his head. "Well, at least now we know what to call them."

They walked on, passing the cave, hearing an occasional peep from the Pachys.

"I wonder what that was all about?" Mike asked.

"I suppose they're territorial," Bertram said. "Their behavior resembles that of mountain goats from our time."

"They might have had young," Candayce pointed out.

Mike shrugged. "I guess we'll never know."

They were halfway around the mountain, staring up at the rear of the high knife-point cliff that tapped the clouds, when a sudden vibration came from around a sharp turn.

"Bertram?" Mike suddenly wished Janine hadn't flown off.

"Oh, no," Candayce said, shoving herself up against the wall, looking around desperately. "There's got to be something to climb, there's gotta."

"What is it?" Mike asked.

Candayce's eyes widened. "Stampede!"

Mike pictured Moriarty and a few new T. rex recruits coming for them. The thunder grew louder, closer.

Bertram yelled, "Mike! Candayce! Get behind me!"

"What?" Mike asked.

"Do it! Quick!"

Mike felt like a coward, but he shuffled back anyway, grabbing at the wall as he slid past Bertram on the narrow cliffside, Candayce already ahead of him. "Bertram, tell me you know what you're doing."

Bertram's club-tail carved a defiant arc in the thin air. "Batting practice."

Mike looked over to see Beanie backing away from him in terror, her tail raised. Candayce touched Mike's hide and said, "You know, if she thinks you're threatening Bertram, she's gonna charge—and I'm in between you two!"

"It'll be all right."

"Oh, yeah. My brave strong man."

Mike looked ahead to see Bertram moving to a wide spot on the ledge, near another cave opening. He brought his tail up and shifted his entire body to the side. *What if it's Moriarty?* Mike thought desperately. *Bertram couldn't—*

Then a blur of shapes came racing around the corner. Pachys! Dozens of them, heads down like battering rams, in rows of four, like soldiers in a regiment.

"I don't suppose you'd stop if I asked you nicely?" Bertram said.

The Pachys thundered on, oblivious of the tank that had been laid in their path. Bertram waved his tail, waited until the Pachys were almost on him, then swung, whipping his tail fiercely. He cut through their ranks. Pachys went flying to the left, piling up at the cave's mouth, or to the right, flopping off the ledge and down the side of the mountain! Bertram's tail struck with a high, sharp *clack,* and Mike could tell he was pulling his punches, doing his best not to actually hurt any of the Pachys. He looked over the edge and saw many of the boneheads lying on ledges below, hugging trees, scrambling to their feet.

Bertram whipped and struck, whipped and struck, until finally the way was clear. "All right, so it was more like bowling. Come on. I want to see this plateau."

Candayce ran ahead and kissed Bertram. "You did it! I don't believe it!"

Beanie *gromp*fed in dissatisfaction and ambled forward.

"Oh, come on!" Candayce returned to Beanie. "Life is nasty, brutal, and short. Ask anyone who's ever been to gym class. So get over it!"

Beanie didn't get over it. She stalked forward.

Candayce backed away and let Beanie take her place right behind Bertram. "Far be it from me to stand in the way of true love."

Mike led them forward. The addled Pachys stacked up near the cave's mouth looked at the group with wobbling heads and dark eyes. "What was their problem?"

"No idea," Bertram said.

"Hey, Bertram!" Candayce called. "Did *that* kiss do anything for you?"

Bertram was silent for a while. Then, "Um, well—"

"Skip it," Candayce said.

"You could try kissing me," Mike said.

"Forget it. You've got fish breath. *He* tastes like peppermint."

Onward they traveled, unchallenged, until a trio of Pachys appeared behind them. "Ook!" "Eek!" "Ack!"

"Ookeekack!"

"We have an escort," Mike said. "I wonder why they're acting this way? Janine scouted the plateau last night. She would have seen if there were nests or something like that waiting there."

"Not necessarily," Bertram said. "It was almost night when she arrived, and she took off again at first light. There's a lot she could have missed."

Like the Standing Stones? Mike wanted so much to share in Bertram's vision, yet…

They walked on. Mike noticed that Bertram had an odd look. "Something the matter, Bertram?" Mike asked.

"No, I...all that talk about luck and things happening for a reason...it made me think of an experiment Mr. London told me about. He said that quantum physicists divided a subatomic particle. The halves were placed in different research facilities, separated by miles. When a clockwise spin was put on one half, its mate, miles away, began to spin at the exact same instant, at the exact same rate, in the exact same way.

"Scientists have put forth the idea that this indicates that there really *is* some underlying force that connects all things. A pattern that gives form and structure to all reality. These same particles they separated are in all of us, in everything that ever was or ever will be. And they're connected to this pattern, which has also existed and will exist as long as time exists in the universe.

"Luck, coincidence, the power of positive thought and imaging, instinct, intuition—even what we feel for one another—it could all be our minds establishing contact on some primal level with this unifying pattern. If the M.I.N.D. Machine made contact with that pattern—tuned in with what has happened, what will happen, what might happen—well, it could explain a lot."

"How does that help us get home?" Mike asked.

Bertram shook his head. "If I'm right, then I guess a lot depends on how badly we *want* to go back."

Candayce laughed. "It's not going to get any argument from me! My bags are packed, I'm ready to go!"

Bertram nodded, wishing it was that simple for him.

Soon, the trail rose higher, and higher still. The rim of the plateau was now only six or seven feet over Mike's head. They were almost there. Janine had said that the outer edge of the plateau rose up like the rim of a bowl. If he could knock the rock away next to his head, he'd be able to see the plateau right now. He waited.

Bertram was the first to see into the valley. He stopped, frozen. "So that's it. Wow..."

"Bertram, what is it?" Mike asked excitedly. "Can you see them? Bertram?"

The club-tail didn't respond. Mike charged up behind him, and Beanie shot him a warning glare. She cracked her tail down on the ledge menacingly. Head down, Bertram led Beanie onto the plateau. Mike saw them scramble through an opening to their left, then slide down and out of view. He looked to Candayce. "You go first. I'll keep an eye on the Pachys."

"Whatever," Candayce said. She gasped when she saw the plateau, then climbed inside.

Mike looked back to the Pachys, who said, "Ook? Ack?"

"Sure," Mike replied. He went forward, his limbs heavy, his thoughts weighed down with the possibilities. He saw the opening in the wall and turned to face the plateau. The sight that greeted him was surprising. There were no Standing Stones. Janine had been right about that much.

But something else was there: Bones. The plateau was the equivalent of an elephant graveyard, with huge ribs and skulls half-buried in the soft earth. There was something else. In the shadows at the far end of the plateau, up against a knife-sharp rise that went up a good hundred feet, he saw—movement. Mike went to stand near Bertram and Candayce. Beanie looked around fearfully.

"Maybe it's the bones," Bertram sputtered, his body quaking.

Candayce sat down hard. "They're not here. They're not here..."

Bertram began to pace. "Maybe, over time, the bones somehow become the Standing Stones. Or maybe the Standing Stones are really insect mounds. That's possible. Insect mounds that haven't yet been erected. Mr. London simply meant the *locale* where the Standing Stones would be, he—"

"They're not here," Mike said. "But there is something..."

He sniffed the air, but the noxious clouds released by Bertram and Beanie all day had again dulled his senses.

"I see it," Candayce said. "In the shadows. More Pachys."

Mike told himself, *Just more Pachys, it's not Moriarty, it's not—you have to let this thing go...* "Bertram, I don't know if we should stay here. It's a long walk down, and with the Pachys and who knows what else here..."

"*We're not all here!*" Bertram cried. "Janine. We need Janine. All four of us have to be here—"

A sharp *caw* sounded and Janine whipped into view, sailing over the group in wide circles.

"Oh," she said. "Didn't see the bones. How could I have missed that?"

Bertram looked around desperately. Mike shared his hopes—but nothing happened. Janine was with them now, but no miracles were taking place. The club-tail looked up sharply and half-sobbed, half-shrieked, "All right! You win. It's not here. It's hopeless, all right? There, are you satisfied? Are you happy now?"

"No." Janine flew toward them, her wings opening wide. "Bertram, I'm sorry, I didn't want to hurt you, I was just—"

Janine's foot touched the ground, and suddenly, a *shape* shimmered into existence before them. Everyone gasped. Candayce fell back, shaking her head. Janine dropped down beside her.

"No," Mike said. "No way. Not a chance."

Facing Mike was an image he'd seen before: Hovering above the ground was a black metal slab. A tall, rectangular obelisk. A *monolith*. Unbidden, the theme from *2001* came to Mike's mind.

"Wait," Bertram said, walking around the floating object. "We're seeing it from the side. From its edge."

Mike followed Bertram around the floating black slab and something else came into view. The slab was long—*very* long—and filled with strange apparatus.

"The M.I.N.D. Machine!" Bertram howled. "Look, it's the M.I.N.D. Machine!"

Mike heard something. Rocks being kicked. Bones crunching underfoot. He felt vibrations. Heard a sharp, ragged breathing.

"We're going home, we're going *home!*" Candayce screamed.

"Yes! Yes!" Janine howled.

Bertram cried with happiness. He trembled and shuddered and howled at the sky. "We weren't all standing. We needed to be *standing,* all four of us, standing here—"

At that moment, Mike saw something stalking behind the monolith. A huge, three-toed claw. Another. A tail.

"No..."

Then a massive shape came out from behind the M.I.N.D.

Machine. A twenty-foot T. rex that had indeed been waiting for them. It was wounded and crazed, its eyes ablaze in the fiery sunlight.

"No," Mike whispered. "Please..."

But he could see the truth: It was Moriarty, and he was charging straight for Janine.

Chapter 37

Mike

Mike froze as he saw Moriarty pluck Janine up in his gaping maw. He held her by one twisted wing, his teeth resting almost tenderly upon her gullet.

"Mike!" she cried. "Mike, please help…"

Bertram backed away. Beanie pounded the ground near the rex with her tail, but Bertram turned and hissed at her. Beanie drew back in confusion.

Mike stared into Moriarty's reddish eyes. "Let her go. Let her go *now*."

Moriarty took a thundering step back.

"Oh, no, I'm gonna die, I'm gonna die," Janine whimpered.

Mike stepped forward. Moriarty drew back again. "Janine, you're not gonna die. You're not the one he wants."

Janine looked down at the six-inch teeth holding her in place. "Oh? You sure about that?"

"Let…her…*go!*" Mike cried, as if he could command the giant rex with the power of his will. Moriarty whipped Janine back and forth. She screamed—then sagged in his grasp. Mike yelled, *"Janine!"*

"I can see her breathing," Bertram said. "She's all right. Probably just the shock."

Mike nodded. "All right. All right..." Ahead, the giant rex stepped back again. And again.

"Why don't you leave us alone?" Mike cried.

"I don't think he can," Bertram said softly. "This isn't normal behavior. I think you've been drawing him here."

Mike couldn't believe he was hearing this. "You think I *want* him here?"

"No," Bertram said. "I don't think it's that simple."

Mike recalled Moriarty's ambush after the earthquake. The name he'd called the giant rex—

Sean, he thought feverishly, *Sean.*

Mike watched the giant rex. Moriarty stepped back. Mike followed. Again. It was like a dance. A terrible, frightening dance, with a horrifying price to pay for stepping on your partner's toes.

Mike stalked after Moriarty. Bertram, Beanie, and Candayce moved to let him go by. Moriarty was backing away from the M.I.N.D. Machine, toward the flat edge of the mountain behind. With a muffled roar, he turned and loped off, toward the dark shadows along the mountain. Mike charged after him.

"Mike, don't!" Bertram yelled.

It was a trap. Of course. It had to be. Moriarty would have other rexes waiting there. Or—

Stop thinking of him as a person, Mike demanded. *He's not!*

The darkness swallowed Moriarty whole. Mike launched himself at his enemy—and struck a wall. "What—?"

He heard Moriarty's growl. Above him, this time. Mike's eyes adjusted to the shadows and he saw what looked like steps. They weren't really steps, just indentations, spaced four or five feet apart, leading up and around to the back of the mountain.

Mike drew back, then leaped toward the first step. He managed it, then hopped to the next, and the next. He circled as he climbed, and came out at the rear. The ground was now far below, and he felt rocks trickling down onto his head. Looking up, he saw Moriarty climbing some new trail along the rear of the mountain. Janine was still cradled in his jaws.

Why doesn't he just eat her? Mike wondered. *If all he wanted to do*

*was make me mad enough to come after him, that would have done it.
Why's he keeping her alive?*

Memories of his first encounter with Moriarty flew into his
brain. The way he hobbled the turtles to make sure they couldn't
get away, going after far more than he could possibly need to eat.
And he thought of Sean, who was no longer happy with simply
tackling an opponent and bringing him down. He'd calculated
blows to cause them *pain*. To take them out. Even if that "opponent" was one of their own, like Lowell.

Mike raced after the rex. Stones fell beneath him, rock gave
way. He leaped and ran faster than he ever had before. He felt as if
he was at a football game, the ball in his arms, racing toward the
goalpost, only this time there was so much more at stake than simply winning a game.

Janine—his friend.

Mike climbed, and ran, and leaped, following Moriarty's trail.
The giant rex was above him now, slowing down. The apex of the
mountain rose into view, and Mike saw two tall forms ahead as his
ascent leveled out. A pair of boulders, like the upraised ends of a
football goalpost, flanked a narrow trail. And—

He stopped, chest heaving, and waited.

Between the stones, he saw a shadow darting furtively on the
ground. It was an anxious preview of something large and dangerous and insurmountable.

Mike trembled. Not with fear. Instead, he felt charged with the
sudden, overwhelming power of understanding.

Moriarty had wanted Mike to run blindly between those posts.
It *was* a trap. Moriarty had been playing him, just the way Sean had
been playing him back home.

Like Moriarty, Sean had to prove that he was the superior
predator. That he ruled without question. That he could inflict pain
without consequence.

Mike had challenged Moriarty's rule when he'd refused to join
in the attack on those turtles. And now the giant rex was using
Janine as bait to draw him to his fall, just as Sean planned to use…

"Lowell," Mike whispered, seeing it all clearly now. "Sure, Sean's

'*Big Event*' was a trap. Only it wasn't just for Lowell. It was for the whole team. And especially for *me*."

A growl came from behind one of the goalpost stones. Mike studied the ground ahead. He saw a crumbling, six-foot shelf of earth, then *nothing*.

Very slowly, he walked between the upright stones. Moriarty was there. Waiting. Perplexed. Janine was in his maw, but the giant rex hardly seemed to notice.

"Okay, I'm here," Mike said. "Just put Janine down, and we'll settle this."

Moriarty took a lurching, thunderous step forward. Mike could feel the fragile layer of rock beneath them quiver. Moriarty's head lowered slightly. Like an opposing defensive lineman, he locked his gaze on Mike.

"Come on," Mike said. "You want to tear me up. I can feel it. That's good, 'cause I want you, too. But you can't fight right with *that* in your mouth. Drop it. Get rid of her."

Moriarty's shoulders bunched. His claws scissored. He roared, opening his maw wide. Janine nearly toppled out, then Moriarty clamped down on her. He could have bitten her in half—but something stopped him.

"Mike...?" Janine whimpered.

Mike's nostrils flared. "Come on! It's better this way. Tooth and claw. Let her go. Let's finish it the way it was meant to be."

A strange light came into Moriarty's eyes. He looked down at the Quetzalcoatlus in his mouth, seemingly in confusion...and tossed her away.

"Janine!" Mike watched as Janine's crumpled form hit the rim of the ledge, bounced, then fell into the waiting abyss.

"*No!*" Mike screamed. He took a step toward the fragile edge, his heart sinking. Only silence greeted him.

Moriarty roared—and Mike threw himself at the rex. They met, maws flashing, claws tearing. They fell together, shoving, ripping, beating. They bit and growled and grunted, pain and fury mixing together, the human part of Mike's brain one with the rex inside him, and he fought with all his heart.

Then Moriarty was sinking back. Mike drew away, his entire shoulder feeling like one exposed wound, and he saw that Moriarty looked even worse.

"Let it go," Mike said. "It can end here and now."

Moriarty's response was to lurch upward, raging, screaming, completely mad now. Mike picked up a rock with his maw and used it as a weapon, smashing it into Moriarty's skull, battering him again and again, feeling his own teeth breaking off and not caring, scraping and stabbing with his claws. *You can't stop, can you?* Mike asked in his head. *Not until you're made to stop.*

Finally, the giant rex sagged beneath him. Mike backed away, horrified, and let the stone fall from his mouth. He shook with exhaustion, with rage...and Moriarty rose. He was shaky, his eyes glazed, but there was still fight in him.

Mike eyed the edge of the cliff. It was a long way down, even if it was just to the plateau. About ten stories.

The words of his friends came to him. Bertram and Candayce had been right, some things were unavoidable—fate.

"What do you say, Professor? It's not the Reichenbach Falls, but... *Wanna flip a coin?*"

Moriarty launched himself at Mike. They met, teeth glistening, spittle and blood flying, two titans roaring and slashing. Mike pulled the monster near, hugged him close, and yanked him to the edge of the cliff. They stumbled, striking the floor of the ledge with a thunderclap, and the fragile rock beneath them shattered!

They fell, the ground that had seemed an impossible distance away only seconds before reaching up for them as they turned and turned, a ten-ton coin flipping and flailing with biting tooth and ripping claw, and—

Chapter 38

Bertram

Bertram saw it all. Janine falling from the cliff, tumbling down, her wings weakly spreading, a current guiding her to an awkward landing—one she'd walked away from on shaky legs before collapsing facedown. And above, at the apex of the mountain, Mike and Moriarty battling, then falling over the brink.

Candayce screamed as they dropped, twisting, ripping, tearing and screaming against all reason, plummeting and disappearing into the shadows at the far edge of the plateau. A horrible explosion sounded, shaking the ground.

"Mike…"

Another crackling sounded from above. Bertram looked up and saw the apex of the mountain shuddering as fissures opened up along its side. The mountain's pinnacle toppled! It fell their way, striking what was left of the ledge and bouncing ahead.

Rocks bulleted their way, boulders twenty feet long, others even larger, smashing toward them.

"Beanie!" Bertram yelled. Then came the explosive force, the ground rippling, rocks striking, screams, clumps of dirt and stone, and—an ending. Silence. Bertram tried to move, but he was pinned. He'd been buried alive by the rockfall!

He felt a sudden, unexpected impact. *Smash! Crack!* The rocks holding him fell away. He struggled—and broke free of their hold. He looked up to see Beanie staring at him with wide, fear-stricken eyes. She moaned and quivered. He went to her, looking all around her spiky form to see if she was hurt. Then he nuzzled her, and soon her moans died away.

"Candayce!" he yelled. "Janine!"

"Present," came a weak voice from the other side of the great pile of rocks off to his right. Candayce wobbled toward him on all fours, her pudgy parrot-headed body looking a little more banged up but still functioning.

"Janine?" Candayce yelled. *"Janine!"*

Nothing. Bertram and Candayce looked to the air. Bertram prayed that she'd taken wing at the last moment, but there was no sound from above.

"We have to find her. Come on!" Bertram said.

He and Candayce dug frantically among the avalanche of rock. At the southern edge, aimed toward the mass of shadows where Mike and Moriarty had fallen, they found Janine. She'd been beaten by the rocks but had managed to avoid the worst of them.

"Again, again, again," she muttered.

Suddenly, a single, thundering footstep sounded. Bertram and Candayce stared at the shadows. A tall figure broke from them and fell onto its side. A rex. He was cloaked too firmly in shadows for either Bertram or Candayce to identify him.

"All right," Bertram said anxiously. "If they hit, with Moriarty underneath, Mike could have—"

Candayce wobbled forward, Bertram keeping pace. She stopped before the T. rex. "It isn't Mike."

Bertram came closer. He watched as the last shuddering breath of air left the giant rex and its chest relaxed.

"No!" Candayce screamed, launching herself at Moriarty, kicking at the giant rex's inert form. *"No!"*

A *caw* sounded from above. Bertram looked up slowly to see Loki glide their way. He dove into the waiting shadows. Bertram moved away from Moriarty's remains. "Hey!"

From the darkness came another sharp cry.

"Get away from him!" Bertram screamed. "Leave him alone!"

Candayce launched herself into the shadows. "Shoo! Get away! I'll kick your scaly backside! I will! I—"

Then silence. Bertram scrambled into the darkness, his eyes adjusting quickly. He saw Loki sitting on a rock beside Mike's still form. Candayce approached Mike slowly. She looked over her shoulder, tears in her eyes. "He—he's..."

Snoring, Bertram realized. Mike was *snoring!* He was alive! Candayce nudged and butted Mike's flank excitedly. "Wake up!"

"Come on, just a little more..."

Mike's tiny arms flailed.

"How do you tickle a T. rex?" Candayce asked. "Someone tell me and I'll do it!"

Mike rolled over and Candayce leaped out of the way, squealing. His eyes opened. "Oh, man. I can't find one part of me that doesn't hurt."

He rolled onto his belly, drew his legs slowly beneath him, then tried to rise. He fell back with a loud crash!

"Mike, is it your legs? Are they broken?" Bertram asked.

Mike shook his head. "Bleaaahhh. Just...everything's spinning. Hold on."

"That's fine," Bertram said. "Take all the time you need."

Soon, Mike was rolling onto his belly again, shuddering, and forcing his legs beneath him. This time, they held steadily and he rose, tail held behind him, chest heaving.

"Bertram," Mike said. "What you were telling me last night. About Sean. I see it now. I know what to do."

"Good," Bertram said. "I—"

"Bertram!"

Bertram turned to see Janine at the edge of the shadows. He considered, from her lack of reaction to Mike's status as one of the living, that she'd been watching for some time.

"You'd better come *quick!*" Janine cried. "The M.I.N.D. Machine. It's starting to fade..."

Chapter 39

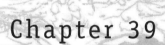

Janine

Janine saw Mike and Bertram hurry out of the shadows. In front of them, the machine hung to one side of the rocks that had fallen from the tip of the mountain. Janine could see through its slightly transparent form. Candayce ran past her and reached the machine first and cried, "What do we do?"

"Do?" Bertram asked.

"To go home!"

"I honestly don't know. Touch it, I guess."

Candayce went to the machine. "All right. Here goes."

She walked right into the machine—and came out the other side. Janine studied her. She looked a little confused, disoriented. Had it worked?

"I don't believe this!" Candayce wailed. "It's too late! We're stuck here!"

"Calm down!" Janine snapped. She looked over to Loki, who sat nearby, staring at them. "Maybe it's what Bertram said. It's got to be all four of us at once."

"Yeah, only you don't *want* to leave," Candayce said. She plopped down on the ground, her back to the rocks. Her head fell to her chest and she wept. "I wanna go to the mall! I wanna eat

261

things that are really bad for me! I wanna sit in front of the television and eat ice cream and expand!"

"There's another problem," Bertram said. "I can't go back, either."

Mike swiveled his giant head Bertram's way. *"What?"*

Bertram shifted his gaze to Beanie. "She's already lost one mate. I can't do that to her."

"Bertram, she's just a dinosaur!" Mike roared.

"So are we."

"It's not the same…"

"No," Bertram said, "it's not. But it means the same to me. I won't do that to her."

"What about us?" Mike asked. "*We* don't want to stay here. Well, Candayce and I don't, anyway."

"Try the machine."

Mike and Candayce walked all around the machine, their claws passing through its levers and switches. Nothing. Janine looked to Loki, then at Bertram. "It really is gonna take all four of us."

"I can't do that to Beanie," Bertram said. "I won't."

Janine was astounded by Bertram's vow. *She* was the one who was supposed to let everyone down, not Bertram.

Loki walked over to her. He tapped her beak with his and studied her. For the first time, Janine knew what it was to be on the other side of someone looking into her, looking deep, and uncovering each and every one of her secrets.

Stepping back, Loki shrugged. He cawed, then took a running leap, dove into a thermal, and was carried up over the rim of the plateau and into the skies beyond.

Janine watched him go. "I think I…just changed my mind. Or I had my mind changed for me."

"What are you babbling about?" Candayce said, pouting.

"I really don't belong here. It's not right, my being here. It's not right for any of us." She looked to Bertram. "You have to let it go. She'll be all right."

Bertram shook his head.

"Listen," she said, "all four of us—we've been changed. What's inside these bodies, the spirits, the souls, whatever you want to call it, of the dinos that were here before us—"

"You're not a dinosaur," Bertram said. "Common misconception. A Quetzalcoatlus—"

"Bertram, stop," Candayce said. "I want to hear this."

"Thank you," Janine said warily. "We've all been changed. Not just by what we've been through, but by the beings who were inside these bodies long before us. Do you understand?"

"And they've been changed by us," Bertram said slowly.

"Yes. When we're gone, Beanie will still have a mate. Look inside and tell me I'm not right."

Bertram looked to Beanie, then hung his head. He straightened up, nuzzled the ever-perplexed club-tail, and said, "All right. We go. But I'm going to miss her."

"You're serious?" Candayce asked.

Bertram nodded. "She's the only person in my life who never asked for anything out of me."

"She can't *talk*," Candayce said.

Mike playfully whacked Candayce with his tail. "Hush."

"She accepted me as I am," Bertram continued, "and she made me feel stronger than Mike even, stronger than anyone or anything I've ever known. This is my loss, my going back. But I know you're right. I don't know how to survive in this world, how to give her everything I'd want to. Maybe I could learn in time, maybe not. I guess the fact is, we don't belong here...but it was a great place to visit."

All four stood beside the machine. They walked into it together—and came out the other side. Nothing had changed.

Nothing.

"Oh, man!" Janine said. "All that and it still didn't work?" She stared at the machine. "What do you *want*, anyway?"

Bertram's eyes opened wide. "Wait a minute," he said softly. "I think I know."

Chapter 40

Bertram

"The monitors," Bertram said anxiously. "I just noticed there's an image on them. It's faint, hard to make out because of the glare from the sun. Mike, can you get close enough and see what it is?"

Mike peered into one of the many computer monitor screens on the phantom M.I.N.D. Machine. "It's a bunch of rocks. Weird-looking."

"How many?" Bertram asked, excitedly.

"Seven."

"The Standing Stones!" Bertram said. "It all comes back to them. But why? It's obvious they're from some later time, that they're..." He looked at the pile of rocks that had fallen from above.

Mr. London's words came to him. Something he said in class all the time: *Remember, everyone, these folks out there telling you there's nothing new, everything's been done? They're full of it. A hundred years ago, people didn't have skateboards, CDs, or video games. Use your imagination. It's the old saying—*

"If it didn't already exist, someone would just have to invent it," Bertram said. "The stones! We have to *make* the stones!"

"What?" Mike asked. "How?"

Candayce trembled. "Janine's the artist. She could tell us what to do."

Janine nodded. "Yeah, it's all there. We just have to move things around and sculpt."

Mike shook his head. "I don't see where this is gonna help us. I mean, why—"

"*Why?*" Janine came forward, shaking her great wings excitedly. "To prove we were here!"

Candayce started trotting in circles. "Janine, Janine, every rotten thing I've ever said about you or might ever say about you, I take back!"

"Or *might* say?"

"Let's be realistic."

Janine laughed. "Okay."

Bertram shuddered. "I don't know about this. What kind of proof can we leave that won't end up throwing our whole future into chaos?"

"It's proof for *us*," Mike said. "No one else would ever believe it."

"That's true," Janine said. "I can't see the scientific community accepting anything we leave here as valid proof of time travel, astral projection, any of it. It would just be looked on as some kind of hoax. Another Bigfoot."

"Yeah, with my dad at the center of it," Bertram said glumly.

"No," Mike said, "what your dad's going to be at the center of is finding that guy over there." He pointed to Moriarty.

Bertram's eyes lit up. "The giant rex! The one he mentioned in the note he left me!"

"I've got an idea," Janine said. "I think I know how to make everyone happy."

They got to work. The day wore on, and the M.I.N.D. Machine faded a little more as the hours stretched away. Mike helped to clear rock away. Janine directed Bertram exactly where to smash the larger rocks. Candayce worked with Janine to chisel the stones into seven distinct forms.

Bertram eyed the sky warily. The sun was reaching its zenith, and the M.I.N.D. Machine was becoming harder and harder to see.

"We're not gonna make it," Mike said.

"Don't be such an Eeyore," Bertram said. "We'll make it fine."

"If you say so."

"I say so."

Soon, the seven forms were nearly completed. Mike stood back and looked at them. "Y'know, if you stare at these things long enough, some of them look like us!"

"I was wondering when you'd notice," Janine said. "It *is* the four of us, plus Loki, Beanie, and Moriarty."

"Cool!" Mike said.

"It's something to prove we were here," Janine said. She bent down and scratched something into the base of a rock. She scraped hard.

"What's that?" Bertram asked.

"My tag. Changed a little."

"I want one!" Candayce said, pointing at the weird little squiggle.

Janine fashioned symbols for all seven. Then she stood back and sighed. "We did it."

Mike studied the image in the monitor and the stones themselves. "I'd say so. Looks pretty close, anyway."

"It *can't* be perfect," Bertram said. "The elements, sixty-seven million years, this whole area being covered in rock…"

"Right. So what do we do now?"

Everyone looked to Bertram. "We go back through the machine."

"Are you sure?" Mike asked.

"Yeah. I can feel it this time."

Mike looked over to Moriarty and whispered, "I'm sorry it had to be like this. And that it's all gotta happen again. But there's no other way, is there?"

The fallen rex gave no reply.

Bertram felt a little guilty at having overheard those very private words. He went to Candayce, who was staring at the dwindling sun.

"It really is pretty, isn't it?" she asked. "Somehow I never really noticed."

Janine looked his way, then said, "Hold on! Forgot something!"

She raced back to the Standing Stones, crouched among them for a moment, then came back. Bertram's stomach tightened. "What'd you do?"

Janine held up her chain. "Good mojo. Luck. We need all we can get right now."

Bertram relaxed.

Janine looked at the sky. "Man, I wish there was time for me to fly again."

Candayce smiled. "You'll fly again."

"What are you talking about?"

"An idea I have. You'll see."

"Hope so."

Mike joined them. Bertram looked back to Beanie. She was staring at him so fearfully that he wondered if he was making a mistake. He hoped the Ankylosaurus who would soon take over this body again would treat her well. "He'd better, or I'll build another machine."

Beanie angled her head inquisitively.

Suddenly, three shapes leaped over the rim and ran toward them. "Ook!" "Eek!" "Ack!"

"Ookeekack!"

Beanie turned to face them. She slammed her tail on the ground, and the Pachys fell. Beanie looked toward Bertram. She was beaming.

He smiled inwardly as a fireball of warmth drifted from him to the club-tail, and he received one in return.

"Now," Bertram said.

Together, they walked into the phantom machine. Lightning struck all around them. Unbelievable energies lifted Bertram up, pulling him away from his heavy Ankylosaurus body. They spun him, and for a moment, he felt lighter than he'd ever felt. Below, he saw something—a cyclone—and at its mouth—

A ferocious T. rex approached a pair of Ankylosaurus. The two tanks banded together, smashing at his legs, narrowly missing them, but driving him back. A tiny Leptoceratops ran away, unnoticed by the predator, and a Quetzalcoatlus hauled herself to the rim of the plateau and leaped into the sky.

Three dome-shaped heads peered into the wind tunnel, obscuring Bertram's view of anything more. Any sounds they might have made were lost among the thunder and the crackling forks of energy that blinded him and—

Dropped him to the floor. Hard. Bertram Phillips grunted as he saw the tendrils of lightning vanish from his hands—

His *hands!*

The world was again a blur. An out-of-focus swirl of maddening activity and human voices. How strange—*human* voices that didn't belong to Mike and Candayce and Janine!

He'd made it. He was home!

"Bertram!" Mr. London said as he dropped to his knees beside the thirteen-year-old. "Bertram, are you all right?"

Bertram grasped at the pair of glasses Mr. London offered. He slid them on, and saw a sea of worried—or at least, curious—faces. He was back in his own body, his own time, and the science fair was still going on.

Behind him, he heard the M.I.N.D. Machine rocking with ferocious life.

"Hey, the geek fried himself. Cool!" some guy shouted.

"Mr. Leonitti, consider yourself on report!" Mr. London shouted. "The next person who says anything like that will get the same. Worse!"

Bertram was barely listening. He was so...puny. So small, so light, so frail. And these things he wore, these clothes, felt so burdensome, so unnatural. Where were his spikes? His tail? Where was his *dad?*

A flicker of electricity struck from behind him.

"I have to turn this off!" Mr. London said, reaching for the machine.

"No!" Bertram said, grabbing the man's arm. "Don't touch it. Cut the power supply."

"Right, right," Mr. London said. "Yes..."

He disappeared around the side of the machine.

Bertram suddenly recalled the blurry shape he'd seen just before his machine had carried him away. He thought it was his dad. But now he didn't see his father.

A man pushed his way out of the crowd. "Janine Farehouse! Where is she? I know she's the cause of this!"

Bertram sighed as he understood his mistake. It was only Mr. Graves, the teacher who'd been getting all over Janine about something that morning.

Janine! Two students were helping her to her feet. About a dozen were clustered around Candayce, who had sat up and was coming around.

What about Mike? Bertram ran to the window. He saw Mike being helped to his feet on the playing field. Over a dozen guys were out there now. Mike approached the tallest of them—Sean—and began shouting. Then he turned and shouted at his teammates. Bertram didn't have to hear what was being said to understand what was happening. Mike was making them choose.

Bertram watched as one by one, the players lined up beside Mike. Soon, only one other guy stood beside Sean, and even that didn't last.

Sean waved his fists in the air. He looked as if he was screaming. Then he turned and ran.

Score one for evolution, thought Bertram. He looked away from the window, smiling. Then he glanced down at his hands, marveling at their dexterous possibilities.

It felt a little dizzying standing upright after all those days as a club-tail. He looked to Candayce, who was now on her feet, coming his way. She was beautiful, and she glided toward him effortlessly, as if she hadn't been trapped at all in the body of a Leptoceratops for the last week or more. Her ease made him question: Had it really happened? Or had he just—

"Bertram," Candayce said. "Bertram Phillips."

"I—"

Candayce was on him then, one hand around the back of his head, the other arm encircling him, her face rushing toward his, her lips drawing near—

I didn't make it back at all, I'm still dreaming!

She kissed him.

It was the sweetest kiss of his life.

A hush fell upon the crowd. A stunned silence.

Candayce murmured in pleasure and they both relaxed, Bertram's strength pouring back into him, his certainty that all they'd been through had not been a dream.

Finally, their lips parted.

Bertram's heart was racing. Candayce grinned. He laughed, and this time he kissed her.

"THAT'S MY SON!"

Bertram and Candayce whirled to face the disbelieving crowd. A man stood at the back, wearing a goofy fishing hat, dark shirt, a brown vest, jeans, and sneakers. His face was covered in fuzz. He bit his lip, his face bright red, but he couldn't stop smiling. "Sorry."

"Dad!" Bertram cried.

Cha-ching!

Bertram and Candayce turned to their right. Janine stood there, whipping her key chain. "The mall. Four o'clock. I'll tell Mike."

"Janine, you look so good," Candayce said, tears welling up in her eyes. Her voice caught.

Murmurs rose from the crowd.

"Did you *see* that?"

"Bertram Phillips?"

"Where'd he learn to kiss like that?"

Suddenly, lightning crackled behind them. Bertram, Candayce, and Janine whirled to see the machine firing up, images playing on its screen.

"The Pachys," Bertram said in disbelief. Suddenly, three guys leaped from the crowd onto a table and started bouncing up and down, yelling, "Ook!" "Eek!" "Ack!"

One head-butted another. They looked around the room frantically. Then, with a sizzle, the power faded, and all three guys shook their heads and looked around in confusion as the crowd erupted with laughter.

"What are we doing up here?" one asked. The other two shook their heads.

Bertram saw Mr. London come around the side of the machine. "It was harder to kill the power than I thought. I had to run and get insulated gloves." He held up his hands. They were covered by clumsy black rubber gloves.

Bertram squeezed Candayce's hand, then broke from her and went to the machine.

"Bertram!" Janine said breathlessly.

"Be careful," Candayce said.

Taking a deep breath, Bertram reached up and touched the side of the M.I.N.D. Machine. His fingers closed over a handful of circuitry boards he'd soldered into place. He yanked them off and stuck them in his pocket.

"That ought to do it," he said.

His dad approached. He looked to Bertram, to Candayce, to Janine, then back again to his son. "So what'd I miss?"

Bertram just smiled—and hugged his father tight.

Chapter 41

Mike

Eight months later

Mike went outside to pick up the mail. It was a perfect spring day. Bright and sunny with only a mild breeze. A moving van went by, and he saw someone looking his way from the cab's passenger seat.

Sean. He didn't wave. Mike watched until the truck reached the end of the street, then made a left and vanished from view.

Mike heard footsteps behind him. He turned to see Bertram, wearing a bulky work shirt.

"Was that who I thought it was?" Bertram asked.

"Yep."

"Oh."

Mike put his hands in his pockets and hung his head as he walked back to the front door. "It's funny. You think you know someone. Your friend. Even yourself. You think people will never change. But everyone changes."

Bertram nodded.

They went inside into the welcome comfort of Mike's house. After dropping the mail on the kitchen table for his parents, he went downstairs with Bertram to the rec room. There was a TV with a VCR, a couch, some chairs, and boxes of stuff piled up in the corners.

Candayce and Janine were already there. Glasses filled with iced tea sat on the small table before them. Mike snagged one and sighed with pleasure as he sipped.

"Oh, look. They're back," Candayce said.

Janine grinned. "I was beginning to think they'd ended up in the Triassic this time."

Bertram peeled off his work shirt, revealing a slightly trimmer, and a shade more muscular, torso. He wore a tight ribbed T-shirt and designer jeans and boots.

Mike watched as Bertram fished out a pair of weights and sat down in a small chair with them, curling without a second thought.

"You better watch it," Mike said. "They're gonna be after you for the wrestling team next."

"Nah," Bertram said. "Baseball's enough for now."

Janine and Candayce sat on either side of Mike on the couch. Candayce ruffled his hair. "Well? Are you going to keep us in suspense?"

Mike reached for a remote control. "I've got it finished. The scrapbook."

Janine propelled herself to the edge of the couch. "Lemme see! Lemme see!"

Mike handed her the remote and smiled at Candayce. Janine hit PLAY as Mike reached back and turned off a few of the lights. He'd borrowed his folks' video recorder for this and put the home movie together in the few stolen moments he'd had recently.

The TV screen lit up. Mike appeared first on the tape, holding a microphone. He stood in a crowded hall at school. "Well, here we are, back at Wetherford Junior High, and a couple of things have changed."

The image shifted to reveal Bertram at his locker, an odd, disinterested, and slightly sad expression on his face as at least four good-looking young women crowded around him. He seemed lost in a memory.

"Come on!" a young African-American girl said as she

bounced near him. "You said you'd think about which of us you'd take to the dance."

"I know," Bertram said. "I just don't know if I'd really be good company, that's all."

Another of the girls issued a muffled scream. "Bertram!"

Candayce walked by. She laughed and said, "I had him first!"

"Yeah, you wish," a third girl said.

"It's true." Candayce shrugged.

Bertram nodded. "Yep."

Candayce grinned triumphantly. "See? See?"

"It's all her fault. Get her!"

The camera swung away as the girls chased after Candayce, who laughed and laughed.

"You're so bad," Bertram said, hauling the weights to his shoulder and breathing hard.

On the television, Janine yelled, "Yo, Candy Striper!"

Candayce turned in her red-striped volunteer's uniform at the hospital. She put her hand up over her face, giggled, and shook her head.

Sitting next to Mike, the Candayce of the present put her hand over her face in the same motion and said, "Oh, man, I wanna die…" Then she giggled, too.

The screen cut to a wicked shot from a cliffside. Then it swung over to show Janine wearing padding and goggles, and standing under the great wing of a hang glider. She drew a deep breath.

"Okay, here I go!"

She ran to the edge and leaped off. The camera followed her as she soared into the air and down toward the valley, screaming with delight.

She flew.

The images cut to a baseball game, Bertram at the plate. His first swing was a strike. His second connected, and the ball was hit past the outfield and into the street beyond.

"Home run!" A voice shouted as Bertram leisurely rounded the bases.

"I told you," Mike said, reaching over and shaking Bertram's leg. "See? What'd I tell you?"

The TV screen cut to an image of Janine downtown at the arts fair, her mom standing proudly behind her as she held up her third-place ribbon for her sculptures.

"Hey," said Janine. "Where's the playoff game stuff? The part I shot for you?"

"It's coming up," said Mike.

The football field appeared with shots of Mike as quarterback in the last game of the season. He let fly a long pass and the winning touchdown was caught and scored by the smallest member of the team.

"Looks like that Lowell guy finished the season pretty well, didn't he?" asked Bertram.

Mike smiled, looking at images of the celebration—of his arms around his teammates, of Lowell being hoisted on their shoulders. "He sure did."

The video scrapbook played on.

Later, when it was finished and all four had gone upstairs, Mike walked in on Bertram and Janine.

"You did *what?*" Bertram asked.

"I've been meaning to tell you," Janine said, averting her gaze. "I couldn't help myself. I just sort of had to…"

Bertram's shoulders sagged and he ran his hand through his hair.

"Hey, that's a trademark move," Mike said. "Watch it."

Smiling sadly, Bertram relayed what Janine had just told him.

"Whoa," Mike said. "Well, I guess there's no running from it. You'll just have to talk to your dad. Make sure it's him, and not any of those guys he hired, who comes across it."

"I guess so," Bertram said. "I guess so…"

Chapter 42

Bertram

Bertram sat at the edge of a small pit with his father. The Standing Stones rose up before them.

"I know I've said it before, but I just can't help it," his dad muttered. "I really don't see the point of all this."

"Then I guess I'd better show you." Bertram climbed down into the pit and knelt before Janine's stone. The odd symbol she had carved was only barely visible. Its lowest reaches were still hidden.

"There's two things we have to go over," Bertram said as he took a trowel and started chipping at the stone.

"Bertram, don't!"

"Relax, Dad. I know what I'm doing. You're not going to find any of the giant rex bones this close to the stones. Take my word for it."

His father sighed and climbed into the pit with him. He watched Bertram carefully.

"First up," Bertram said, "we need to talk about the household chores and responsibilities."

"Do we have to?" his dad asked in a low voice.

"Yes, we have to. Now, I'll admit, things have been better since the find, the book deal, all that. But lately, you've been slacking off. You haven't been holding up your end. Last week I had to do the

276

laundry, the cooking, *and* the bills."

"Right. I know. Sorry. I got swamped."

Bertram chipped away. "I understand. But you've got to accept that I have a social life now. Things to do. Responsibilities."

"You're right, you're right...I'll be better. I promise."

"Good. Now the second thing..." Bertram saw the rock beneath him crack wide open. "The other thing is the story I told you. About my going back to the Late Cretaceous with Mike and Candayce and Janine—you know, the one you don't believe." Bertram smiled.

"Bertram," his dad said sternly.

"You've had security out here twenty-four hours a day. I know. I tried to get in without you knowing about it and I couldn't. Neither could a couple of my friends. That's what made this necessary."

"I don't see—"

"This whole layer of rock wasn't even excavated until last fall, right? Just before the freeze."

"Yes."

"And today is the first day you've reopened the site. So there's no chance of tampering."

"None."

Bertram stood away from the cracked rock. "Read it, Dad."

His father leaned forward and stared at the rock. His eyes narrowed. His brow furrowed. He began sputtering. "I—I—"

Bertram nodded. Beneath her tag, Janine had scrawled two words: WAS HERE.

"English," his father whispered. "English! But that's impossible, unless..."

"Yep," Bertram said. He picked up one half of the stone and smashed it against the writing.

"Bertram!"

Ignoring his dad, Bertram cracked the stone into pieces and destroyed the fragile layer of rock into which Janine had made her mark.

"How about we just keep it our little secret, okay?" Bertram asked.

"But—but—the information you must have in your head, the

things you've seen! We need to talk about it. We need to explore. We need—"

"We need to rent a movie."

"What?"

"We need to sit back, have some popcorn, watch some stupid flicks, and just have some fun. Like we used to. I need that. What about you?"

Bertram's dad shook his head. He looked down at the rocks.

"It'll keep, Dad." Bertram put his hand on his dad's shoulder. "It's the past. It's not going anywhere. But in a couple of years, we're going to be talking about college for me, and you could be on a dig who knows where."

Bertram watched as his father stared at the broken fragments of stone. The older man kicked at the rocks, then looked away and started to climb from the pit. Bertram followed him.

They stood before the Standing Stones, looking at them as the sun hung low in the sky behind the obelisks.

"A movie?" his dad asked. "Do you have any ideas?"

"Nope. Do you?"

His dad put his arm around him. "Seven stones. The seven of you...how about *The Magnificent Seven*?"

Bertram took one last look at the stones then turned away. "You're on!"

For the first time since he was a little kid, Bertram held his dad's hand as they walked away.

And his dad held *his*.

Epilogue

Bob London sat in the basement of Wetherford Junior High, staring at Bertram Phillips's M.I.N.D. Machine. He'd swore to Bertram that the machine had been dismantled and hauled away as junk, but somehow, he just couldn't bring himself to do it.

There was something…*unusual* about this machine. Something Mr. London couldn't remotely begin to explain.

For weeks after the science fair, Mr. London had been unable to sleep. All he could think about was the machine. It couldn't have done half the things he'd seen it do. The machine simply didn't have the capability.

Yet he knew what he'd seen. Dead computer monitors flaring to life. Images broadcast upon them that resided nowhere on the CD-ROM Bertram had written. Lightning and other strange, inexplicable energies rising out of the machine's depths, while, at the same time, the machine remained chill to the touch.

There were, of course, the circuit boards Bertram had taken from the machine the day of the accident. But it simply didn't seem reasonable that those boards, which were meant strictly for show, could have made any real difference.

Mr. London had soldered other boards into the machine, just in case. He'd powered it up, run a dozen tests, but all that occurred were the functions it'd been designed to perform. Nothing else.

Overhead, Mr. London heard the sound of hundreds of feet. It was Friday and the kids were rushing around, excited about their weekend. But Mr. London remained, laboring over an impossible cause.

Maybe on the day of the fair, *he'd* been struck by the odd electrical impulses, too. They could have messed with his memories, somehow scrambled his perceptions.

Suddenly, a crackling came from all around. Mr. London rose, startled, and looked to the machine. It was off. Unplugged.

Lightning whipped about him. He heard a voice in his head.

"Listen to me. You must listen to me. My name is Robert London. I am you some sixty years into what you would consider the future. I'm sending this message because I don't know if the one I've already sent to Bertram in the Late Cretaceous has reached him or not. If I've failed, then you're their only hope of making it back!"

Mr. London clutched at his head as the lightning struck him, filling his mind with schematics, advanced knowledge and theories—more information than he'd ever dreamed possible!

Then it stopped. The lightning vanished. The crackling faded.

He looked to the M.I.N.D. Machine. It was so simple now. He understood it. The genius of it. The *power.*

"I can see any age. Any time." His hands trembled as he plugged the machine in and pulled Bertram's keyboard close. It would be better, of course, with the circuit boards Bertram had taken away and certainly destroyed, but the replacements he'd installed would serve.

He activated the program, keyed in dozens of strange sequences that he understood on only the most instinctive level. As lightning kicked up around the machine, he placed the sensors on his forehead and considered all the possibilities.

A door opened. "Mr. London?"

Students. Mr. London stared in shock as a small group of them skipped down the stairs and came toward him.

A boy he could barely recognize beyond the blurring light of the electrical fire surging and snapping around him said, "Mr. Graves sent us. You're supposed to take over study hall for him, and—"

The students froze. Mr. London turned, panicked, and his hand mashed the keyboard. The machine hummed. It roared!

"Wait!" Mr. London yelled, thinking wildly, *The age of dinosaurs, why did Bertram choose the age of dinosaurs*—

The lightning shot from his hands. It encircled the group of students—and rocketed upward, toward the ceiling! There were screams. Blinding lights!

Mr. London gasped and felt himself falling away from his body. He'd done something wrong. He knew it! He reached for the keyboard, but his hand passed through it. Then he was yanked upward and back into a cyclone of energies beyond all reason, beyond terror and doubt. From somewhere distant, he heard the sound of thunder, of ancient roars, of primal creatures that roamed the earth long before the age of man. The screams of the students he'd dragged with him—so many—echoed in his mind, then were swallowed up by the howling, incessant winds.

With a last, desperate effort of will, Mr. London cried, "Bertram! *Helllllllllllp! Berrrrrrtraaaaaam!*"

Then…he was gone.

And the M.I.N.D. Machine sat roaring and trembling, shuddering, raining lightning around the darkened basement.

Waiting.

In a classroom three stories above, Bertram Phillips was overcome by the strangest urge to run down to the basement and see what was wrong.

Wrong? What could be wrong?

Suddenly, he heard it. Screams. Crackling energies.

Tendrils of light burst up from the floor. They struck two students ahead of him, a boy and a girl he hardly knew. They shouted, then sank to the floor. Others screamed.

Bertram saw more tendrils approaching. Then—

The power cut out. The harsh, glaring overhead lights faded. The lightning vanished.

"What…what happened?" someone asked.

Bertram ran from the classroom, rocketed down the stairs, one flight after another.

Somehow, he already knew.

The journey was over. But the adventure had just begun.

Acknowledgments

First and foremost, I must thank my wife, Denise Ciencin, M.A., National Certified Counselor. For four solid months, she worked on this project with me, offering invaluable ideas as she sifted through texts on not only dinosaurs, but the history of the earth, climate, and so much more.

Denise also supplied many brilliant scenes and likewise amazing insights into the stresses, strains, and joys of adolescence, drawing not only from her own childhood memories but also her sterling work with children.

I would also like to thank Dr. Thomas R. Holtz, Jr., Vertebrate Paleontologist, Dept. of Geology, University of Maryland, for serving as project advisor and supplying wonderful new information and interpretations regarding the lives of dinosaurs.

Special thanks also to Alice Alfonsi, my amazing editor. Working with Alice has been, without a doubt, the high point of my career. For years of friendship, dedication, insight, and unrelenting, passionate support and guidance, words really cannot suffice. I am grateful, too, for the incredible efforts and unswerving support of Kate Klimo, Harold Clarke, Kristina Peterson, Craig Virden, Kenneth LaFreniere, Doby Daenger, Georgia Morrisey, Gretchen Schuler, and Randi Machado of Random House.

Thanks to Jonathan Matson, who, as a great author once referred to him, is more than an agent, he is a true friend.

Thanks also to Mike Fredericks, for bringing Bertram and his pals to amazing and intensely satisfying life.

Thanks to Jim Gurney for allowing me to fall so deeply in love with the dinosaurs of his wondrous *Dinotopia* that I simply had to build a playground for myself! And to Alan Dean Foster, Dr. Kenneth Carpenter, Ray Bradbury, Raymond E. Feist, Janny Wurts, Jeff Mariotte, and Bob and Bryan Salvatore, for their encouragement and inspiration.

Finally, thanks also to Lynn Pyle and Sonia Simpers of the International Readers Association; Dr. Judith Totman Parrish, Dept. of Geosciences, University of Arizona; Dr. Jerry Wermund, Bureau of Economic Geology, University of Texas; Dr. Stephen Reynolds; and Dr. Ronald Blakey, Dept. of Geology, Northern Arizona University, Flagstaff.

Dinoverse Glossary

Ankylosaurus (ANG-kih-luh-saw-rus): One of the last armored dinosaurs and largest of the club-tails. Built low to the ground, Ankylosaurus walked on all fours and weighed three to four tons. Even Ankylosaurus's eyelids were armored!

Ankylosaurus

Carnivores (KAR-nuh-vorz): Meat-eating animals.

Cretaceous (krih-TAY-shus): The last of three distinct periods in the Mesozoic Era, 145 million to 65 million years ago.

Crocodilians (krok-uh-DILL-ee-unz): A sizable collection of reptiles that spawned modern crocodiles and other now-extinct creatures, some larger than any carnivorous dinosaur.

Herbivores (HUR-bih-vorz): Plant-eating animals.

Ichthyosaurs (IK-thee-uh-sorz): Water-dwelling, fish-eating, air-breathing reptiles.

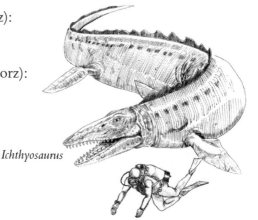

Ichthyosaurus

Invertebrates (in-VUR-tuh-braytz): Animals without backbones, like jellyfish.

Leptoceratops (lep-tuh-SER-uh-tops): The name means "slender-horned face." It was a Protoceratops of the same family as Triceratops. Leptoceratops was distinguished by its smaller size (the size of a pig), absence of horns, and beaked face. Leptoceratops was found only in North America.

Leptoceratops

Mammals (MAM-ulz): In the Cretaceous, they were small hairy animals.

Mesozoic Era (mez-uh-ZOH-ik ER-uh): The age of dinosaurs, 245 million to 65 million years ago.

Pachycephalosaurus (pack-ih-SEF-uh-luh-saw-rus): The name means "thick-headed lizard." These plant-eaters used their dome-like heads for defense, ramming opponents with them much like present-day mountain goats.

Pachycephalosaurus

Paleontologist (pay-lee-un-TAHL-uh-jist): A scientist who studies the past through fossils.

Parasaurolophus (par-uh-saw-ruh-LOH-fus): Plant-eating crested dinosaur that was thirty feet long and stood sixteen feet high. Parasaurolophus's crest was a long, hornlike tube that curved backward from the head to beyond the shoulders and produced sounds.

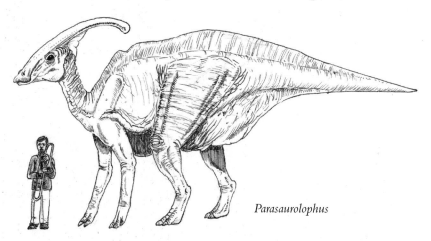

Parasaurolophus

Protoungulatums (proh-toh-UNG-gyuh-lah-tumz): Tiny mammals that were the forerunners of horses, antelopes, camels, and so on. They appeared to be part cat, part rat, and part horse.

Pterosaurs (TER-uh-sorz): Sizable and varied flying reptiles.

Quetzalcoatlus (ket-sahl-koh-AHT-lus): A pterosaur, a flying reptile that was not actually a dinosaur. A full-grown Quetzalcoatlus had a thirty-six- to thirty-nine-foot wingspan. It was the largest flying creature of all time.

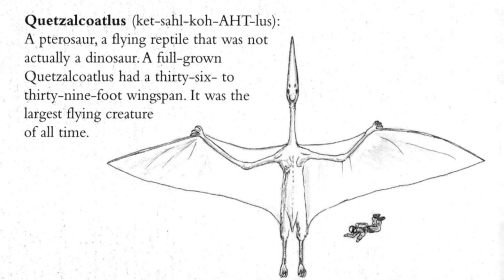

Triceratops (trye-SER-uh-tops): "Three-horned face." Triceratops weighed up to eleven tons and traveled in great herds near the end of the Late Cretaceous period in North America.

Triceratops

Tyrannosaurus rex (tye-RAN-uh-saw-rus recks): "King of the tyrant lizards," a large meat-eating dinosaur with tiny but enormously powerful arms and muscular jaws filled with fifty teeth. Paleontologists differ on whether the T. rex was a predator who attacked live prey, a scavenger who lived on carcasses, or both.

Tyrannosaurus rex

Vertebrates (VUR-tuh-braytz): Animals with backbones, like fish, mammals, reptiles, and birds.

The world: The continents and the seas of Earth sixty-seven million years ago were different from those in our present day. North America was subdivided by an inland sea, and water also prevented movement between North and South America. Mexico was under water, India was a separate island, South America and Africa had begun to separate, and Europe and North America were moving apart. Seaways also divided Europe and Asia.

References for Dinoverse

Benyus, J. M. *Beastly Behaviors: A Zoo Lover's Companion*. Reading, Mass.: Addison-Wesley, 1992.

Bloch, M. H. *Footprints in the Swamp*. New York: Atheneum, 1985.

Czerkas, S. J., and S. A. Czerkas. *Dinosaurs: A Global View*. New York: Mallard Press, 1991.

Dixon, D. *Dougal Dixon's Dinosaurs*. Honesdale, Pa.: Boyds Mills Press, 1993.

Dixon, D., B. Cox, R. J. G. Savage, and B. Gardiner. *The Macmillan Illustrated Encyclopedia of Dinosaurs and Prehistoric Animals*. New York: Simon & Schuster/Macmillan Company, 1988.

Dodson, P. *An Alphabet of Dinosaurs*. New York: Scholastic, 1995.

Eyewitness Visual Dictionaries. *The Visual Dictionary of Dinosaurs*. New York: Dorling Kindersley, 1993.

Fastovsky, D. E., and D.B . Weishampel. *The Evolution and Extinction of the Dinosaurs*. New York: Cambridge University Press, 1996.

Glut, D. F. *Dinosaurs: The Encyclopedia*. Jefferson, N.C.: McFarland & Company, Inc., 1997.

Hanson, J. K., and D. Morrison. *Of Kinkajous, Capybaras, Horned Beetles, Seladangs, and the Oddest and Most Wonderful Mammals, Insects, Birds, and Plants of Our World*. New York: HarperCollins, 1991.

Horner, J. R., and D. Lessem. *The Complete T. rex*. New York: Simon & Schuster, 1993.

Lambert, D. *Field Guide to Prehistoric Life*. New York: Facts on File, 1985.

Lambert, D. *The Ultimate Dinosaur Book*. New York: Dorling Kindersley, 1993.

Lambert, D. and Diagram Visual Information Ltd. *The Dinosaur Data Book.* New York: Avon Books, 1990.

Lessem, D. *Dinosaur Worlds.* Honesdale, Pa.: Boyds Mills Press, 1996.

Lessem, D. *Ornithomimids: The Fastest Dinosaur.* Minneapolis: Carolrhoda Books, 1996.

Masson, J. M., and S. McCarthy. *When Elephants Weep: The Emotional Lives of Animals.* New York: Bantam Doubleday Dell, 1995.

Norman, D. *Dinosaur!* New York: Prentice Hall General Reference, 1991.

Norman, D. *The Illustrated Encyclopedia of Dinosaurs.* London: Salamander Books Limited, 1985.

Retallack, G. J. "Pedotype Approach to Cretaceous and Tertiary Paleosols, Montana." *Geological Society of America Bulletin,* vol. 106, no. 11, 1994.

Stanley, S. M. *Earth and Life Through Time.* New York: W. H. Freeman, 1989.

Walker, C., and D. Ward. *The Eyewitness Handbook of Fossils.* New York: Dorling Kindersley, 1992.

Wellnhofer, P. *Pterosaurs: The Illustrated Encyclopedia of Prehistoric Flying Reptiles.* New York: Barnes and Noble Books, 1991.

Wilford, J. N. *Riddle of the Dinosaur.* New York: Knopf, 1985.